WAYNE STINNETT

RISING TIDE

A JESSE MCDERMITT NOVEL

Caribbean Adventure Series
Volume 20

2021

Published by DOWN ISLAND PRESS, 2021
Beaufort, SC

Print Edition

Library of Congress cataloging-in-publication Data
Stinnett, Wayne
Rising Tide/Wayne Stinnett
p. cm. – (A Jesse McDermitt novel)

ISBN: 978-1-7356231-4-6 (print)

Cover photograph by Alexandr Gerasimov
Graphics and Interior Design by Aurora Publicity
Edited by The Write Touch
Final Proofreading by Donna Rich
Audiobook Narration by Nick Sullivan

Dedicated to the memory of Ed Robinson, a great storyteller, friend, husband, and father, whose final voyage came far too early.

#sailonbreeze #cancersucks

"Shit always works out."

–Meade Breeze

If you'd like to receive my newsletter,
please sign up on my website:

WWW.WAYNESTINNETT.COM.

Every two weeks, I'll bring you insights into my private life and writing habits, with updates on what I'm working on, special deals I hear about, and new books by other authors that I'm reading.

The Charity Styles Caribbean Thriller Series

Merciless Charity
Ruthless Charity
Reckless Charity
Enduring Charity
Vigilant Charity

The Jesse McDermitt Caribbean Adventure Series

Fallen Out
Fallen Palm
Fallen Hunter
Fallen Pride
Fallen Mangrove
Fallen King
Fallen Honor
Fallen Tide
Fallen Angel
Fallen Hero
Rising Storm
Rising Fury
Rising Force
Rising Charity
Rising Water
Rising Spirit
Rising Thunder
Rising Warrior
Rising Moon
Rising Tide
Steady as She Goes

THE GASPAR'S REVENGE SHIP'S STORE IS OPEN.

There, you can purchase all kinds of swag related to my books. You can find it at

WWW.GASPARS-REVENGE.COM

MAPS

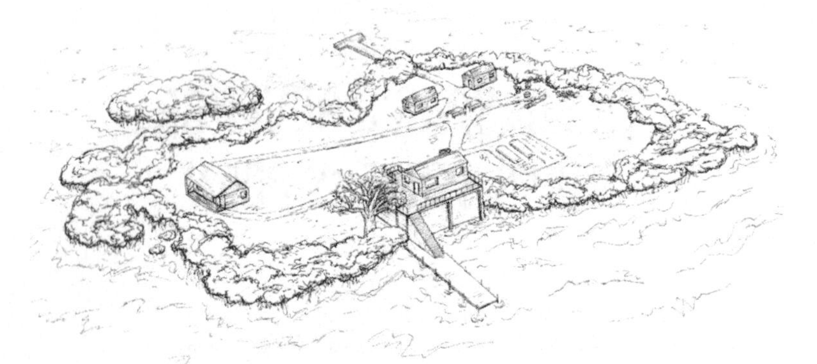

Jesse's Island in the Content Keys

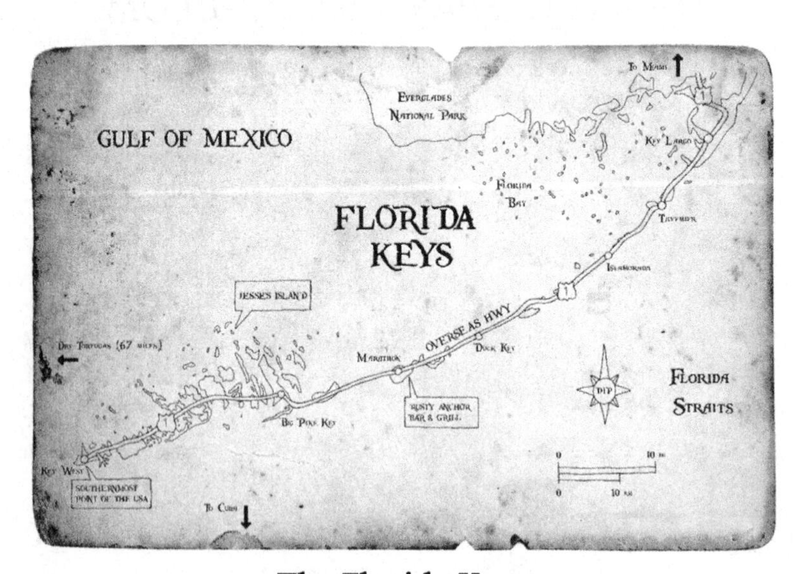

The Florida Keys

PRELUDE

January 5, 2021

I was on Singer Island, prepping for a billfish tournament, when Buck Reilly called me. He'd told me a couple of weeks earlier that he'd help me find a flying boat. I was surprised that he was calling so soon.

He wanted to make a deal: trade my services for a plane he found. The problem was, he needed me in the Bahamas with *Floridablanca* on Monday, two days after the tournament ended. I explained to my crew—Jimmy, Rusty, and Tank—what Buck wanted me to do. Tank and Jimmy were up for the adventure, but Rusty had reservations.

"I tossed him and another man outa the Anchor a few years ago," he said. "Is what he's asking you to do legal?"

I thought about it a moment. "It's a fine line," I said. "But I don't think any laws will be broken."

"Ethical?"

"You're talking ethics about the people he's trying to swindle?"

"Point taken," he said. "Okay, I'm in."

Six days later, after having had a great time in the tournament, we skipped over to Bimini, swapped boats, and met up with Buck and his partner, Ray Floyd. The meeting place was at a predesignated spot on the edge of the Bahama Banks, west of Andros Island. Checking my chart, I found that the location was in international waters. Barely. Buck and Ray arrived in a pair of Grumman flying boats—a Goose and a Mallard.

We'd dropped the hook on a dive site and anchored nearby, floated the two flying boats—one of which was soon to be mine. All we had to do was hoist some heavy cannons off the sea floor and move them somewhere else. I didn't ask any questions. It was Buck's find.

We'd already raised three of them onto the foredeck. They were heavy, but *Floridablanca* was all steel and displaced fifty tons when fully loaded. The water and fuel tanks, eighteen hundred gallons each, were half empty, so the weight of the cannons was negligible. We just weren't going to be running real fast with them up near the bow, which was the only place they'd fit and the only place the large forward crane could reach.

Buck surfaced and gave me the signal to hoist. I used the controls in the pilothouse to allow Jimmy to maneuver the cannons onto the deck without having to deal with the remote control.

As he guided the cannon to the deck, Jimmy called to Buck over the side, "Dude, how many more of these pirate sticks you got down there?"

"Last one," Buck yelled back. "Come get me at the plane once you have that one set."

As Jimmy and Rusty covered the last cannon with a tarp, Buck swam back to his plane to get out of his dive gear.

A moment later, Jimmy started the outboard on the tender and headed over to the Goose to get Buck. We still didn't know where he wanted us to take the cargo.

Jimmy killed the engine as he came alongside the Goose's hatch, where Buck was waiting for him.

"Cool old planes, *hermano*," I heard Jimmy say. "Like stepping back in time."

Buck got into the dinghy and the two started back over. I went back through the salon and stepped outside to the covered cockpit, where I opened the transom door.

After Buck tied off the painter to a cleat, he stood in the dinghy, smiling up at me. "Permission to come aboard?"

I waved him on.

"Gentlemen," he said, shaking hands with Tank and Rusty.

"Reilly," Rusty said.

"Are we talking the Goose or the Mallard?" I asked, point blank.

"The Mallard," Buck replied.

I turned to look at it and saw Ray Floyd seated in the hatch, watching us. He waved. Ray sometimes worked on my old deHavilland Beaver.

"That Ray Floyd?" I asked.

"Yeah, he's my partner at Last Resort," Buck replied.

"Let's go check it out," I said.

"Now isn't the best time."

Buck and I were the same height, though I probably had over thirty pounds on him. I peered straight into his eyes. "Then when?"

"Few days," he replied. "Either you can come to Key West, or I'll bring it up to Marathon. Ray wants to clean it up pretty for

you."

"Well, I've got your cannons," I said. "But our deal was to drop them off today, not in a few days. So, you want me to drop them back in the water?"

"As a matter of fact, I do." He lifted his phone and tapped the screen a few times. "I just sent you the numbers where I'd like you to drop them, just north of Vero Beach."

"In the water?" I asked again.

He nodded. "Three thousand feet offshore in thirty feet of water. As soon as possible."

I nodded slowly and glanced from Buck back over to the Mallard. I raised a pair of binoculars and studied the old flying boat. "Okay," I agreed. "Vero Beach is nearly two hundred miles away, but the cannons will be dropped in a tight pile there by this time tomorrow. I'll see you to collect the Mallard next week."

We shook hands.

Buck glanced at Tank and gave a little two-fingered salute.

"Ooh-rah," Tank grunted.

"Thanks, guys," Buck said. "Let me know after you make the drop."

Jimmy took Buck back to his plane as I started the engine and hoisted the anchor. Once Jimmy was back on board and the tender stowed, we were underway. The next few days would be busy and I didn't want to wait around.

The two planes took off and were soon nothing but specks headed southwest as we headed northwest. My plan was to drop the cannons where Buck had asked, then head straight back to Bimini to pick up the *Revenge* before heading back to the Keys.

The whole trip would be nearly six hundred nautical miles and would easily take three days, running all night and taking

watches for the next few nights.

The next day, we arrived at the prescribed spot and, with no other boats around, we quickly hoisted the cannons off the deck and lowered them to the sea floor.

For the return to Bimini, we disengaged the main engine and fired up the twin Mercedes powerplants, so the return crossing took half the time.

Upon our return to the Rusty Anchor, since it was still early enough, I climbed into *Island Hopper* for the short flight to Key West to meet with Buck and Ray.

Buck had warned me that Ray was less than thrilled about the deal to trade the Mallard. He'd asked me to sweeten the pot for his partner by asking Ray to do the restoration.

Ray was professional and walked me around and through the bird, pointing out the many things he'd already spotted that would need major attention or upgrade. He also pointed out locations where a stash might be hidden with a little modification.

I nodded my understanding. "You restored Buck's other planes, right?"

"That's right."

"Would you be interested in restoring the Mallard for me?"

Ray's face lit up. "Absolutely. I've done a lot of research on where I…er…you, could get parts, and the optimal updated specs that should be included."

I nodded at his enthusiasm. "I'm more interested in quality than speed, so why don't you come up with a plan and budget, and then give me a call?"

He agreed and we shook hands. No contracts to sign, or lawyers to involve. That was just the way things were done in the Keys.

As Buck and I walked back over to *Island Hopper*, he covertly pulled something from his pocket and palmed it into mine as we shook hands.

"Thanks again for your help," Buck said. "And for hiring Ray to restore the Mallard."

"He's the best there is," I replied. "I would've hired him anyway but appreciate the token."

What he'd put into my hand was small but heavy. I had a fairly good idea what it was.

"You got off easy anyway, Reilly," I said, discreetly putting the coin in my pocket. "Or, should I say, King Buck, redux?"

After taking off and getting out over the water, I dug the thing out of my pocket. It was an eight-escudo Spanish gold coin.

I chuckled and put the $30,000 "token" back in my pocket.

CHAPTER ONE

April 13, 2021

The aging Ford Taurus drove slowly south on US 41 toward Pine Manor, an older neighborhood in the southern part of Fort Myers. The driver scanned the shadows, as if looking for someone.

Most of the homes in the half-square-mile neighborhood—known locally as Crime Manor—were small, one- and two-story apartment dwellings built in the late 1960s and early '70s, though a few dated back to the early 1940s. A fourth of the residences were vacant; some abandoned and used as crack houses. The majority of the people who resided in Pine Manor were renters.

The businesses fronting the highway reflected the downward trend of the neighborhood. The old Ford rolled past a Mexican restaurant, a check-cashing place with bars on the windows and door, a used car lot full of older model cars, a florist, a pawn shop, and a convenience store, all with security bars. The car slowed at one of the few up-scale businesses, a furniture store that offered rent-to-own pricing.

The Taurus had been blue at one time, but the driver's door

and left front fender were white, having been replaced after a wreck. The rest of the car's paint was faded and peeling. The hood, roof, and trunk were coated with surface rust, making the car look anything but blue under the orange glow of the street-light on the corner.

"I'm hungry," a small boy said from the backseat of the car.

"Me too, Alberto," his mother replied, turning right at the furniture store. "We'll eat in the morning. I just need to make some money first."

The woman looked around nervously, but not because of the high crime in the neighborhood. She knew it well and was known by people in the area.

Her twitching and scratching were the result of heavy drug use.

The street she turned on was dark. Shattered streetlight housings gave blind testament to what happened below them. Lee County Electric Co-Op had given up repairing the lights a long time ago. The residents of this street preferred the darkness, and the lights were shot out as soon as they were replaced.

Carmel Marco pulled into a vacant spot at a one-story row of studio and one-bedroom apartments. She could feel eyes on her as she shut off the engine and turned to the boy in the backseat.

"You stay in the car," she said. "And don't open the door for anyone."

Alberto Marco slumped in the seat, casting his eyes down to the floorboard. "Yes, Mama."

Carmel got out and locked the doors. She looked back at the boy for a moment, then turned and followed the sidewalk along the left side of the water-stained, concrete block building. She'd only be a few minutes; then she'd drop Alberto off at a friend's so

she could work the streets.

At the door to apartment six, she knocked twice, then twice more. There was a faint blue light coming from a gap in the heavy curtains, which was quickly extinguished. She heard movement inside.

Finally, she heard the sound of the locks clicking and the rattle of the security chain. Then the door opened slightly, revealing a lean Hispanic man, shirtless, with gang tattoos from the neck down.

"What choo want?"

"The usual," Carmel replied. "Just enough to get me through the night."

The man, known on the streets as Razor, grinned lasciviously at her, revealing a gold-capped front tooth. He stepped back and waved her in.

"You know I don't like doing small sales, Car."

"I need it, Enrique," she replied, stepping into the darkened room. "I didn't see Bones out on the street."

Razor was a member of the ruthless MS-13 gang, which had chapters all over the globe. He sold drugs, and Bones was his street dealer. He and Carmel had known one another a long time and he didn't mind her using his given name when they were alone.

The television came back on, but no other light emanated from anywhere in the apartment.

"How much cash you got?"

"Well, see—"

"You don't got no *varos*?" Razor said, flopping down into a worn out recliner. "This ain't no charity I'm runnin' here."

"I'll get money, man," Carmel pleaded. "But I gotta pay the

sitter so I can."

"We did this a few times before," Razor said. "And I had to hunt you down to get my money more'n once."

"She won't let me leave Alberto unless I pay her up front," Carmel said, eyeing the crack pipe on the table with a hunger that bordered on lust. "You know I'm good for it."

Razor looked her up and down. They'd known each other since high school. Back then, she was *buenota*, a hard body, but now, at twenty-five, she looked twice her age, weary and worn out. Having a kid at sixteen would do that. Dropping out, living on the streets, and getting strung out on crack cocaine before eighteen would accelerate it and make a girl do things she never thought she'd do.

Razor took a small rock from his little sample bag and put it in the pipe. Then he handed the pipe to Carmel along with a lighter. "A little cloud to get your night started."

She took it greedily and fired the end of the pipe with his miniature torch. The clouds swirled in the glass tube and she inhaled deeply.

The change was instantaneous. Her nerves settled and the light and low sound coming from the TV seemed different, as if she could see and hear it better. Even Enrique's grin seemed inviting.

"Just leave the boy here," he told her. "Then you can buy more."

Carmel, her mind now swimming from the huge release of dopamine in her brain, thought that was an excellent idea. Alberto wouldn't be in the way; he'd just curl up somewhere and go to sleep. She could come back two or three times throughout the night to check on him.

Later that night, after Carmel had turned a couple of quick tricks, she felt as if things were looking up. She'd gone back to check on Alberto around midnight. And to buy more crack.

Carmel knew that eventually the sun would come up and she'd crash. Then the miserable feeling would return, the desperate despair. But if she could keep it at bay long enough, if she rationed the crack wisely, she'd have enough money by morning to feed her son for another day.

She stood in the shadow of a telephone pole, waiting. Occasionally a cop would pass by. Carmel was always careful to keep the thick, wooden pole between her and their prying eyes.

Other cars whisked past, drivers intent on getting home from work, or to a bar to meet a friend. She didn't hide from them, knowing they had other things on their minds. She stayed in the open. They might remember later.

Then a car came slowly down Cleveland Avenue. The driver was obviously looking for something. Or someone. It was an older model Chevrolet, nothing like what the unmarked cop cars usually looked like.

Carmel stepped out of the shadow.

The car slowed and came to a stop.

"Wanna party?" a young black man asked, smiling at her.

"I'm working," she replied back.

"Twenty bucks says your mouth can do more than talk, *chica.*"

Carmel stepped over to the open window and looked inside, checking the backseat. "Are you a cop?"

"What the fuck you mean am I a cop?" the man said. "I'm a horny muthafucka is what I am. You getting' in or what?"

She opened the door and got in the car.

"Name's Tavarius," he said, taking a hit from a joint and offering it to her. "Tavarius Carter."

She took the joint and pulled on it, inhaling deeply. She didn't like weed, but it was sort of a custom on the streets. By sharing it, they both knew that the other wasn't a cop. Besides, he was offering twice what she usually charged for a blowjob and unlike the last two, this guy wasn't fat or ugly.

"There's a parking lot just around the corner," she said. "Lots of cars there. You can park there and nobody will see."

"I meant what I said about partying," he offered, as he started to drive away. "I got a few dawgs comin' over, 'bout six or seven. Could be twenty a pop for a hot little *mamacita* like you. And all the rock candy you can smoke."

Over a hundred dollars, she thought.

Carmel slid closer and rubbed his crotch. "I like parties."

Tavarius, known among his Lake Boyz brothers as "Bumpy," smiled at how easy it'd been. Other gang members were busy picking up more hookers who worked the MS-13 controlled part of south Fort Myers.

He drove north, headed back to Lake Boyz turf. He took his time, letting her work magic on him with her mouth, knowing that once they got to the clubhouse, she and the others who were being rounded up would be used as sex toys and eventually killed.

MS-13 was new to Fort Myers, and though they had a reputation in bigger cities, they were still small-time on the southwest coast. Lake Boyz had been around for as long as Bumpy could remember.

It was time to put MS-13 in its place in Fort Misery and that started with eliminating one of their sources of income.

CHAPTER TWO

The rhythmic sound of my running feet on the pavement had lulled me into an alternative state after the first mile—the runner's high. The first mile is always easy and quickly brings on an almost euphoric state.

It was the second mile that always made me think, *why not just go for a swim?* As a means of keeping fit, swimming was by far a better total body work out. And it was a lot easier on the joints.

It's not that I couldn't run—I just chose not to. At six-three, my long legs could eat up miles effortlessly.

My elongated shadow stretched thirty feet in front of me and the morning sun was warm on my back. Each step was in harmony with the cadence I always heard in my head when I ran.

I used to run a lot. Back when I was an active-duty Marine, our morning PT always consisted of at least a three-mile run, usually more. Rain or shine, hot or cold, that's how we started our day in the infantry. And it usually wasn't on nice, flat concrete with running shoes. We ran the same way we trained to fight; in boots and utes, running through the woods or on a sandy beach.

The sing-song cadences we used while running in formation

were often colorful, to say the least. They were downright profane on other occasions—not meant for politically correct ears. But Marines are Marines. The ditties, as we called them, were used to keep the troops in step and motivated, but they served a purpose beyond that. Singing while running also helped to regulate breathing, as the platoon or squad would sing the song back to the leader.

My particular favorite, learned while I was in boot camp, told the mythical story of the Corps, as if it were one person. It could be sung in a quick-time march or a double-time run.

He was born on Parris Island,
The land that God forgot,
Where the sand was fourteen inches deep,
And the sun was blazing hot.

But that was just a one-mile cadence and I'd already chanted it twice in my head, including the sing-back.

I knew many others, and as I searched my memory for another favorite, the voice in my head—that of my boot camp senior drill instructor, Staff Sergeant O'Lowny—defaulted back to the minimalistic *Lo-right-a-lo-right-a-LO-right-a-layo.*

"What are you thinking about?" Savannah asked, running steadily right beside me. This morning's seven-mile run was her idea.

"I'm trying not to think," I replied. "It makes it hard to keep from running into people."

She laughed. "It's thinning out a little. I swear I got bumped a dozen times there at the start."

We were running on the world-famous Seven Mile Bridge,

currently closed to vehicular traffic on a beautiful Saturday in the middle of April.

Savannah had signed us both up for the 40th Annual Seven Mile Bridge Run. The race was held by a local running club every year. It started on Knight's Key, at one end of the longest of forty-three bridges on the Overseas Highway, and it ended on Little Duck Key at the other end. There would be a grueling half-mile stretch before the midpoint of the race, as the bridge rose from twenty feet above the water to nearly seventy. A fifty-foot climb doesn't sound like much, but it's the equivalent of running up to the fifth floor of a building. Except it's stretched over a much longer distance than five flights of stairs. The high arch over Moser Channel would reduce a lot of the runners to walkers.

There were at least a hundred people running ahead of us, and fifteen times that number behind us. We weren't running to compete, but the leaders *were* in sight, running together in a line from one side of the bridge to the other, about two hundred yards ahead of us.

"I can tell you want to move up there and beat them," Savannah said. "You're so competitive."

I looked over at her and smiled. "No way. Those guys are half my age and far more competitive than I ever was."

"All the more reason to beat them," she said, lengthening her stride just a little.

I grinned and matched her gait as we passed two much younger athletes.

Fifteen hundred runners participated every year, chosen randomly from perhaps 10,000 entrants. Most were from South Florida but there were always runners from countries all over the world competing in what was likely the longest footrace held

entirely over water.

There were dozens of professional athletes in the mix. They'd mostly started at the front of the pack on Knights Key and would likely stay in the front throughout the race. I figured that somewhere around the highway's forty-one-mile marker—about a mile from the finish line—the leaders would start lengthening their strides in a one-mile kick to pull away from the others. Starting too early would burn a runner out before the finish line. And starting too late, though you might finish at a faster run, meant the leader could already have crossed the finish line. It was all about knowing your body's ability and durability.

Pigeon Key lay off to the right, just a little ahead of us. It was at the end of the old bridge. A section had been removed just past a ramp going down to the island. The rest of the old bridge still paralleled the new one, just off to the north, but with a section removed at both ends, the middle part was completely inaccessible and slowly deteriorating from the elements and the steady march of time.

Ahead of us about a mile, the new bridge curved to the left and the high arch over Moser Channel was visible in the distance beyond. I knew that about a mile past the arch, at the halfway point of the race, the fire department had what they call a "quint," or quintuple combination truck staged with its ladder extending across both lanes. As the runners approached, they'd turn on the pump, sending water through misters to cool the runners. The firefighters also handed out drinking water.

The race had started at 0730, only thirty minutes after sunrise. But being the Florida Keys, even at an early hour in the spring, eighty degrees wasn't uncommon. And it looked like this day was shaping up to be a scorcher.

"How soon will I be able to join you again?" Savannah asked.

We'd only been married for four-and-a-half months, and I was scheduled to take the helm of *Ambrosia* on Friday for two weeks of intense familiarization with retiring Captain Nils Hansen. I'd worked with Nils before as his acting first mate. He and I both held the same unlimited sea captain's certification, but he had dozens of years at the helms of large ocean ships. I'd already learned a lot from the old Norseman.

"End of the month," I replied. "But you already knew that."

"Will you miss me?"

I glanced over at her. It wasn't like Savannah to doubt herself.

"You know I will," I said. "I don't know how I ever got along without you."

We continued running, and another cadence came into my head.

Momma told Johnny not to go downtown,

Marine Corps recruiter was a hangin' around,

Suzy told Johnny go serve your nation,

Take a cab down to the MEPS station,

Suzy's in the bedroom, Jodie's at the window,

Johnny's got his bags and he's ready to go,

Put Johnny on a Greyhound bus,

Then there came the bends and thrusts,

Drill Instructors trained him rough and hard,

They taught him to fight, they taught him to march,

It was short but long it seemed,

Johnny had earned the title Marine.

"What's going on up there?" Savannah asked, pointing ahead.

Several runners, none from the front of the pack, had stopped and were standing at the left side of the bridge, some pointing down into the water.

We moved over to that side of the bridge for a better view, and as we approached the group, I could see a boat just a hundred feet or so from the bridge. It looked like a beat-up old derelict, maybe fourteen or fifteen feet in length.

"Just another boat adrift," I said, slowing my pace a little.

After Hurricane Irma, there had been reports of abandoned boats drifting on the currents all over South Florida and the Keys. Many were still afloat three years later and occasionally one would wash up on shore or be found lodged in the mangroves or aground in shoal waters.

We'd found one on my island in the Content Keys just two weeks earlier. It'd been pushed up on shore during a squall, and we came across it the next morning, wedged solidly against the north pier. It had a trailer still strapped under it. Finding the owner turned out to be pretty easy. He came out and towed it to a boat ramp at Old Wooden Bridge Marina.

There was something odd about this boat, though. For one, it didn't look like a typical boat you'd see around here. It was crudely built and made of wood.

"There's someone in it," a woman yelled.

Savannah and I moved quickly to the concrete guard rail. It was an incoming tide, and the boat was drifting toward the bridge. Just as the woman had said, I could make out a small form lying on the deck in the middle, covered by a piece of canvas. A bare brown foot stuck out from under the cloth.

I looked down. The water was maybe eight or ten feet deep and the current was moving pretty fast. The boat was coming right toward where we stood.

"Rafter!" I shouted.

Without thinking, I put one hand on the rail and vaulted over it, pulling my legs up and wrapping them with my arms.

Diving into shallow water from a height of twenty feet was suicide, and going feet first would put both my legs in casts for months. Tucked into a cannonball position, it didn't matter how I hit the water; it was going to hurt. But a cannonball lessened the depth I'd descend and I might avoid hitting the bottom.

I smacked the water on my side. The impact against my thigh was like that of a big wooden paddle and the sting almost caused me to kick my legs out early. But I didn't. I waited until my body stopped descending, then unfolded and pushed off the bottom.

Running shoes are good on pavement but not so much in the water. I kicked them off as I rose from the bottom.

When I broke the surface, it was just in time to see someone else smack the water ten feet ahead of me. I'd already drifted back under the bridge a little. When they surfaced, I was surprised and then angered to realize that it was Savannah.

"Come on," she shouted. "We have to keep it from hitting the bridge pilings."

She was right. The boat was in poor shape, and though it wasn't moving *fast*, if it got sideways against one of the concrete bridge piers in the right position, the weight of the water could break it in half.

I started swimming against the current, which was probably moving at close to two knots. I knew Savannah and I could swim faster than that, but not much, and the boat was moving toward

us at the speed of the current. At best, we'd reach it twenty feet from the piling.

"Get to the stern," I shouted, as we reached the boat. "We can be its engines."

At the back of the boat, I could see over the half-rotted transom board. The figure lying on the deck hadn't moved.

"Pull this way," I yelled, then started tugging the stern to the right, swimming with one hand.

Once we got it turned, we both moved to where the low gunwale met the transom on either side and started swimming hard with one hand. We managed to steer the boat safely around the big concrete pilings just in time.

As we disappeared under the bridge, I yelled up to those looking down at us. "Call 911! We'll get it to Pigeon Key."

"Get aboard," I ordered my wife. "See if there's a rope or anything."

Savannah submerged, then pulled and kicked herself up, climbing into the little boat. She moved past the inert body to the bow.

"There's a bow line," she said.

"Toss it out and I'll tow. Then get back in the water and keep the bow angled to starboard so the current helps push."

The old bridge was only two hundred yards away. Drifting with the current, it wouldn't take the boat more than three minutes to pass it. Then the next land would be the southwest coast of the mainland—Cape Sable—nearly thirty miles away.

Pigeon Key lay beneath the old bridge, about a hundred yards west of where the little boat was headed. We needed to move it sideways in the current to reach the tiny island.

It doesn't take much to hold a boat against a current if the

bow's pointing into it. The bow line was about twenty feet long. I quickly tied a bowline knot with a large enough loop to fit over my head and one shoulder, then slipped it on.

Without waiting for Savannah to signal she was ready, I started swimming against the current, angling just to the right a little. The weight of the boat hit my shoulder as the line went tight and I dug in, breathing every third stroke in a power swim.

I could tell by the feel of the boat on the line that Savannah was at the stern, pushing as she worked to keep the current on the boat's port bow.

Swimming hard, I could feel the burn in my shoulders and legs. I kept at it for five solid minutes, knowing that it would take quite a while to drag the boat sideways as the current pushed us steadily northward toward the massive concrete piers the old bridge's arches were built on.

Those foundation piers were twenty feet wide and rested on a bottom that was mostly less than fifteen feet deep. They were cracked and crusted with barnacles. We could easily get the boat to one of them and let the water hold it against the pier, which we could then climb out onto while waiting for some help.

But I wasn't sure of the legalities of a bridge piling versus dry land. If the person in the boat was a Cuban rafter, and still alive, being on dry land used to mean they could stay in the country. I just wasn't sure if a hundred-year-old concrete bridge pier counted as dry land.

Finally, I heard Savannah calling out to me. I stopped swimming and saw that we were just south of Pigeon Key and the current was taking us straight toward shore, less than a hundred feet away now. It would change before we reached shore, as the water parted to go around the island. I wanted the sweet spot

right in the middle.

"Get in and check on them," I called out as I moved back to the boat.

As she did so, I turned the boat, then started pushing it toward the rocky shoreline, where a solar panel farm provided power for the island. I hoped I'd gotten the sweet spot right and didn't get caught in a faster current to one side or the other.

Giving up my shoes might have been a bad move on my part. I wasn't sure how far out the rip-rap of rocks extended.

"It's a little boy," Savannah said. "He's alive, but unconscious."

A Cuban boy alone on a boat? There'd been a storm two nights before; we'd seen it from my island, lightning flashing across the sky to the south, way out on the Gulf Stream. Had this boy lost his family on the treacherous ninety-mile crossing in a rowboat?

"He's been beaten, Jesse," Savannah said. "At least a couple of days ago, by the looks of his injuries."

I winced a little at the analytical sound of her voice. She shouldn't know how to tell how long ago a person had been hurt.

There was a crowd of people moving toward shore. Vehicles weren't permitted on the two-mile section of the old bridge connecting Pigeon Key to Knight's Key and Marathon, but I could see an ambulance stopped on the span just before the ramp.

"Is anyone alive?" I heard a man shout.

Savannah looked up. "Yes. A boy about six, maybe. But he's been hurt badly and looks malnourished and dehydrated."

Once we were in shallower water, I stood and pushed the boat toward the people waiting on shore.

The man who'd spoken was wading toward us. He was a big man. I'd seen him around Marathon quite often. He worked for the foundation that ran the island-turned-museum. The whole island appeared just as it had in Flagler's day.

"Jesse McDermitt?" he asked, recognizing me, and then helping to pull the boat ashore.

"Sorry to drop in like this, Brian," I said, remembering his name.

"Did y'all just jump off the bridge? Were you in the race?"

"Yeah," I said, as the boat hit a rock.

We moved to opposite sides and muscled the little skiff onto dry land. Well, dry rocks anyway.

It'd probably been fifteen or twenty minutes since we'd entered the water. I could usually swim for three times that long, with little effort, but towing the boat against the current had sapped the strength in my arms and legs.

The paramedics from the ambulance were quickly beside the boat, and Savannah got out, allowing them room to work. I could tell she wanted to stay and hold the boy's hand, even though he was still unconscious.

One of the paramedics looked up. "Does anyone know who he is?"

"A Cuban rafter, drifting on the tide," I replied. "Can he be moved off the boat? You could probably work better over there on the sand."

The paramedic, a guy I only knew as Drew, looked at me. "That policy ended three years ago, Jesse. We're just here to get him to the hospital. What happens after that is up to the courts and whether this boy has family here in the States."

"Everybody's got a cousin in Miami," I said, quoting the

popular Jimmy Buffett song. “Mind if my wife and I ride with you?” I jerked a thumb toward the Seven Mile Bridge. “It looks like we’re out of the race, and neither of us is wearing shoes.”

CHAPTER THREE

Brian and I helped the EMT guys carry the backboard over the rocky shoreline and sand to where they'd left the stretcher at the foot of the ramp. A uniformed deputy was standing there.

"Are you the one who found him?" the deputy asked.

"My wife and I," I replied, nodding toward Savannah, still holding the boy's hand.

"I'll need to get a statement."

"A boat was adrift with a little boy on it. We jumped in the water and brought the boat to Pigeon Key. Jesse and Savannah McDermitt. End of statement."

He joined us, jotting our names on a simple, spiral-bound notepad as the paramedics strapped the boy and the backboard to the stretcher and began wheeling it up the wooden ramp to the waiting ambulance.

I looked at his name tag—Deputy B. Fife.

I couldn't help but grin. "Anything else, Deputy Fife?"

"Before you ask, yes, that's my real name and no, my first name isn't Barney. It's Bradford."

I was sure he got that a lot, so I decided against asking if he

had one bullet in his shirt pocket.

"Anything else, Brad?" I asked instead.

"I'm going to need more than that simple statement," he said. "Like who is he and where did he come from."

"I don't know what else we can tell you, Deputy," I said. "Look at him. Then look at that boat and the ninety miles of open water across the Gulf Stream. Where do you think he came from? What do you think happened to his family? Your guess is as good as mine."

The boy was strapped to the gurney with a white sheet over him. He had dark features, and hair as black as night. There was a bruise around his left eye.

As we wheeled him up the ramp, the boy stirred and moaned. When he opened his eyes and looked around, I could see the fear etched on his face.

Savannah leaned over the little boy and spoke softly in Spanish, holding his hand reassuringly. "*Estás seguro. Estamos aquí para ayudarte,*" she said, telling him he was safe and we were helping him.

"What?" the boy murmured. "Where am I?"

Savannah and I looked at each other, confused. He not only spoke English, but with no accent.

The deputy and paramedics looked just as confused.

"What's your name?" Savannah asked. "Where are you from?"

The boy looked totally bewildered. "I don't know?" he whined, as we reached the waiting ambulance. "Are you my mom?"

We stood there in disbelief as they loaded him in. How does an American kid end up on a homemade Cuban boat?

The deputy turned to face me. "Now I have a lot more questions, Mr. McDermitt."

I looked at him, then at Savannah, and finally at the boy. His eyes were closed again.

"Can my wife go with him, deputy? I'll stay with you and answer any questions I can while we look at the boat. Something's not adding up here."

He nodded to Savannah, who climbed into the back of the ambulance, accepting a blanket from one of the paramedics.

"I'll meet you at the hospital in a little while," I told her.

Then the doors were closed, and the ambulance drove away.

"So, he's not Cuban," the deputy said.

"I was sure he was a Cuban refugee," I said, as we turned and started down the ramp.

"Understandable," Fife said, looking at the boat on the rocks. "He's definitely Hispanic and that boat looks like others I've seen rafters come over on."

At the bottom of the ramp, Fife stopped and pulled his notebook out again. As I watched, he quickly sketched the scene before us.

"During my rookie year, my partner always made me sketch what I saw," Fife said. "He told me it trains the eye to look for more details."

He finished and we crossed the sand to where Brian stood, keeping tourists away from the boat. Though the bridge was closed to private vehicular traffic, tourists still visited the island by ferry.

Fife wore jungle boots, typical for a lot of Florida cops. They had drain holes to let the water out. There weren't many places in the southern half of the state more than a stone's throw from

water.

Together, we waded around the rocks to the side of the boat.

"Oarlocks, but no oars," Fife said, taking his notepad out and jotting something down.

"And that transom has never seen an outboard," I added. "No markings from the mount."

Fife pulled the small piece of canvas out. There was nothing at all under it. No empty water bottles, no food containers, nothing.

"I wonder how long he'd been out there?" Fife asked, rhetorically.

"No more than three or four days without water," I replied, studying the canvas closer. "Check this out."

He leaned over the boat and I showed him a label sewn into the edge of the canvas cover.

Fife looked over at me. "Ray's Custom Canvas?"

"I know a place called that up in Fort Myers," I said.

"That's a hundred miles away."

"More than that," I said, as my mind calculated the currents. "A hundred and thirty to Fort Myers Beach."

"But a boat can't get this far without some means of propulsion."

"The Loop Current," I said. "It flows into the Gulf between the Yucatan and Cuba, then curves around to flow south along the Florida coast before it joins the Gulf Stream in the Straits."

"But that's still a long way," Fife offered, bending low and checking the boat's exterior hull.

"It flows at about three knots," I said, looking south across the new bridge, to where the two mighty currents converged. "If a boat drifting off Fort Myers was caught in the Loop, it could be

right out there in less than three days, allowing for twice daily tide changes that slow the current. Less if the Loop Current moved farther north."

"It moves?" Fife asked, obviously curious.

"At times, it barely flows into the Gulf before turning east," I replied. "Other times, it brushes the coast of Louisiana, the Panhandle, and the west coast. I never looked into why; maybe it has to do with how much flow is coming out of the Mississippi River."

"You sound like a cop," Fife said. "Or a scientist. What do you do for a living, Mr. McDermitt?"

I grinned at him. "I live," I replied. "And call me Jesse. Everyone around here does."

"What's that supposed to mean? I live?"

"I'm retired military. And I own a fishing and diving charter business. Savannah and I live on a private island I bought twenty years ago. We don't work for a living. We live for a living."

It was something my old friend, Tank had told me. He'd come to the Keys just before my and Savannah's wedding and stayed on. He'd told me then that he was dying of cancer and he just wanted to live for a living.

"I'm pretty sure the boat was made in Cuba," Fife said. "I've seen more than my share, not always with living passengers."

"A Cuban boat," I began, thinking out loud, "with an American kid on board, covered by a tarp made in Florida? One of these things doesn't match the other two."

"You sound like my lieutenant."

"Then he's a smart man," I said. "Always look for patterns and just because one thing doesn't fit, doesn't mean it's not a part of the pattern. Just like the Loop Current. It changes location and

anything floating on it is affected by the tides and wind. But its existence is a constant and the changes are anomalies."

"You sure you're not a cop?" he asked, peering closely at the transom board.

"I also own part of a security firm up island," I replied. "And over the years I've done some 'consulting' with federal and local law enforcement."

He bent over and examined the inboard side of the transom. "Hey, look at this."

I went back to where he was standing.

"It looks like a word is sort of carved or etched in the wood," he said, holding his smart phone up and trying to shield the sun to take a picture.

Leaning over, I picked up the canvas. When I held it up, it reflected some of the sun's light sideways across the transom, giving the markings more definition.

"Alberto Mar?" Fife asked, snapping several pictures.

The wood was soft and it looked like the name had been scratched into it with a small knife or something.

"Can you radio the ambulance?" I asked. "And see if the boy has a pocketknife?"

He pressed the button on his lapel mic and asked his dispatcher to contact the ambulance and find out. Then he continued to examine the little boat, scanning every part of it in turn.

A few minutes later, the dispatcher said that yes, the boy had a small, antique-looking, folding knife in his pants pocket.

"So, the kid's name's Alberto Mar," Fife said, rubbing his chin. "Ties in with his appearance. Not so much with his very American accent."

"Mar means sea in Spanish," I said. "Could be more to it that he didn't finish. Martinez, Marina, Martin… Probably a lot more."

Fife scribbled on his notepad again.

"I'd go with the notion that he's from the Fort Myers area," I offered. "Like you said, boats like this have drifted ashore many times. Maybe this one ended up on Florida's west coast somehow."

Fife nodded his agreement. "That makes more sense than an American-made tarp and an American kid ending up in Cuba and drifting back."

"What should I do with the boat?" Brian asked.

"Let's get it up on the sand," Fife replied. "At least until we find out who the kid is and where he and this boat came from."

Brian pointed to three other men, ordering them into the water. Together, the six of us easily lifted the boat over the rocks and carried it up onto the beach.

"Can I give you a lift to the hospital?" Fife asked. "I'm going there anyway."

"Thanks," I replied. "It doesn't look like there's anything more to learn here."

We went up the ramp to where his cruiser was parked, the engine idling. There was a large K-9 stencil on the rear fender, and I could see a dog in the back of the patrol car.

Fife unlocked the car and opened the passenger door. "Major gets less excited if I hold the door for someone," Fife explained.

I got in. Barely. The passenger seat had been slid forward about as far as it would go and there was a plethora of gadgets situated within easy reach of the driver's seat, but they encroached on the passenger side.

The dog looked at me, his ears up and alert to my every move. He was a shepherd of some kind.

Fife got in and turned a rugged-looking laptop toward him. "Give me a minute to file a preliminary report," he said, taking his notepad and phone out. He propped the pad on the dash and plugged his phone into the laptop, and then began pushing keys and typing.

"Is Major a Belgian shepherd?" I asked, deciding the dog was too small to be a German shepherd.

"Collectively, there are four breeds of Belgian shepherd dogs," Fife explained, as he pushed the laptop away and put the cruiser in gear. "Major's a Belgian Malinois, which literally means made in Mechelen, Belgium in French. They're not as big as German shepherds, but every bit as smart and maybe a little faster, due to their more compact size. They're definitely more agile."

"How long have you been working with him?"

"Since K-9 school when he was six months old," Fife replied. "He's almost nine now and will be retiring soon."

"What happens then?"

Fife glanced in the rearview mirror, which I noticed was angled down, so he could see the dog. "Hopefully, I'll move to a desk job about then and Major will just retire to my home. But if I'm assigned a new dog, Major will be put out for adoption. They usually get adopted by someone within the department, which is good. But a handler with a working dog isn't permitted to adopt another."

"That would make sense," I said. "At least you could see him sometimes."

"To be honest, Mr. Mc—Jesse, if I don't get the desk job

when he retires, I've been thinking of leaving the department so he can stay with me."

I knew that police dogs, like most working dogs, were extremely loyal to their handlers. Apparently, it went both ways.

Once off the bridge, it was a short ride to the hospital—less than two miles. The new hospital wasn't complete yet and the doctors and nurses were still using the modular ER facility erected in the parking lot adjacent to the new building. The original hospital had been damaged so badly during Irma, more than three years ago, that it had to be closed.

"Any word on when the new hospital will open?" I asked as we got out of the cruiser.

"They say they're still on track for a fall opening," he replied, then leaned in to tell the dog, "*Bleibe.*"

I grinned. "We use German commands for our Rottweiler, too. Since he's Belgian, why don't you use French?"

"We have several breeds and use German commands for all of them," he said. "My first dog was a German shepherd. He died in the line of duty."

I'd heard about a police dog being killed by a knife-wielding man strung out on meth, about eight years ago.

"Was he the one who rescued the little girl from the meth monster?"

Fife nodded as he pulled the door open. "You heard about it?"

"Everyone in the Keys did," I replied. "I was at his funeral with my dog, Finn."

"A Rottweiler named Finn?" he asked, following me in.

"No. Finn's our yellow Lab. Woden's our Rottweiler."

"Cool names."

Savannah rose from a chair and came toward me. I held her in my arms for a moment before asking if there was any news about the little boy.

"Nothing yet," she replied.

"We think his name might be Alberto," I said.

"I'll go to the desk and get them to relay that to the doctors," Fife said. "Maybe it'll jog the boy's memory."

Savannah was still wrapped in the blanket from the ambulance and her clothes were damp. Having been outside in the sun, my clothes were almost dry.

A man in scrubs came through the restricted door and looked around. Seeing Fife talking to the admitting nurse, he went over to him.

Savannah and I followed.

"Are you the policeman who found the boy?" the man asked.

"Deputy Fife," he replied, then nodded to me and Savannah. "They were the ones who found and rescued him. The boy's name might be Alberto. Any idea what happened to him?"

The man turned toward me, and I could see his nametag. "I'm Jesse McDermitt and this is my wife, Savannah. How is the boy, Doctor Reynolds?"

"He's alive," the doctor replied. "But he wouldn't have survived another day. He's severely dehydrated and seems to have been malnourished for quite some time. But that's not what worries me. We're treating him for that."

"What else?" Savannah asked.

"Maybe three days ago, this boy received a beating. He has two fractured ribs. He's awake but doesn't know who he is or where he comes from."

CHAPTER FOUR

"So, you both jumped off the Seven Mile into skinny water?" Rusty asked. "You coulda broke your necks."

There'd been school buses on Little Duck Key to bring the runners back, but Rusty had driven to the other side of the Seven Mile Bridge before the race to see the finish and bring me and Savannah back. When we didn't arrive, he started asking some of the runners he knew, and someone told him what had happened.

"It seemed like the thing to do at the time," Savannah said.

We'd walked from the hospital to the Anchor, hoping that Rusty would be back soon, because we'd left a change of clothes in his truck. Now that he'd returned, we were in dry clothes, but since we hadn't anticipated losing our shoes, our feet were bare.

Savannah was the barefoot type anyway.

Rusty just looked at her a moment. "Seemed like the thing to do, huh? You coulda just called 911 and let the water cops handle it."

Savannah shook her head. "That little boy needed help, Rusty. So, we helped."

He looked across the bar at me and shook his head. "I can understand you doing something dumb like that. You're just a

grunt. But why'd you make her jump, too?"

I opened my mouth to speak, but Savannah beat me to it.

"He doesn't *make* me do anything," she said.

"That's true," I agreed, turning toward her. "In fact, I was a bit pissed that she did. But as it turned out, I needed her there."

"Is the boy gonna be okay?" he asked.

Amy slipped past Rusty and picked up the TV remote, turning up the sound on the TV over the bar. The image on the screen was from a helicopter that had been covering the race. As the camera zoomed in, I watched myself leap the safety barrier, Savannah right behind me.

"Earlier today, in the middle of the Seven Mile Bridge Race, two unidentified runners jumped off the bridge to rescue a boy who was adrift in a small boat. Authorities speculate that the boy is a Cuban refugee who'd been adrift for several days. A spokesperson at Fishermen's Community Hospital said only that the boy is alive and will recover but will remain hospitalized for observation. More tonight at six. This is Camilla Crawford, ABC Action News, reporting."

"Sounds like he'll be okay," Amy said, answering Rusty's question. "But didn't you say the little boy didn't speak Spanish?"

"He only said a few words," Savannah replied. "But he spoke English, and I didn't detect any accent."

We were alone in the bar, but I leaned in conspiratorially. "I think they're saying that because the kid had been beaten. They probably don't want whoever did it to know he's alive."

Rusty shook his head sadly. "Somebody beat him up, then set him adrift in a leaky boat to die. Animals."

There were other scenarios.

"Maybe he got in the boat himself," I said. "To get away. The doctors think his amnesia might be temporary. Until he

comes out of it, nobody will know."

The door opened and Deputy Fife strolled in, followed closely by Detective Clark Andersen, who I'd met back in December.

"Mr. and Mrs. McDermitt," Fife said, approaching us. "This is—"

"Detective Andersen," I said, rising from my stool.

I shook hands with them both and introduced the others.

"Any word on the kid?" I asked.

"He'll pull through," Andersen said. "I've been assigned the investigation."

"Like I told Deputy Fife, we don't know anything more about him than you do."

Andersen shifted his feet, then looked over at Savannah for a second. He was uncomfortable. "The thing is, I want to ask you a favor."

Andersen had been the lead investigator when Cobie Murphy had gone missing before Thanksgiving. He didn't progress much beyond finding her car and it was parked at the place where she worked—the *first* place they looked. Since she'd been found, he and I had talked a few times.

"A favor?" Savannah asked.

"Yes, ma'am," he said, swallowing, and causing his Adam's apple to bob. "We're completely blind here. The victim can't even tell us who he is, much less who did this to him. It could be almost anyone."

"What's the favor?" I asked.

"The doctor said he could be healthy enough to leave in just a few days. The kid's already eating everything in sight. The temporary hospital isn't set up for long term, non-emergency care and he doesn't warrant being transferred to another hospital up

island. Apparently, his amnesia is psychological and doesn't have anything to do with being beat up."

Savannah's hand went to her mouth as she gasped audibly. "Where would he go? He can't be any more than five or six."

"The doctor said he's closer to eight," Andersen said. "He thinks the kid's been treated badly for most of his life. He said he looks younger than his teeth show. That's how they tell the age of a kid's bod—um—he just thinks he's older than he looks."

"Bless his little heart," Savannah said softly.

"The thing is," Andersen began, "we don't want him to go into foster care until we know for sure who he is."

Rusty leaned on the bar. "I wouldn't want my worst enemy's kid to go into South Florida's foster system."

Andersen looked over at Rusty. "That's why I'm here."

"What do you mean?" I asked.

Andersen turned to face me, squaring his shoulders with his hands clasped in front, almost like what Pap would have called "hat in hand" or contrite, except Andersen didn't have a hat.

"I'd like to ask you if the boy might be able to stay with you," he said. "I know you live off the grid up in the Contents, and I checked you out. The kid'll be safer there than anywhere I know of."

"Wait just a sec—"

"We'll do it," Savannah blurted out, cutting me off. "You can bring him up or we'll come get him, whenever he's ready."

"Savannah," I said, looking over at her.

When she turned my way, the look in her eyes froze any further words that were forming in my mouth.

"He'll stay with us, Jesse. And that's all there is to it."

"But—"

"Was there something I said that you didn't understand?" she asked, fierce conviction in her words. "That little boy has been through enough. If he needs a place to stay or someone to help guide him, we can do it."

I started to open my mouth again, and she put a finger to my lips.

"Hush now. It's decided."

A smart man knows when he's been beat. Savannah rarely insisted on anything. Though I knew doing this could bring trouble to us, there was no chance of my overriding her decision.

I turned toward the detective. "Okay."

"This is completely unorthodox," he said. "But I know what you're capable of and this is the only idea I could come up with."

He looked over at Rusty and Amy. "This can't go any further."

"It'll have to," Rusty said. "I'll tell my wife but that'll be as far as it goes. We don't hide things from each other."

I shook my head. "It'll go beyond that," I said, turning to my wife. "If we do this, I'm asking Deuce to send a couple of guys down to stay with us."

"Tony for sure," she said. "Obviously, Paul, and maybe Andrew?"

I grinned at her and nodded. "GMTA." Then I turned toward Andersen. "Men I trust and have worked with at Homeland Security."

Andersen looked at each of us in turn. "Let me have your number. I'll call you when I know anything."

I handed him a *Gaspar's Revenge Charter Service* card. One that I kept in my wallet. "My cell number's on the back."

He took it and flipped it over. "It might not come to pass," he

said, putting the card in his wallet. "If the kid regains his memory, we might be able to find his parents."

"But you said he'd been abused most of his life," Savannah said.

"We can investigate that," he replied. "But if his parents want him, it'll be difficult not to return him. Being the victim of poverty isn't abuse."

"We'll do whatever is needed," I said, putting my arm around my mama-bear wife. "He'll be safe and well-cared for with us."

"I believe you," Andersen said.

Then the two cops turned and walked out.

"We'd best be getting back," I said. "Jimmy has a charter scheduled for tomorrow and we have to get *El Cazador* ready."

"Reef-fishing charter?" Rusty asked.

"Yeah," I replied, not sounding very enthusiastic. "Three guys from Atlanta."

"Jimmy can't handle that himself?"

"He can," I replied. "Until about the second case of beer."

"That kind, huh?" Rusty said. "Happens every April. Where ya fishin'?"

"G Marker," I said. "It's close enough they can swim to Big Pine if I decide to toss 'em overboard."

CHAPTER FIVE

When Savannah and I returned to our island in the Content Keys, Jimmy had *Cazador* out from under the house and tied up to the south pier.

"Everything okay?" I asked, as we tied up the little Grady in front of the much bigger thirty-two-foot Winter.

Jimmy's head appeared from where he was bent over the raised center console. "Yeah. All fine now. I just wanted to do a good engine inspection and cleaning. She hasn't been out in a while."

He was right. Most of our charters were aboard *Gaspar's Revenge*, my big forty-five-foot offshore machine. She was built for blue water fishing, going after mahi, tuna, or billfish in the Gulf Stream. *El Cazador* was a diesel-powered center console, with lots of room to walk around her decks from bow to stern—ideal for stationary reef fishing with larger groups. The downside was she had only a single engine, where the *Revenge* had two. Jimmy was always nervous about going offshore on one engine.

I looked down into the Winter's engine bay, which occupied most of the space below the console. The whole console was hinged at the helm area and the console and T-top were in the

raised position.

"Looks brand-new," I said. "What time did you say we were picking the charter up?"

"Sunrise," he replied. "At the Rusty Anchor."

"Where are they staying?"

"Old Wooden Bridge Marina," Jimmy replied. He'd worked for me for a long time and knew what I wanted to know. "I talked to Old Jason last night, man," he continued. "Just to check in on what's where offshore. You know how he likes to gossip."

I did. Old Jason wasn't old. But he was older than another guide by the same name, and he was a good source of information about the goings-on in the northern part of Big Pine, as well as what was happening offshore.

"He told me he met our clients this morning," Jimmy continued, "after they apparently tore up Key West last night."

"Having second thoughts?" I asked.

I was particular about who I took out. We didn't charter because we had to. Everything we owned was paid for, free and clear. I just didn't like being around unpleasant people. And when you were miles from shore on a small boat with unpleasant people, it got damned crowded.

"Nah. Nothing like that," he said, lowering the console. "Dink and Ash put them on a big tarpon run yesterday afternoon. Dink said the three guys were rowdy and boisterous, but not a problem."

"I'm going to go up and put together something for lunch," Savannah said. "Any requests?"

Jimmy and I looked at each other, then back at Savannah. She turned before we could say anything.

"Lobster salad it is," she said, turning, and heading up the

steps.

"With melted garlic butter on the side!" I called out.

She tossed her hair over one shoulder and looked down at me. "Not happening. Too much cholesterol."

I turned back toward Jimmy and shrugged. "At least it's lobster."

"We're both kinda lucky, man. Know what I mean?"

"Yeah," I replied, as Savannah reached the top of the steps and disappeared into our house. "In a lot of ways."

He stepped up on the dock as Finn came down the steps. "Neither one of us is getting any younger, man. And our ladies will see to it that we live a damned long time."

Jimmy was more than a decade younger than me and had been with a woman named Naomi for quite some time now. She was Sid's niece and a part-time model. Like Savannah, Naomi kept Jimmy on a healthy diet and had even gotten him to cut down on smoking pot.

Not that either of us were gluttonous slobs before they came along—we ate mostly seafood and I'd had an aquaculture garden for many years. We worked hard for exercise and were fit and healthy, for the most part. But Jimmy was right; we weren't getting any younger.

Finn came trotting toward me, his big head bobbing and his tail smacking his flanks. He melted on top of my feet, nudging my hand for an ear scratch.

"Where's Woden?" I asked, as I rubbed the fur on Finn's neck and head.

"Last I saw him," Jimmy said, "he was lying in the sun out on the end of the north pier. How'd the race go?"

"I guess we're not the only ones growing old," I offered. "We

didn't finish the race."

"Huh? You and Savannah are great runners, man."

"We jumped off the bridge," I replied, then went on to tell him about the boy in the boat and the visit by Detective Andersen.

"So, the little guy's gonna come and stay here?"

"Maybe," I replied. "We'll just have to wait and see."

"We have two bedrooms," Jimmy offered. "Be no problem for him to shack up with us, man."

"I hadn't even thought about where he's gonna stay," I said, as we went up the steps to the deck.

Naomi was just coming out of the house when we reached the top.

"Savannah told me what happened," she said. "I was just coming to get you guys. She wants to move the little bed from our spare room into your living room after lunch, Jesse."

The three of us went inside. Savannah had the table set and was at the stove, heating up small chunks of lobster tail left over from the previous night to add to a big salad bowl of greens and tomatoes.

"We don't have to take Jimmy and Naomi's spare bed," I told her. "We can pull one of the bunks out of the bunkhouse. It's time to turn it into something else anyway."

"It's easier to get to," she replied, hurriedly dumping the lobster bites into a strainer, "and it doesn't have to come apart. We can move it after lunch."

"Slow down," I told her, taking the strainer from her hand as it dripped coconut oil on the deck. "We have a couple of days, at least."

When she turned to face me, I could see that her eyes were

red and rimmed with tears. "We can't let them send that boy back to his parents."

There'd been signs over the last nine months since Flo'd gone off to college—signs I should have paid better attention to. Savannah had been nervous at times, worried. She and our daughter had been inseparable for eighteen years, living on a boat, moving from port to anchorage, just the two of them. She was a fantastic mother; of that I had no doubt.

Was she experiencing withdrawal over not having a child to look after and care for?

I moved her to the table and sat her down in a chair, then knelt in front of her. "He's still at Fishermen's," I said. "We can bring him up here as soon as the doc says he's okay enough. But legally, if his parents want him back, there isn't much the police can do."

"There has to be, Jesse. That little boy has been starved and abused all his life."

"We don't know that," I said. "Yes, he suffered a beating. But the malnourishment could have just been in the last year or two. It might not even have been his parents who did it. Remember how frail Cobie looked when we brought her home?"

She nodded and started to say something, but I put a finger to *her* lips this time. "We don't have to rush," I told her, moving my hand to her cheek, and cupping it. "Jimmy and I will go to the bunkhouse and take one of the bunks apart. Maybe all of them. We can have one of the uppers here before nightfall."

She leaned into my hand and the tears started as she fell into my arms. "I just can't get the thought out of my head of what he might have had to endure."

Naomi moved beside us and put an arm around Savannah.

"Or he can just stay with me and Jimmy and have his own room."

Savannah nodded, wiping her eyes with my shirt. Then she looked up at me. "Yeah, I know you're right. I don't know what came over me."

"I do," I said. "Flo hasn't been home in over a month."

"Let's eat," she said, nodding and going back to the little kitchen area.

The four of us sat down and ate quickly. There was always something to do on the island, and adding another chore was just something we took in stride.

Later, as Jimmy and I were taking one of the bunkbeds apart in what for twenty years had been a "bunkhouse for fishermen," he stopped and looked out the window.

"Is something wrong with Savannah?" he asked.

I shrugged, though he had his back to me. "Women sometimes have anxiety after giving birth—postpartum depression, they call it. Maybe it's some sort of separation anxiety from Flo going off to school in Gainesville."

He turned and started taking the slats out of the bed. "Empty nest? Yeah, man, that makes sense. She seems to have lost her direction lately. Like a boat without a rudder."

Together, we lifted the frame of the upper bunk off the lower one and set it down.

"You noticed it too?" I asked, leaning against the frame. "For years, she's had the double stress of raising a child alone and living on a boat. After long periods in a high-stress environment, I think people get used to it some, adapt, and then, when the pressure's gone, they go into a slump. I'm just not real sure what to do about it."

"Dude, you fix things when they break," Jimmy said. "It's what you do. Hell, it's what most men do. But she ain't broke, man. So, you can't fix her."

"What's that leave?" I wondered out loud.

"Maybe she just needs a project," he said. "Something to give her direction."

I shook my head. "I hope bringing the kid here doesn't make things worse."

"Think we can get the frame through the door without taking it apart?" Jimmy asked.

"Should be able to," I said, pushing off the frame. "We'll need to turn it sideways and keep it level as I go down the steps backward."

Who would beat up a little kid after starving them? I wondered, as we lifted the frame and maneuvered it to the door.

The cops didn't have much to go on. The boy couldn't tell them anything. All they knew was that there'd been a tarp on the boat that was made in a shop in my hometown. I decided that I'd give a friend a call who lived near there and see if he knew about any missing kids.

My phone vibrated in my pocket. "Hang on, Jimmy. Set it down a sec. I have a phone call."

"I remember a time when you didn't even know where your phone was," Jimmy said, as we set the frame down. "I remember finding it once in the cockpit fridge on the *Revenge*."

I fished my phone out and looked down at the screen. "The times, they are a changin'."

"Dude, you can't quote Dylan when talking about a cell phone."

I stabbed the *Accept* button. "Scott, it's been a while."

Scott Bond was a former Navy lieutenant, and like my friend and partner, Deuce Livingston, a SEAL. He'd worked for a couple of years with Deuce's Caribbean Counterterrorism Command.

"Hi, Jesse. Yes, it has. How are things down in Florida?"

"I wouldn't know," I replied, grinning. "I haven't been up there in a while. I remarried a few months ago and we're very content down here in the Keys. What's up?"

"Congratulations!" he said, sounding genuinely enthusiastic. "Listen, I got a call from a friend up in the Windy City—a PI named Kevin Grainger. He was asking for a referral in the Fort Myers area to do some discreet protection work."

"Why didn't you call Deuce?" I asked.

"Well, Fort Myers is your hometown, right? I figured you might be interested, and you're more likely to know someone there than he would."

I'd moved away from Fort Myers when I was seventeen and joined the Corps. While it was my hometown-of-record, I'd only returned there a handful of times since I'd left the Marines. But there it was, popping to the surface twice in one day.

"Do you have any details?" I asked.

"He wouldn't give me much. A former client, a wealthy woman by the sound of it, has a teenage niece who got into a scrape with some gangbangers down there. The rich aunt wants to protect the girl and her family without them knowing it. Can she contact you directly?"

I thought about it for a moment. I disliked giving my number to people I didn't know. "Yeah," I said. "Tell him to have her call me at the *Rusty Anchor* tomorrow evening. You still have the number there?"

"I do. What time's too late?"

After the charter, Jimmy and I had decided to stay aboard *Salty Dog*, rather than try to get back to the island in the dark. Lobster season was over, but there were still six weeks left in stone crab season and the traps' buoys were just as dangerous to a prop as any other.

"Any time after nineteen hundred," I replied, figuring we'd have the Atlanta bubbas back to the dock before sunset.

"Will do," Scott said, as we ended the call.

"What was that all about?" Jimmy asked.

"That was Scott Bond," I replied. "You remember him. He used to be part of Deuce's team and has a friend who's in trouble."

Jimmy looked at me with real concern in his eyes.

"Don't worry," I said. "It's just a little protection job, which I never did much of anyway. He was just looking for a referral. But don't say anything to Savannah about it. Or Florence when she comes home."

"Uh-oh."

"What's that supposed to mean?"

"You're in operational mode, man. You just called Flo by her full name."

CHAPTER SIX

After setting up the bed in the living room, it looked more cluttered than it ever had. My little house was only a thousand square feet or so, and the living room and kitchen were more than half of that. My friend Tank had recently bought a house on Grassy Key that had a master bedroom nearly as big as my whole house.

"Why don't I move my workbench into the bunkhouse?" I said. "Then we can move the bed up against that wall under the window."

"I thought you were going to make it a place for Flo," Jimmy said.

Savannah took my hand. "He was. But now Kim and Marty are house hunting on the mainland. They plan to settle in Everglades City or maybe Goodland."

"Really?" Jimmy asked. "That's cool. So, that means the west bunkhouse will be Flo's permanently?"

I nodded. "At least as permanent as it had been for Kim."

The west bunkhouse had undergone many changes over the years. Initially, it had been a simple bunkhouse, just like the other one—six sets of bunkbeds and a small desk. It came in handy

when Deuce's counterterrorism team needed a secluded place to stay and train. But his team had included three women, so it'd quickly turned into two rooms, basically overnight, with the smaller half having two sets of bunkbeds, as well as a desk—sort of a command-and-control center for Chyrel Koshinski, the team's computer and communications tech.

Then Kim came to live with me, and she turned the larger half into a small studio apartment. When Hurricane Irma destroyed it and just about everything else on the island, we'd rebuilt it into a home for her and Marty. But by then, they were working for Fish and Wildlife up on the mainland.

"I have an idea," Jimmy said. "Let's leave two sets of bunkbeds for whenever we have people on the island and use the rest of the space as a workshop. Tearing down an outboard in the hot sun is getting old."

He had an excellent point. I could rebuild a carb or rewire a dash at my workbench but working on one of the many outboards we had meant mounting it to a sawhorse and working outside.

Having a full shop would be great, but it'd be an ambitious project, to say the least. And to what end? I was scheduled to fly over to Bimini in just six days, to take command of *Ambrosia.*

"I'm leaving next week," I reminded him.

Savannah's face went kind of pale. "But what about Alberto?"

"We're not even sure that's his name," I said. "And we don't even know if the police will be bringing him here. They might have already found his parents."

She eyed me cautiously. "We should go on the assumption that he'll be staying with us. What is it you always say? Better to have it and not need it than to need it and not have it."

I hated when she used my own logic against me.

Taking her shoulders, I looked into her eyes. "Yes, we should. But we have obligations. If he does come to stay with us, and it extends beyond next weekend, you may be taking care of him on your own."

"Me and Naomi will be here, man," Jimmy added. "If it comes to pass, we'll help take care of him."

I looked from Jimmy back to Savannah. "And what about when I finish the familiarization cruise and you come to join me? We were planning to live aboard, for the most part, coming back here once a month or so. Remember? You wanted big ocean adventures."

"We can bring him with us," she said defiantly. "You should call Jack and tell him now."

"I can't insist—"

"Yes, you can," she said, cutting me off. "We already told him that if he wants you at the helm, it was a package deal."

She had me there. Jack Armstrong had already agreed that Savannah would be joining us as part of the crew and that our kids could visit from time to time. But this wasn't quite the same.

"We don't know anything at all about him," I argued. "For all we know, the boy might be a pickpocket or an arsonist."

"He's just a little boy," she scolded. "And he needs help."

"Okay," I conceded. "I'll call Jack."

"Now."

"Yes, right now." I turned to Jimmy. "Start clearing my bench. We'll move it tonight."

Savannah smiled as I dug my cell phone from my pocket and turned to walk out onto the deck. Outside, I pulled up Jack's number and tapped the *Call* button.

"Good evening, Captain," Jack said, his voice almost jovial. "Nils and I were just talking about you. We're both looking forward to your arrival next week. *Ambrosia* is nearly ready to sail."

Nils Hansen had delayed his retirement long enough. He was in his seventies now and still as sharp-minded as ever, but he was tired of being at sea all the time. I'd already delayed taking command twice.

"Yeah, Jack. About that," I began.

Then I went on to tell him about the events of the day and Savannah's idea.

"How old is the boy, again?" he asked.

"We're not really certain," I replied. "The doctor thinks he's about six or eight."

There was a long pause before he spoke again. "You know I grew up on oil exploration ships and platforms," he finally said. "It won't be easy—not for him or you."

I remembered him telling me that once. I also remembered him telling me about his own son, who had been killed along with his wife in the World Trade Center attack.

"This isn't my idea," I said. "Savannah insisted after the detective told us the boy would go into foster care."

"I happen to agree with her," Jack said. "A kid could do a lot worse than having you and her as parents or foster parents."

"That's just it, Jack. We're not foster parents. Hell, I'm a grandfather and our youngest is in college. I'm sure this arrangement will only be temporary. The detective just needs a safe place for the kid until he can get to the bottom of things."

"Bring him," Jack said. "And bring Savannah on Friday. I'll get the crew busy converting Nils's quarters into a two-bedroom

suite, joining it with the cabin next to it."

"Whose cabin is next to it?" I asked, surprised that he'd agreed so quickly.

"That's the first mate's cabin," he replied. "Sara is flying home tomorrow. You'll have a new first mate, and he can take a cabin on the main deck."

Sara Patrick had been Nils's first mate for more than ten years. We'd had a long-term, long-distance relationship that ended some years ago, but the split had been amicable—neither of us had ever been emotionally committed—and I'd just assumed we'd move into an awkward working relationship.

"She's leaving?" I asked.

"First flight out tomorrow. She's getting married, Jesse."

Married? I hadn't even been aware that she was seeing anyone.

"Well... good for her," I said. "Who's the lucky man?"

"He's an Englishman by the name of Brent Tumlinson. They met when we were doing that project in the Seychelle Islands."

"I'm happy for her, Jack."

"And she was happy for you," Jack replied. "So, bring Savannah and the boy on Friday. We'll have things ready. If the police need him to go back, you and he can fly back in less than a day."

We ended the call, and I went back inside, a little bewildered.

"What did he say?" Savannah asked.

"He said to bring you and the boy on Friday. He's having Nils's cabin converted into a two-bedroom suite."

"His cabin's on the bridge deck," she said. "I remember from the tour Jack took us on. The only other cabin on that deck is Sara's."

"Sara Patrick will soon be Sara Tumlinson," I said. "She's

leaving *Ambrosia*."

"She's getting married?"

"Apparently so," I replied. "A British guy she met in the Seychelles last year."

I helped Jimmy finish boxing things up from my workbench. It was a heavy piece, so everything had to be removed.

"Let's just get it over there," I said, as we lifted the bench and started toward the door. "We can remove the other beds tomorrow, then set things up how we want later."

With the bench out on the deck, Jimmy and I went back inside and moved the little bed under the window. Savannah slipped down to the *Revenge* and got some extra linens from the guest cabin, which had two single bunks. While she set about making the bed up, Jimmy and I went outside and started to lug the bench across the clearing.

"What if the boy doesn't come?" Jimmy asked. "All this work would be for naught."

"No, it won't," I replied. "It's what Savannah wants."

We got the bench inside and returned for the boxes of fly-tying equipment, tools, and the other odds and ends that had accumulated on it and in its cabinets and drawers.

By the time we finished around 2100, the first quarter moon was already past its zenith and heading toward the western sky. The air was a little on the chilly side, so I started a fire in the ring. We'd worked right through sundowners, so I figured a couple of beers might be in order.

The fire ring was one of the few things left after Hurricane Irma. It'd been on the island long before I bought it. The thick, heavy steel ring had had some rust back then, but I'd been able to clean it up and maintain it all this time. It was too heavy for the

hurricane-force winds to blow away, but the storm surge and waves that had put the whole island under water had moved it a few feet.

Within a few minutes, bright colored flames were dancing in the center of the ring. Savannah must have seen it, because when I looked up, I saw her coming down the back steps carrying a small cooler.

We make a good team, I thought.

Savannah and I had been finishing each other's sentences and anticipating one another's wants and needs very soon after we'd left on our Western Caribbean cruise over a year ago.

As she approached, Jimmy and Naomi crossed the short distance from their house. He was also carrying a small cooler.

I took my usual seat on a low bench we'd made from a cypress tree that'd washed up over the winter.

Savannah sat beside me and opened the cooler, handing me a stubby brown bottle of Red Stripe and an opener.

"You can have two," she said. "You need to get up early."

Jimmy and Naomi sat silently on a couple of worn beach chairs. He pulled a bottle of mango juice from his cooler and set it aside. Then he took a bottle of wine out and looked over at Savannah.

"Wine?" he asked.

"I'll just have one of Jesse's beers."

He poured wine into a plastic cup and handed it to Naomi. Then the four of us sat quietly for a long moment.

Jimmy finally broke the silence. "It ain't gonna be the same around here, man."

"How so?" I asked.

"Y'all being gone," he said.

"We were gone for most of last year."

"But we knew you were coming back, dude," Jimmy said, "This feels a lot more…permanent, I guess."

"We'll be back once a month or so," I offered, then took a long pull from my beer.

"At first." Jimmy sighed and took a drink of his juice. "But that ship goes all over the world, man. How's this little island ever gonna compare with living on a two-hundred-foot yacht?"

"It's not a yacht," I replied. "At least not anymore. It's a working research vessel." I looked around the island's interior, bathed in the light of the dancing orange and green flames. "This is home," I said quietly. "No other place will ever compare. Look at it this way; you and Naomi will have the whole island to yourselves."

He reached over and put a hand affectionately on Naomi's knee. "I know, *hermano*. I'm just gonna miss you. That's all."

CHAPTER SEVEN

The charter the following day was, for the most part, uneventful. At least nobody had to swim to shore. The guys from Atlanta caught a lot of fish; grouper, snapper, a few Spanish mackerel, even a big amberjack, a species we called reef donkeys because of their enormous strength and durability. It took two of the Atlantans to boat it.

At sunset, we had them back at the Rusty Anchor, where we'd picked them up. By then, they were drunk and happy as clams. Jimmy cleaned their fish for them, and they tipped him well. By 2030, he and I were at the bar and the bubbas were headed back to their hotel.

"Sounds like quite a day," Rusty said, after Jimmy recounted the events.

"Yeah," I agreed. "I think they had a good time. I know they caught a lot of fish."

"Beer?"

"Nothing for me, man," Jimmy said, spotting his girlfriend coming through the door. "Naomi's here. We're going out for a while, then back to her condo."

"Sure," I said to Rusty, checking my watch.

"You expecting someone, too?"

"Phone call," I replied.

"You done called Savannah when you first got here," he said. "She s'posed to call you back?"

"Someone else," I replied.

"Well," Jimmy said, slipping an arm around Naomi's waist, "we're off to a party, *amigos*. We'll probably be back to the island by mid-morning."

I nursed a few beers after Jimmy left and ate a blackened grouper sandwich. It'd been a long day and I was tired. I should have specified a time for the woman to call.

Just after 2200, the antique rotary phone Rusty kept under the bar rang and he picked it up. "Rusty Anchor."

He listened for a moment, then looked across the bar at me. I nodded, expecting the call.

"Hang on," he said, holding the receiver against his chest. "Some woman for you."

"I'll take it."

He pulled the phone's base out and set it on the bar, passing me the receiver. I put the clunky device to my ear.

"This is Jesse McDermitt," I said. "Speak."

"Mr. McDermitt, my name is Nancy Liddell. I'm sorry for calling so late, but it was the only time I could call for reasons I'll explain in a moment."

Although I was expecting the call, I had to know it was the right person. "How did you know where to find me, Nancy?"

"A private investigator who did some work for me back in Chicago named Kevin Grainger found you for me. Kevin used to work for DHS with an associate of yours and that associate gave Kevin your name and where I might reach you."

"The associate's name?"

"Scott Bond."

"Fair enough," I said. "Scott's a good man and I know him well. How can I help you, ma'am?"

"Please, just call me Nancy."

"Okay, Nancy, how can I help you?"

"First, I'd like to apologize again for calling so late. I'm in Boston right now with my niece and I had to wait for her to go to bed before calling you. I don't want her to know I'm doing what I'm doing."

"No need to apologize. What's going on?"

"I wanted to see if I could contract you to do some personal protection work."

"That's not something I do. I'm not sure why Scott gave you my name."

"Part of the reason is that I specified that the person or persons needed to be highly discreet. I don't wish my niece or her family to know that I've arranged this protection."

"Still not ringing any bells on my end, Nancy. I have on occasion done some consulting for DHS, but I've never done any PI or personal protection work. I'm afraid you got some bad info."

There was a pause, but I didn't hear the tell-tale click of her hanging up. Even if she were on a cell, there would be an audible click as the landline connection broke.

"Mr. McDermitt, I have a sixteen-year-old niece that I absolutely adore. She's one of the brightest, most ambitious, talented girls I've ever met or known and I'm terrified that she and her family might be targeted and killed by MS-13."

There was a pause. Then, as if she were not just asking but admitting something to herself, she added. "I need some help.

I'm fearful of what these animals might do to them."

MS-13? I thought, sliding my empty beer bottle toward Rusty.

He picked up the bottle with a questioning look. I nodded that I'd have one more.

"Are you still there, Mr. McDermitt?"

"I am. I was thinking. I'm not a big fan of the gang. Tell me a little more about your situation."

"Thank you, thank you!"

"Slow down, Nancy. I'm not saying I can help, but you've piqued my interest. What's the story with the niece and why are they after her?"

"I gather from what she told me that she interrupted an attempted kidnapping one evening about ten days ago. In the process, she beat up two of the gang members, grabbed the girl from them, and escaped with her on the back of her motorcycle."

"I thought you said she was sixteen?"

"She is."

"How big is she?" I asked, a bit incredulous.

"Tiny, maybe five feet, if she's lucky."

"I'm missing something here, Nancy. This doesn't jibe with what I know about the gang."

"I know, I know," she said. "I had the same questions, and I would have dismissed what she'd told me out of hand if I hadn't seen what she's capable of myself."

"What did you see?"

"As I mentioned, we're in Boston right now looking at colleges. Yesterday we stopped at a friend's jewelry store to have something appraised. While we were in there, a masked man wielding a shotgun broke in, disabled the armed guard and held all of us at gunpoint." She paused dramatically. "For about one

minute."

"Why just a minute?"

"That's how long it took for my niece to disarm him, knock him out, and then get him in cuffs."

"Miss Liddell, no offense, but that sounds like what we used to call a sea story in the Marines. Others might use the term bullshit."

"Swear to God. She disarmed him, hit him in the jaw with the butt of his own gun, and when that wasn't enough, she drew some sort of telescoping pipe out of her jacket and cracked him alongside the head and he went down."

"Sounds like a police baton. Has she had martial arts training or something?"

"Yes. Something happened to her last year—an altercation. After she told me about it, I introduced her to an Israeli friend who teaches self-defense. She was excited about it, so I paid for her membership for a year. She went almost every night. I gather she's gotten quite good at it over the last several months."

Israeli? I knew of only one martial art form from that region of the world, and the term martial art could only be applied to it in a very loose way. It's a combat fighting technique; not really for self-defense, but used to kill the enemy with whatever is available, including bare hands.

"Krav Maga."

"Yes, exactly. How did you know?"

"You said the instructor was Israeli. I know a little about it."

"Anyway, since she took down those two gang members, they've been actively looking for her and have already made three attempts to try and capture or kill her. I'm terrified that they're going to succeed."

"Where do you and she live?"

"I live on Boca Grande and Callie lives just outside Fort Myers on the Caloosahatchee."

"That's about 120 miles from me by boat."

"You'll help me!"

"No, sorry. I was thinking out loud. I need to give this some more thought. You said you're in Boston right now?"

"Yes, we're looking at colleges and we'll be here till Sunday."

"You said your niece was sixteen. Isn't she kind of young to be looking at colleges?"

"Not really. Callie's a high school senior right now. She started school young and she also skipped a grade."

"So, she's a brain, too. Why is it so important that she and her family be protected without their knowledge? It's much simpler to protect someone if they're compliant and following some basic rules."

"Is why really important?"

"It is to me," I replied, nodding to Dink as he headed for the back deck. "I never work with anyone unless all the cards are on the table."

"The main reason is that I'm afraid my sister and her husband will blame me for getting Callie involved with martial arts in the first place and forbid me from seeing her or allowing her to go off to an out-of-state college. They're prideful people and would resent the rich sister thinking she can buy their protection. From Callie's point of view, I just don't want to undermine her self-confidence."

"I see. Listen, I need to think about this. Your niece sounds like a good kid and she's likely in considerable danger. I want to do some research on MS-13 in Fort Myers. I want to know what I

would be up against before I give you an answer."

"What would you typically charge for an assignment like this?"

I grinned. She seemed honest and didn't dodge around. "I don't *do* assignments like this," I replied. "I'm sort of retired. If I were to somehow help you out with your problem, I would simply ask that you pay it forward and help someone else who needs it at a later date."

"I can't thank you enough, Mr. McDermitt."

"As I said, I'm not sure I *can* help, due to some other obligations, but I'm not without resources and contacts with others who might be able to help if I can't. Let me make a couple of calls. What's the address of your niece's home in Fort Myers? Also, you and I should exchange phone numbers. You were pretty lucky to have reached me here."

I signaled Rusty for a pen and he produced one from his pocket, along with his ever-present order pad, which he ripped a sheet from.

I flipped the paper over and scrawled Nancy's name and number on the back, along with her niece's address.

"Thank you so much, Mr. McDermitt. Call me back as soon as you know whether you can help."

"I will. And just call me Jesse."

Once Nancy disconnected, I held out the phone to Rusty so he could put it back under the bar. He had a quizzical look on his face as he passed me another Red Stripe.

"Who was that?" he asked.

"I don't know the woman. Scott Bond put her on to me."

He leaned over the bar. "Scott's a straight shooter. But you look worried. What'd she want?"

"She seemed nice," I said. "She's got a sixteen-year-old niece that she's very worried about. According to her, the niece stumbled onto an attempted MS-13 snatch of another young girl and the niece took out two of the gang members and saved the girl they were trying to abduct. Now MS-13 wants to put her in the ground or worse."

"*There's* a story with no happy ending."

"No kidding," I agreed. "You know how I feel about gangs. Every last one of their members is a skin-bag, wasting precious oxygen."

"You got that right. So, what did the woman want?"

"She wants me to provide protection for the girl and her family."

Rusty put down the glass he'd been polishing and looked up. "That ain't something you do."

"I know, but it sounds like this young girl has a ton of heart. What teenager puts her own life at risk to save a stranger these days?"

"She must be a big girl."

I shook my head, still a bit perplexed. "Nancy said she's just five feet tall. Told me the girl's had some Krav Maga training."

"My kind of lady," he said. "So, what are you going to do?"

"I'm not sure. Her niece is three years younger than Flo and going off to college in the fall. She sounds like a really good kid and I know that if Flo were in the same kind of trouble and someone could help keep her safe, I'd be eternally grateful to that person."

"There's a lot of worthy causes out there, Jesse," Rusty said, putting the glass away and wiping a bar that was already clean. "You can't save them all."

"I know. I've got to give it some thought and talk it over with Savannah tomorrow." I rose from my stool. "I'm going to head down to the *Dog*."

"You'll figure something out," he said. "Oh, Jesse, Rufus wanted me to give you a care package for Savannah." He reached under the bar and handed me a small paper bag, the top folded over neatly.

"What's in it?"

"I think it's some of that secret rub he puts on the fish. He won't give anyone the recipe, but he obviously thinks highly enough of Savannah to part with some of it."

I opened the bag and breathed in the incredible combination of allspice, nutmeg, ginger, garlic, cloves, and several other Caribbean spices I couldn't identify. Just the smell made my mouth water and I suddenly craved a fish sandwich.

"Man, does that smell good," I said, closing the bag back up. "Be sure to thank him for me. Savannah will love this."

"I will," he said. "Have a good night."

"You too, brother."

Outside, I walked around to the far side of the canal, where Savannah's boat was tied up. The warm night air was fragrant and rich with the scent of jasmine, frangipani, oiled deck planks, and exposed mudflats. The complex combination smelled familiar to me and was unique to the Florida Keys.

I stopped at *Sea Biscuit*, Savannah's Grand Banks trawler. No one was aboard, but I wanted to check her lines to make sure she was secure.

MS-13 gang activity in Fort Myers?

I had no idea they'd spread to that small town. So many changes were taking place. But the last thing I needed was

another project.

I caught myself as I walked back around the barge. Since when had helping to save the life of a sixteen-year-old girl become just another *project* to me?

"Come on, Jesse. Priorities!" I chided myself.

As I strolled back along the dock, I reviewed the conversation with Nancy in my mind. I had a lot going on. I was in the process of renovating the bunkhouse and I wanted to make the island more like a home for Savannah and less like a DHS training facility. Savannah and Flo had lived on *Sea Biscuit* for eighteen years. After returning from the cruise, we'd decided to create a land-based residence that felt like a home to both of us. That was my top priority. We'd even put up a tree on Christmas, a first for my little island.

I was also preparing to take the helm of *Ambrosia* with my new wife and possibly a little boy, who couldn't remember his name. *Ambrosia* was scheduled for sea trials next week, and by the summer we'd be on station off the coast of Brazil.

I figured Chyrel could probably provide some insight about gang activity in Fort Myers, but I wanted information about them from someone with boots on the ground.

When I stepped up to *Salty Dog's* deck, I unlocked the companionway hatch and switched on the lights, then went down to the navigation station, where my laptop was located.

I knew a guy by the name of Phil Tucker up in Miami. He was a corporal when I retired from the Corps, ending my active service, and I'd kept in touch with him off and on, since he was also from Florida. He'd EASed after four years, gone home, and taken a job with Miami-Dade PD. The last time I'd talked to him, he'd been promoted to detective.

I pulled up his name on my phone and he answered on the first ring.

"Phil, it's Jesse McDermitt."

"Semper Fi, Gunny. How're they hanging? Or should I ask are they still hanging?"

I chuckled at the dig on my advancing years. "They're hanging like the American Flag, brother—with dignity and pride."

"Of course, they are! What can I do for you? Are you in town?"

"Not right now," I replied. "I'm wondering if you can share any intel about MS-13 in Fort Myers?"

"Is this a DHS assignment?"

"You know I haven't worked for the government in years."

"Right...whatever you say, Gunny. Listen, I don't personally know anything, but I'd be happy to make a few calls. Will you be around an hour from now?"

"Sure. I'll listen for the phone."

"Give me an hour."

I set about doing some boat chores to kill time. Owning a boat meant constant upkeep and maintenance. Owning several compounded that. I rarely idled away minutes, much less hours.

Phil called back fifty minutes later.

"Found what you're looking for, Jesse. The gang in Fort Myers is run by a banger named Diego Alturaz. His number two is someone who goes by the name of Esteban. They've got about twenty-five regular, full-time members and probably half that again they can call up if they've got something going on.

"Pretty standard banger shit; they sell meth and weed mostly—blow, when they can get it. But here's where it gets a little different. Lately, here in Miami, and probably over in Fort Myers

and the rest of the country, for that matter, they're getting more and more into sex trafficking. They've got this horrific new business model where they kidnap young girls, do the gang initiation thing with them, then addict them to drugs and put them to work as prostitutes. The girls don't last long, as you'd imagine, but the bangers don't care—they just grab more. They used to snatch up primarily young, homeless women with drug habits who wouldn't be missed. But lately, they've also been taking straight girls right off the street."

This dovetailed perfectly with what Nancy had told me.

"What have your gang people been doing to push back?" I asked.

"Not much, I'm afraid. We try, but for all their incompetence as criminals, they've proven to be masters at witness intimidation and murder. Every time we put together a good case against one of them, our witnesses either die a gruesome death or develop memory problems right before trial. It's incredibly frustrating."

"Must drive you nuts."

"It does." Phil replied. "It's like every one of them knows and accepts that their life expectancy is around twenty-one years and none of them seem to care about any life outside of the gang. They'd rather go down in a blaze of glory when backed into a corner. Fort Myers has had a series of incidents lately. The local PD thought they finally had a really good case against Diego Alturaz for the murders of two young gang members he shot and then chopped up. They also had him cold on the kidnapping and rape of two innocent thirteen-year-old middle schoolers."

I felt the tension in my brow move to my jaw, clamping my teeth together like a vice. "What happened?"

"Once again, the gang got to the primary witness. He was in

jail. And get this: they killed him with a jar of wasps."

"What? How?"

"They must've known the mick had a serious allergy. Someone walked by his cell, threw in the jar of wasps, and bang; he gets stung like twelve times, blows up like a fucking piñata, and he's dead ten minutes later.

"In another recent incident in Fort Myers," he continued, "the gang went after some teenage girl on a motorcycle. The police set a roadblock to catch the guys, and because one of them had an immigration beef, he gets out of the car, pulls a cannon, and tries to shoot it out with like ten cops! How can you fight against people who have so little regard for their own lives, let alone the lives of others?"

I knew the answer. But Phil, just like Detective Andersen, had strict rules he had to abide by. I paused a moment before responding. The teenage girl on the motorcycle sounded like Nancy's niece.

"The rulebook you guys are forced to play by only works if both parties play by the rules. Obviously, these guys don't."

"What're we going to do, Jesse? You know what it's like out there right now. It's all over the news. When a cop pulls his piece, he gets totally screwed by the press. Doesn't matter whether his life is in danger or what the perp was doing. If he's a minority, it's hands off. It's like a get-out-of-jail-free card for whatever these punks want to do."

Rules of engagement were motivated by politics. Our troops were hampered, the cops were hindered, and even a private citizen in his own home risked jail time if he shot an intruder. And because of that, good people died, because they were slow to act.

"I don't envy you, Phil, with your hands tied the way they are. At some point, the media's got to wake up. But it's tough to fix stupid. It can be done, but like they say, it's going to hurt."

"You got that right, brother."

"Okay, thanks for the intel, Phil. It's just what I was looking for."

"Anytime, Gunny. Keep one on ice for me."

"I will," I replied and ended the call.

It was obvious that Nancy Liddell's niece and her family were all in serious danger. Something like this would take more time than I had. But I wanted to do something, and I had an idea.

I pulled up Billy Rainwater's number. He'd be perfect to discreetly keep an eye on the girl and her family. If Billy didn't want to be seen, he wouldn't be. It was just a matter of whether he was available.

The phone rang twice.

"Billy Rainwater, original and authentic American Indian. How may I direct your call?"

"It's Jesse."

"No kidding, Kemosabe. You think I'd actually answer the phone that way if I didn't know it was you?"

Billy and I had become blood brothers when we were kids. We'd grown up together, hunting and fishing the Caloosahatchee River and the Ten Thousand Islands area. Later, we'd served side-by-side in the Marine Corps. We'd been covering each other's six for over forty years.

By blood, Billy was, in fact, the acting chieftain of the Calusa people, the first settlers of Florida's southwest coast. Roughly translated, Calusa means "fierce people." Even the *conquistadors* sailed wide around Southwest Florida after Juan Ponce de León

first landed in Charlotte Harbor and got an arrow in his gut for the discovery.

Few had ever seen Billy's fierce side. But I had.

Since leaving the Corps, he'd guided hunting trips in the Everglades and built incredible 4x4s that could go anywhere. Later, he'd received a law degree and worked to secure a place for his people. He'd helped Deuce on occasion with legal matters. And he'd helped me dispose of a body once. He was an odd mix, but I trusted him implicitly. We'd put our lives on the line for each other more than once.

"I've got a situation," I began. "And I'm hoping you might be free and willing to help. A woman called me earlier tonight. She sounds like a nice lady and tells me this story about her sixteen-year-old niece, who's gotten herself jammed up with MS-13 in Fort Myers."

"Why would that be something you'd get involved in?"

"Couple of reasons," I replied. "From what the aunt tells me, the girl sounds like a really good kid, but I also think it's because this gang is so clearly out of control. Apparently, they're going around these days thinking they can kidnap innocent girls off the street, gang-rape them, addict them to drugs, and then run them as prostitutes, all without fearing retribution of any sort. The police are powerless over them because they're so effective at intimidating and killing anyone willing to testify against them. Apparently, this girl, Callie, interrupted one of their kidnappings and, in the process, took down two members of the gang. That obviously made them look like fools, so they've been going after her hard. The aunt's worried about the girl and her family."

"How did the woman hear about you?"

"A PI she knows up north knows a guy I once worked with. I

agreed to have her call me at Rusty's, thinking I might be able to help, but I'm leaving at the end of the week."

"I don't like MS-13, Jesse. They make the whole human race look bad."

"I was hoping you'd feel that way."

"I've got some time," he offered. "Want me to go down there and scalp a couple of them?"

I explained the situation with as much detail as I knew, including the part about how he would have to basically offer invisible protection to the girl's family for the next three days and then to the girl herself once she got back from Boston.

"So, I have to provide this protection silently? Like a ghost?"

"Yup," I replied. "You'll need your moccasins, for sure. But don't put your life in danger over that aspect. I'd much rather the girl and her family find out that her aunt arranged protection than have anything happen to you."

"You said the girl drives a motorcycle?"

"That's what her aunt said."

"I recently treated myself to an Indian and have been looking for an excuse for a road trip."

"Vintage?" I asked, knowing Billy's dislike of most modern things.

"No, not this time. She's a brand-new 1200cc, blacked-out, Indian Roadmaster. She's even got a GPS nav system built into the fairing."

"Jeez, Billy, what happened to *old school*? Your ancestors are probably rolling over in their middens."

"You forget; I'm chief of the Calusa. It's called executive privilege. Iron horse is heap powerful."

I chuckled.

"Text me the girl's address after we hang up," he said. "I'll head over to Fort Myers tomorrow. You said the girl will be back on Sunday?"

"That's what her aunt said. And thanks, Billy. I'll owe you another one. Give me a call once you get settled in and keep track of your expenses. I'll pick up the bill on this."

"You can't afford me, brother. I'll put it on your tab, though."

CHAPTER EIGHT

In a darkened motel room in Fort Myers, Manuel "Bones" Bonilla patiently waited, though he was excited at what the night might bring. The motel was on MLK, just a few blocks from Harlem Lakes.

Bones's gang, MS-13, had sprung up in Los Angeles, ostensibly to protect Salvadoran people and businesses. It had quickly turned to more lucrative and illegal activities and soon spread across the globe. But unlike most of his MS-13 fellow gang members, Bones was of mixed heritage.

His mother was Salvadoran and his father, whom he never knew, was black. His darker skin and African-American features allowed him to move around in the Lake Boyz-controlled part of Fort Myers as if he were invisible. And Harlem Lakes was the center of the other gang's territory.

Having been raised by a devout Catholic mother, Bones couldn't wait to get out of that confinement. By the time he reached thirteen years of age, he'd already had numerous run-ins with the law. At fifteen, he moved out of his mother's house, quit school, and lived with friends under a bridge, or in one of the many abandoned crack houses nearby. He soon started selling

crack, but he never used it. The roots of Catholicism ran deep.

Bones was bigger than most of the Hispanic people who lived in his neighborhood, and he took care of those who lived on the streets. While they slept or smoked, he was armed and alert. Left to their own devices, most would end up dead or in jail, and they couldn't very well buy more drugs from him if they ended up in those conditions. He didn't care about them. They were a means to an end, nothing more. Over time, he'd gained a reputation for dealing fairly with suppliers and customers, and people liked and trusted him. He quickly rose from selling dime bags of skunk weed to moving several ounces of meth every night.

But a chance encounter with a man called Razor had changed things. Razor worked for a Salvadoran named Diego Alturaz, who'd come to the west coast of Florida from Miami to organize the many street gangs in the predominantly Hispanic communities. Razor and Diego were MS-13, and soon grew the gang to a couple dozen members.

Given the choice of remaining on his own and competing against the notorious gang or joining it, Bones had agreed to work for Razor. He still made the same money, maybe a little more, even though he was now moving over half a pound of product every night. The upside was, he no longer had to babysit his customers, which suited Bones just fine.

In just the last two weeks, his customers, mostly hookers, had begun to disappear. Five days earlier, Razor had learned that the disappearances were caused by a rival gang to the north—the Lake Boyz of Harlem Lakes. He and Diego began making plans.

MS-13 had been providing protection for a number of crack whores, in exchange for a fee. They'd started there and then expanded their extortion to legitimate businesses in the area. The

disappearances of the prostitutes they were protecting was an embarrassment to the new chapter of the gang.

The disappearance of one of the hookers hit close to home for Bones. His cousin, Carmel Marco, had vanished earlier in the week. While Bones and Razor were out looking for her, a bunch of the Lake Boyz had kicked in the door of Razor's place and trashed everything. Carmel's little boy had been staying there while she worked the streets, and he had also turned up missing.

With the hookers gone, MS-13 lost an income stream, and acquired the shame that loss brought from other chapters. The answer was simple. Get more hookers. Diego came up with the idea of just making them, instead of finding them.

Bones had been assigned to sit on several new girls that other gang members had snatched up from more affluent neighborhoods in the suburbs and surrounding towns.

The girls the gang kidnapped had been taken to one of the many crack houses in the area, where they'd been gang-raped repeatedly. All the while, they were shot up with meth until they'd become as addicted as the average street whore.

Bones's job was to keep them as high as he could without killing them, until it was determined they were loyal to the gang. If one got out of line, he raped and beat her until she became submissive. Bones enjoyed that part of the training and was good at it.

Razor had come up with the idea to strike back at the Lake Boyz in the same way. That was why Bones was sitting in a motel room, waiting.

With his African-American looks and Salvadoran heart.

The first time, he'd been nervous. Bones had picked up a black hooker on MLK four nights earlier. He'd taken her to a

crack house a few blocks away, where he'd offered her a rock of crack cocaine, which she'd greedily smoked. When she'd lain back on a dirty mattress, he'd simply fallen on top of her and strangled her.

She'd struggled, but not much. Her brain had been so fried, she'd thought he'd just wanted rough sex and even urged him on. The excitement of killing her and avenging his cousin had stayed with Bones for the rest of that night.

The second murder was even easier, but Bones took advantage of the moment and *did* have rough sex with the *puta*, waiting to choke her to death until the end.

There was a knock on the motel room door.

Bones rose slowly from the bed and moved quietly to the door, like a jungle cat stalking its prey.

He looked through the peephole and just outside, a black woman stood, fidgeting nervously.

There wasn't anyone with her, so he unlocked the deadbolt and opened the door.

"You the guy who called Tavarius?" she asked.

She wore a simple blue tank top with a square neckline and short, cutoff jeans, both of which she filled out quite well. Bones could tell by the way she kept shifting her weight from one foot to the other and rubbing her arms that she was a tweaker.

"Yeah," he replied. "If that was who I talked to. Never got his name till now. I got a number from a brother—a number I could call if I wanted to party."

"Let's get this party started," the hooker said, as she came into the room. "You got any party favors?"

Bones closed and deadbolted the door. "Yeah, I got a little weed."

She turned and rubbed at both forearms. "Just weed?"

Bones grinned, as the rubbing of her arms caused her boobs to bounce up and down. "I got a little ice."

The woman eyed him cautiously. "How do I know you ain't a cop?"

Bones just shrugged and took a small vial from his pocket before unfastening his pants and pulling them off.

Inside the vial was a dime rock of meth. He placed the container next to a cheap crack pipe and a fat joint lying on the table. Then he picked up the joint and lit it. The pungent smell of marijuana quickly filled the room.

"Cops don't get high 'n' naked with someone they about to bust."

CHAPTER NINE

Lying on my bunk in the aft stateroom, I thought about what I'd asked Billy to do. Sure, it could get dicey, but knowing him, if anyone got hurt, they'd have had it coming.

I knew the area where Callie and her family lived. I'd grown up not far from there. It was a rural area, just up the river from Fort Myers. Billy knew that part of the Caloosahatchee better than anyone, except maybe his dad. He'd be in his own element and able to keep an eye on things. If he had to intervene, I knew it would be swift, silent, and from a distance.

I drifted off to sleep around midnight, the sounds from the marina and bar reaching my ears through the open hatch.

When dawn came, I was well rested and ready for the day. Instead of going to the galley for coffee, I just locked up the *Dog* and went up to the bar, carrying my Thermos. It was more than a one-mug ride back to the island.

To say that the Rusty Anchor Bar and Grill was just another bar was an understatement. Rufus and his niece made breakfast, lunch, and dinner for all the liveaboards in the little marina, as well as many of the locals and a few fishing guides and their clients. Information was shared over coffee about what was biting

where, who got drunk and fell off a pier, or what boat was down for repairs. And whenever trouble came, like a hurricane, the Anchor was a rally spot for volunteers and displaced locals.

It'd been that way since before Henry Flagler's railroad had arrived to build the long bridge beyond Vaca Key and what would later become the city of Marathon.

I had a quick breakfast and filled my Thermos before going back down to the dock, stepping aboard *El Cazador*, and starting the engine. While it warmed up, I called Savannah to see if she needed me to bring anything out, though I doubted she would. Our little island home was quite self-sustaining.

"How was your night alone?" I asked.

"I'm hardly alone," Savannah replied. "These two are a handful when you're not around."

"Finn and Woden? All they do is lie around and watch me work."

"That's their favorite thing," she agreed. "But you're not here. So, they were both bugging me all day and pacing the floor all night."

"Need anything?"

"Just you," she replied.

I smiled. "Oh, I almost forgot. I have something for you from Rufus. A bag of his "swimmer" spices."

"How'd you get him to part with that?" she asked.

"I didn't. Rusty handed it to me and said it was a gift for you."

"That's sweet," she said. "Be sure to thank him for me. Have you heard anything from Detective Andersen?"

I spotted Rufus walking toward the dock.

"Nothing yet," I replied. "I'll give him a call before I leave."

We said goodbye and I stepped back up to the dock.

"Savannah says thanks," I said, holding up the bag.

"I and I hear what yuh and Miss Savannah did yestuhday," Rufus said in his lyrical island accent. "She a brave woman, dat one."

"No big deal," I said. "The kid needed help, so we just swam the boat to shore."

"Not talkin' bout dat, Cap'n," he said, looking all around. Then he lowered his voice, conspiratorially. "I see and hear tings, Cap'n Jesse. And not jest from udduh peoples. Whut yuh and Miss Savannah are gwon do will bring trouble, mon. Dat boy will bring trouble to yuh." Then he smiled broadly, his teeth like white Chicklets against his dark features. "But di gods smile on peoples like yuh and Miss Savannah. Everting gwon work out. When tings look bad, jest remember dat."

Without another word, Rufus turned and crossed the lawn toward the deck and his kitchen.

I scratched my head. Rufus always talked in riddles and often spoke of hearing from the gods. He was Rastafari, which was a monotheistic religion, but he once told me that the souls of his ancient African ancestors dwelt within him and he often spoke to them and their gods.

Shaking my head, I scrolled through my contact list and called Andersen's cell number.

"Detective Andersen," he answered.

"This is Jesse McDermitt. Any word on the boy?"

"I was holding off calling you until a respectable hour," he said. "I should have figured a man like you would be up with the roosters. Yes. I spoke with the doctor who's treating the kid just a few minutes ago to see if there was any change."

"Has he remembered anything?"

"He's doing great, physically," Andersen replied. "The doctor said he could be released later today or tomorrow morning. But no, he hasn't regained any of his memory." There was a pause. "Are you sure you want to do this, Mr. McDermitt?"

"My wife wouldn't have it any other way, Detective. Which means it's what I want."

"Happy wife, happy life," he said. "I get that."

"She's already had me move a bed from the bunkhouse to our living room."

"I should have word this afternoon," Andersen said. "If he's ready to be discharged, I can have him up there before nightfall. How do I find your place?"

"Got a pencil?"

"Shoot."

Put these numbers in your GPS," I said. "24.788714 degrees north and –81.452636 west. That'll bring you right to my dock. Just don't try going between Howe Key and Water Key unless you have a skinny boat and know the area."

"Got it. I'll phone as soon as I hear anything."

We ended the call and I untied the lines.

Idling out of Rusty's canal, I continued at slow speed through the channel until I reached deep water. Then I brought the beefy center console up on plane and swung a wide turn around East Sister Rock, headed toward Moser Channel and the high arch of the Seven Mile Bridge.

This whole notion of kidnapping girls and turning them into drug-addicted prostitutes was unsettling.

I'd learned that Cobie Murphy had undergone a similar experience during her captivity. Willy Quick had shot her and

several other women up with what was later learned to be a barbiturate cocktail. The effects of the drugs, in his captives' cases, was a depression of the central nervous system, making them completely compliant, but still conscious. When he'd used them up, he'd just dumped them, semi-conscious, for the gators to finish off.

What Quick used wasn't nearly as addictive as heroine or crack cocaine, but the two survivors did have to go through treatment.

I feared that the drugs MS-13 was hooking their abductees on would be a lot more addictive. Enough so that a morally upright young woman with a fantastic future ahead of her would do anything to get more.

Including selling herself in back alleys.

I shuddered as I slowed down a little to pass under the bridge. Clearing it and the remnants of the old Seven Mile Bridge, I opened the throttle again and turned slightly east of due north to follow the natural deep channel.

The idea of an innocent girl like Cobie or Nancy's niece being transformed into a near-lifeless shell of a human, to be rented out by the hour to the sickos that frequented those dark alleys, disgusted me. But I'd seen firsthand what certain drugs would do to a person. A crack monster would sell their children for another rock.

I also thought about the kid, Alberto, if that was his name. He'd been starved most of his life, beaten, and put on a leaky boat to die slowly under the baking sun or drown in the Gulf.

These things angered me—a deep, seething rage that I knew I wouldn't be able to just shake off. It was an irritation to a primal part of my brain, the part that society has tried to bury for

thousands of years.

If you boiled down the animal kingdom to its very base, there were really only two kinds—prey and predator. The two were easily identified by the location of their eyes.

Animals that fell into the prey category—like mice, rabbits, deer, and horses—had eyes on the sides of their heads, giving them greater side vision to watch out for predators all around them. Some of these animals had eyes that evolved to have long, horizontal pupils, allowing them even greater peripheral vision. Horses and other animals of the plains became ridiculously hard to sneak up on.

Predators, like wolves, lions, owls, even humans, had eyes in the front of their heads, which could focus on a single object. That gave them a three-dimensional image, allowing them to judge distances better. Cats' pupils are long and narrow, also, but vertical, allowing them a greater field of view above their heads.

Predators kill prey to survive. It's the law of the jungle.

But there are some animals that will murder their own kind. A male lion will kill male cubs to maintain dominance. Many species of fish will devour their own young. It's a natural part of the evolution of a species.

Only humans will kill one another without reason.

Those humans who preyed on weaker people, using them for their own sick purposes, or for financial gain, only to toss them aside when they were finished with them, were at the bottom of the evolutionary scale.

Then there were animals like me.

That deep, dark part of the human brain that society has pushed down for centuries is in all of us. The will to hurt, maim, and kill can be honed, trained, and, as we are thinking creatures,

redirected.

Right now, my hostility was directed at an unknown, unseen enemy—a group of people who kidnapped, tortured, and murdered others, whose only mistake was in passing before the forward-looking eyes of a predator.

With a following current, I made good time and was soon idling up to the south pier, packing away the rage I felt; that need to seek animalistic justice.

Clicking the key fob button, I reversed *Cazador's* engine, and stopped her alongside the pier as Savannah came down the steps from our house, Woden and Finn following dutifully behind her. There was a time when they'd have run down the steps.

I stepped up to the dock and into Savannah's embrace, holding the bow line in one hand. The dogs tried to wedge their heads between us from either side, but Savannah wasn't allowing it. Finn actually whined.

She kissed me, then stepped back. "I know it's only been a little over twenty-four hours, but I missed you."

"Me too," I said, as Finn and Woden vied for my attention. I gave them both a good neck rub, then bent to tie the line off to a cleat. "Being alone in that big bed on the *Dog* was like being adrift in the middle of the ocean. Only the ocean smelled like you."

I kissed her again as the dogs moved to the end of the pier to lie in the sun.

"Next time," she said, "we'll all go together, or you won't go at all."

I laughed and pushed *Cazador's* stern away from the dock. She drifted slowly in an arc and, when she'd moved out far enough, I untied the bow line and pulled it the other way, turning her around. With a single inboard engine, it was easier that way.

"I'll go inside and help you get her into her slip," Savannah said, then climbed quickly up the steps.

With the outboard boats, backing into a slip was easy—point the back of the motor in the direction you wanted to go, and that's where it went. *Gaspar's Revenge*, with her twin inboards, was even easier. By using the thrust from each prop separately, she could be turned around almost within her own length.

But *El Cazador* had a single inboard and the rudder was several inches behind the prop—of little use in reverse.

We managed to get the boat tied up alongside the *Revenge* and I shut down the engine.

"I spoke to Andersen," I said, handing her the bag from Rufus. "He said the boy might be released this afternoon and he'd phone before he brings him out."

"What are they calling him in the hospital?" she asked, opening the bag, and inhaling the fragrant mix of herbs and spices. "Mmmm."

"I didn't think to ask. I'm sure it's not 'boy'."

"He looked like an Alberto," she said, referring to the name Deputy Fife and I had found on the transom of the boat he'd been in.

"Names don't have a look."

She looked up at me. "Oh? If I mention the name Waldo, what mental image do you get? How about Brutus?"

I clicked the key fob again and the hydraulic pump began to whir, pulling the doors closed.

"Fair enough," I said. "But I've met guys named Alberto who were tall, short, thin, or fat."

We went upstairs to the living room, where I discovered she'd done some more redecorating. Beside the bed was a table and

lamp, which I recognized from Flo's house. There were two books on the table. One was a children's book with a cartoon boat on the cover. The other was a picture book for identifying tropical fish.

"Are you planning to teach him to dive already?" I asked.

"That was Flo's favorite," she replied, picking up the fish ID book. "She memorized every fish in Paul Humann's books on Florida and the Caribbean."

She put the book back down. "We don't have much in the way of reading material for little boys."

I went to the kitchen and poured the last of the coffee from my Thermos into a clean mug, then pulled out one of the chairs. "Come and sit down a minute."

"What's wrong?" she asked. "You have that look."

"Look?"

"You're upset about something. I can tell."

We sat down and I told her about the phone call from Nancy Liddell the previous night and my conversations with Phil Tucker and Billy Rainwater.

"And he just agreed to do it?" she asked.

"Billy has a very strong sense of right and wrong," I said. "If he can help someone out of a bad situation, like Nancy's niece is in, he will."

"It could be dangerous. I've heard that gang is quite ruthless."

"So were the *conquistadors*," I said. "And even with their more advanced weapons and armor, they steered clear of the Calusa people. Besides, Billy's also a Marine. If anyone's in danger, it's the gang, should they go after the girl."

"But that's not all you wanted to tell me, is it?"

"Something Barney Fife said," I began.

"His name's Bradford."

I grinned. "I bet all his cop buddies call him Barney," I said, then got serious. "We know three things—Alberto Mar is an American kid, he was covered by a tarp made in Fort Myers, but the boat was most likely Cuban. Throw out the odd thing and Alberto's from the Fort Myers area. I can't explain how or why I know this. I just do. And you know I don't believe in coincidences."

"The Blancs are all gone," she said. "Either dead, in jail, or hiding in the swamp."

"That wasn't what I meant," I said, taking a sip of my coffee. "You and I jumped into the water to save a kid. He was covered by a tarp made in Fort Myers and he'd been beaten. The very next morning, I get a call from a woman who lives in that area, asking for help in protecting her niece."

"And what? You think these two things are…connected somehow?"

"Call it an aligning of the planets," I said, running the fingers of both hands through my hair, "or call it Rufus's gods manipulating the strings of humanity, but yeah, I do think they're connected somehow."

CHAPTER TEN

Savannah stared at me. Her big blue eyes gave away nothing of what was going on behind them. She blinked twice. "Call Tank and Deuce. You're not going up there alone."

"You think you know me that well already?"

"You mean you weren't planning to go 'recon' the area?"

I grinned. "No. That you'd think I'd go alone."

"The dogs and I will be going with you, too."

"Oh no—"

"Oh, very much yes," she said, cutting me off. "And we're not going to miss the boat on Friday."

"What about Alberto?" I asked.

"He'll come too."

"No," I said. "No way. Forget about it."

"We'll take two boats," she insisted. "You, Tank, and whoever you can get from Deuce can go on *Gaspar's Revenge*, and Chyrel and I will meet you there on *Sea Biscuit* with Alberto."

"It could be dangerous," I said. "There's no way I'm taking a kid to where we're going."

"He'll be perfectly safe, Jesse. Once we're there, we won't even have to acknowledge each other. Chyrel can run things

from my boat and I can assist her."

I had to admit, having Chyrel there would make things easier, as would having Tank and maybe Tony come along. I didn't have any idea what I could do against the gang in just four days, but I was going to do something. Savannah and I both knew that.

Billy was likely already in place, providing protection to Callie and her family, should MS-13 make a move against them. We could discourage them from another angle.

"Okay, we'll take both boats," I conceded, digging my cell phone from my pocket. "But the dogs are staying with you."

I called Tank first. He wasn't in the best of health and he was in his seventies, but there wasn't a better strategist on the planet. He'd been diagnosed with cancer several months ago and given less than a year to live, so he'd chosen to live it well and moved to the Keys. Chyrel had kept him on an extremely healthy diet and they exercised daily. For a seventy-year-old man with cancer, he was surprisingly fit.

"Whatever you have planned," he said, answering the phone, "you can count us in. Marlin, snook, diving, flying…I'm ready."

"What do you think about taking on one of the most ruthless gangs in the world?" I said bluntly.

There was a pause, and I could hear him whisper something, though I couldn't make out what it was.

"When and where, Gunny?"

"Before dawn," I said. "We're going up to Fort Myers to look around."

"Chyrel's coming."

"So is Savannah," I said. "We'll be taking two boats. And Tony, or one of Deuce's other men will be coming along."

"Have whoever it is come to our house," Tank said. "You can

pick us up here."

I agreed and we ended the call. Then I called Deuce, to see who he had available.

"Tony and Paul are both here," he said. "Drinking all my coffee and not making a fresh pot."

"Have them both meet us at Tank and Chyrel's place on Grassy Key at zero seven hundred."

"Will do," Deuce said. "DJ Martin stopped by yesterday. He's up in Miami this week, going over the progress on a house he's renovating in Coconut Grove."

"Think he's available?"

"Probably," Deuce replied. "He seemed bored."

"After that dust up in Puerto Rico? How could he be bored?"

"You know those Ranger types," he said.

"Thanks. I'll give him a call."

Ending that call, I searched for DJ's number and hit the *Call* button.

"Jesse McDermitt," he said. "I was just talking to your partner yesterday."

"I know. He told me you were in the States. You busy for the next couple of days?"

"Nothing I can't get out of," he said, his voice dropping an octave.

"Can you meet me across the state in Fort Myers tomorrow?"

"Where and when?"

"There's a place called Landings Marina on the east side of the Caloosahatchee River, just south of the Cape Coral bridge. We'll arrive there by ten hundred. Don't you even want to ask what for?"

"Why bother?" he said, his tone flippant. "If you're involved,

it definitely won't be boring."

I ended the call and put my phone back in my pocket.

"Who is DJ Martin?" Savannah asked.

"A one-legged pirate," I replied with a half grin. "Tony and Paul are both in, too."

"A one-legged—never mind, I'll find out tomorrow. How do you do that?"

"Do what?"

"How do you get people to do things," she began, "without them even knowing what you want them to do? Billy, last night, and Tank and this DJ just now?"

"DJ's a door-kicker, too," I said. "He lost a leg in Afghanistan, but that barely slows him down. The world of spec-ops is pretty small."

"That still doesn't explain why someone would volunteer to put themselves in harm's way without even knowing what they were up against."

"What can I say?" I offered a grin. "I'm just a likable guy."

She laughed. "Okay, Mr. Nice-Guy, why don't you go pull some traps? And take one of these pests with you."

"Come on, Finn," I said, rising from the table. "The admiral wants stone crab claws for lunch."

He rose and trotted after me.

Woden sat waiting for his command.

"*Bleibe und bewachen*, Woden."

The big Rottweiler rose from where the two had settled on the rug and positioned himself between the door and where Savannah sat at the table. He'd remain on alert and move to keep himself between her and the door until I returned.

The traps out in the channel had been in the water for just a

couple of days, so Finn and I headed across the clearing and out onto the floating pier on the north side of the island. I had four crab traps that'd been soaking there for three whole days. There were four more tied to the north pier, but they'd only been in the water for a little over a day.

As I pulled up the first trap, Finn started barking in anticipation.

"Calm down," I told him.

Clam season had closed just a few weeks earlier. Finn would usually catch a few in the shallows between the main island and the little one just a few yards off the northern shore while I pulled the traps.

Hefting the trap to the pier, I saw that it had a couple of crabs with at least two big claws between them.

Pulling the remaining three traps, I quickly removed the legal-sized claws and put them in a small bucket before letting the crabs go back into the water. Crabs regenerate lost appendages when they molt, which they do up to twice a year for juveniles and at least once for adults.

As I carried the bucket back to the house, my phone vibrated in my pocket. I pulled it out and saw that it was Detective Andersen.

"McDermitt," I answered.

"Detective Andersen here," he said. "Alberto Mar is being discharged now. I'm outside waiting for him and have a boat at the dock."

"We'll be waiting," I said. "He'll have fun here."

I ended the call as I hurried up the steps.

"How many did you get?" Savannah asked as I came through the door.

I retrieved a colander from a cabinet. "Over a dozen. But I only checked the four traps on the north pier. Andersen and Alberto will be on their way soon."

She looked up. "Now?"

"Andersen's waiting for him to be wheeled out," I replied, dumping the claws into the colander. "I better go check the traps on the south pier and see if we have some more."

"Jesse, wait."

I stopped at the door and turned around.

"He won't have any clothes."

"Hmm, yeah, that's a problem. But not an insurmountable one. I can call Chyrel and have her run to the Kmart this afternoon."

"Do that, and then check the other traps," she said. "We'll ask the detective to stay for lunch, also."

I called Chyrel's cell as I started down the steps. When I explained what the problem was, she was eager to help and asked what size he was.

"I don't know. The doctor figured he was about six or eight, but he looks on the small side."

"In comparison to Deuce's kids or your grandson?"

"Yeah! He's about as big as Trey. Can you call Julie and ask her what size clothes he wears?"

She agreed and promised to buy sizes both larger and smaller, just in case. We ended the call, and I stuffed the phone back into my pocket.

Finn sat by the end of the pier and cocked his head, watching me pull up the first trap.

"You know there's some in there, don't you?" I said. "Don't worry, you and Woden will get a little, too."

We ate a lot of seafood on our island, and both piers had cleaning stations. The fish waste was just dumped into the water and attracted all sorts of marine life. We caught quite a few lobsters, stone crabs, and even a few blue crabs in our traps. But the season for blue crabs was only two weeks in early fall.

After pulling up the fourth trap and breaking off three more claws, I rebaited each one and dropped them back in the water. When I turned to head back up to the house, Finn barked an alert.

He was standing at the end of the pier and looking off to the east toward Mac Travis's island. His ears were up, or at least as up as a Lab's ears can get. I'd learned long ago to trust Finn's hearing and his sense of smell.

After a moment, I heard the drone of twin outboards. I scanned the water in the direction of the sound. Far out in the wide, natural channel, I could just make out a large center console. It had some kind of marking on the side, but it was too far away to tell what it was.

"Come on, Finn," I said, heading toward the steps.

When I opened the door, Savannah was looking sideways out the south-facing window. Woden must have alerted her to the approaching boat. If anything, his hearing was better than Finn's.

"Is that them?" she asked, hurrying back to the kitchen.

I dumped another ten claws into the colander. "I think so. It has markings on the side, but it was too far away to be sure."

Grabbing the binoculars that were hanging by the door, I went back out onto the deck and around to the southeast corner. Savannah was right behind me, with both dogs trailing her.

Looking out past Mac's island, I saw the boat. "It's a Monroe County Sheriff's boat," I said. "Four people aboard—Andersen, a

uniformed deputy, a woman, and the boy."

"Stop calling him that," Savannah said. "His name's Alberto Mar."

"We think that's his name," I corrected her. "For all we know, that could be the name of the guy who built the boat."

Savannah shielded her eyes with her hand, looking out toward the far waters. "It's *his* name."

I lowered the binos and glanced over at her. She looked anxious.

Then she turned and caught me staring at her. "I need to get lunch ready," she said, and started to turn.

"Savvy, wait."

She stopped and faced me, her blue eyes a little glassy with moisture.

"I don't think it's a good idea for you to get too attached to this kid. He's probably only going to be with us for a little while."

"He just needs a little stability," she said.

"Stability? We're taking him with us tomorrow. *And* when we fly to Bimini on Friday. That's not stable."

"Stability doesn't mean stationary," she said. "I'm talking more about people than places."

"Still, I don't want you to get too attached."

"He's not a puppy, Jesse."

I dropped my head in defeat. It was too late. "Go ahead and get lunch ready. I'll go down and give them a hand tying up." I slapped my thigh. "Come on, Finn."

As I turned, she touched my arm. "You saw his face, too. You saw how terrified he was."

"Yeah," I replied. "I saw."

"We have what it takes to help him," Savannah said. "Two

rational, stable people. And we have this beautiful place with so much for him to do here. Good things."

"I just don't want you to get hurt," I warned. "Like I said, he probably won't be staying with us for very long."

"I know you don't want me hurt," she said, hugging me tightly. "That's just one of the many things I love about you."

Savannah went back inside, and Finn and I started down the steps, taking our time. Finn was tall enough that I could scratch the furry spot behind his ear without bending over.

"Why'd you let me get into this?" I asked him.

CHAPTER ELEVEN

I stood at the end of the pier as the patrol boat turned into my channel. The driver looked hesitant until he saw the deep turning basin in front of the house and the massive doors below the deck.

Alberto sat with the woman in front of the console, on the forward-facing seat. He looked hesitant, but unafraid. She looked overbearing.

"I didn't know you owned a dog," Andersen said, handing me a line.

"Two dogs," I said, then looked at the boy. "This one's called Finn, like Huckleberry Finn. Do you like dogs?"

The boy shrugged.

The woman looked at Finn with some trepidation.

"Finn likes everyone," I said to Alberto. "And both of our dogs are highly trained. Tell him to sit."

Alberto looked at the woman, who just kept staring at Finn. Then he looked at Andersen, who nodded.

"Sit, Finn," he said.

Finn glanced up to me and I nodded, releasing him to obey the boy's command. He promptly sat on my foot, which made

Alberto laugh.

That broke the woman's stare and she looked down at Alberto.

"I think he likes you," I said. "And our other dog, Woden…well, he likes anyone Finn likes."

The woman rose and extended a hand. "My name is Emily Delgado. I work for the Florida Department of Children and Families."

I looked at Andersen, arching an eyebrow as I shook her hand.

"The Sheriff's Department had to involve them," he said. "Miss Delgado just wanted to check for herself that the conditions are adequate."

I squelched my normal response to authority.

"Well, our house is a one-bedroom," I told her. "But my wife has made a few changes and Alberto will be quite comfortable. We're having stone crab for lunch. Will you join us?"

"Thanks, no," she replied, stepping up to the dock a bit unsteadily. "I have other appointments." She turned to Alberto. "Come along, young man."

Maybe they hadn't been calling him Alberto at the hospital.

I winked at the kid. "That just leaves more for us."

Finn punctuated my remark with a bark, which startled Emily. "Are you sure it doesn't bite?"

"*He* bites a lot," I replied. "But he only bites people if I tell him to."

Her glare told me she didn't appreciate my wit.

"Finn and Woden are protection-trained," I said, then looked down at my big yellow lab. "Take Alberto up to the house, Finn."

He rose and moved alongside the boat, waiting.

Alberto climbed over the side, a lot less clumsily than the welfare lady. He put his hand on Finn's head and Finn leaned into him, turning his big head so the boy's hand was on his ear.

"He likes to have the area behind his ears scratched," I told him.

Alberto gave Finn an ear scratching, then Finn took a slow step. When Alberto moved to go along with him, he picked up his pace, and the two of them started toward the steps.

"That's a pretty good trick," the uniformed deputy said.

"No trick," I replied. "Dogs understand a lot of words, besides simple commands, and ours are intelligent enough to put words they understand together and figure it out. He knows the words take, up, and house, and I guess he just figured out on his own which one of you was Alberto."

"Your house is very pretty," Emily said. "But I will have to inspect."

"Welcome to our island," Savannah announced from the top of the steps, Woden standing beside her. "Please come on up and get out of the sun."

"I'll wait on the boat," the deputy said, taking a pack of cigarettes from his pocket. "Okay to smoke here?"

"Your lungs," I said. "Pollute 'em all you want, just don't put anything in the water."

The other two joined me and we followed Alberto and Finn up the steps, catching up to them quickly. The boy stopped halfway up and looked at Savannah.

"Are you the lady who found me?"

Savannah's face registered her surprise, and she squelched a gasp. "You remember that? Yes, yes. Jesse and I found you and got your boat to land."

He looked back at me and I nodded.

"Come on," Savannah said. "I want to show you something."

He hurried up the steps, with Finn right at his side.

Woden must have picked up on Finn's attitude toward Alberto and his little stub of a tail wagged a welcome.

"That's a Rottweiler," Emily said, hesitantly.

I knew there were people who had irrational fears of big dogs, and even some whose fears were rational. The sight of a large Rott was all it took to send them into a panic.

When Alberto reached the top of the steps, both dogs danced around him, vying for attention.

"You don't have anything to fear about our dogs," I reassured the woman. "They're like toddlers, just a little bigger."

Once we reached the deck, Savannah put a hand on Alberto's shoulder and guided him to the other side, which looked out over the island's interior.

"Wow!" he exclaimed, climbing up on the rail for a better look.

"You're free to explore anywhere you want," Savannah said. "Finn and Woden can show you around."

"Can I go look now?"

"Sure," I replied. "Just be careful out on the other pier. Can you swim?"

I realized it was a dumb question, even as the words were coming out of my mouth.

Alberto turned and looked at me, a sadness in his eyes. "I don't know."

"No problem," I said. "We can find that out later easy enough. Finn's a great swim coach. Go ahead and look around."

He and the dogs disappeared down the back steps and I

turned to Emily. "He's perfectly safe. And you probably have some questions he doesn't need to hear."

"Shall we go inside?" Savannah asked. "You're staying for lunch, right?"

"I'm afraid not," Andersen said. "Miss Delgado needs to get back and I have a lot to do."

"And Miss Delgado is…"

"I'm with the Florida Department of Children and Families," Emily replied, extending her hand.

Savannah shook it and we went inside. The welfare lady looked around. I wasn't worried she'd find any fault, other than the bed in the living room.

"This will be the boy's bed?" she asked, walking toward it.

"Yes," Savannah replied. "Alberto can stay as long as he likes."

"I'm only agreeing to this because Detective Andersen thinks the boy might be in danger."

I could see Savannah's jaw muscles tighten. She obviously didn't like this woman. I knew I didn't much care for her institutional manner, myself. She might have gotten into her line of work to make a difference, but that had likely worn off.

"His name's Alberto," I said, saving Savannah the confrontation. "At least that's what we'll call him until we know better. I can assure you, he's perfectly safe with us."

"Detective Andersen gave me a brief bio on you, Mr. McDermitt, but it only went back twenty years. He said you were a charter fisherman, but you don't look like one, and if you don't mind my saying, this island looks a lot more substantial than a fisherman could afford."

I knew what she was angling toward. A lot of boat captains

scored big bucks bringing contraband into South Florida.

"Did he also tell you that I retired from the Marine Corps about twenty years ago, or that I worked with Homeland Security after that?"

"Er—no, he didn't."

"And I bet he didn't say anything about my dad and grandfather also being Marines, did he? My dad was killed in Vietnam when I was Alberto's age."

I was getting angry and needed to dial it back.

"Look, Miss Delgado, I was raised by my grandparents and was their sole heir. I inherited enough to buy this island and my charter boat. I'm partners in a security firm in Key Largo, which does some training and consultations with Miami-Dade PD. I don't do drugs and I certainly don't smuggle them into the country."

"I wasn't implying—"

"Perhaps not," I said, cutting her off. "But you *were* thinking it."

She looked toward Andersen for support.

"To be honest," he said, "I didn't dig very deep into the McDermitts' backgrounds. The sheriff himself vouched for them."

"Then I guess there's no problem with them," she said. "But a bed in the living area is out of the question."

"By the end of the day, I'll build a wall around it," I said. "It will be a small room, but Alberto will have privacy."

"We're not placing him here permanently."

I grinned at Savannah. "Then my wife will have that walk-in closet she's wanted. Look, there are four houses on my island, and just below our feet is a boat with two staterooms. Alberto has

plenty of room for privacy."

She looked at each of us in turn, ending with Andersen. "Then I suppose he can stay."

Andersen turned toward me and offered his hand. "Thank you, Mr. McDermitt. We'll get out of your hair now."

I walked them down to the waiting boat as Savannah went down the other steps to find Alberto.

"One last thing, Mr. McDermitt," the welfare lady said, when we reached the patrol boat.

"What's that, Miss Delgado?"

"If someone found out the boy was staying with you and your wife, and wanted to hurt him, how hard would it be to find this place?"

"Look around," I said, waving a hand to the south. "From the water, all these keys look the same. Unless someone had my GPS coordinates, they could search for days and not find this place."

"I can attest to that," the deputy added. "I know these waters very well and had no idea anyone lived out here. I didn't even see this dock until we got within a quarter mile."

"Besides," I said, "finding my island and getting ashore are two vastly different things."

CHAPTER TWELVE

After Andersen's boat left, I went to the foot of the pier and waded through the ankle-deep water to shore. I found Savannah in the middle of the clearing with Alberto and the dogs.

The boy was throwing sticks for Finn and Woden to fetch. Finn was better at the game than Woden, who liked to hang onto the stick and play tug-of-war instead of dropping it at the thrower's feet.

"Are y'all hungry?" I asked.

"I am," Savannah replied. "How about you, Alberto?"

"I guess so," he replied, shrugging his shoulders.

Then let's go up to the house and have lunch," I offered. "When I was your age, I was always hungry."

He frowned up at me, his brows knitted in thought. "I don't remember anything before they took me to the hospital. But I've been hungry since I woke up there."

I noticed that he spoke quite clearly and used proper grammar. That was unusual in kids today. Wherever he came from, someone had taken the time to teach him well.

That made me think of something else. It was April. He

should have been in school. Savannah had home-schooled Flo. They'd called it boat-schooling. I made a mental note to make sure that there was learning material on *Ambrosia* if he was still with us at the end of the week.

Alberto didn't pay a lot of attention to the salad. He nibbled on some carrot sticks and tried a couple of slices of cucumber. But after I showed him how to crack open the big crab claws, he murdered half a dozen of them.

"Did you call Chyrel?" Savannah asked, as Alberto and I helped move the plates and utensils to the sink.

"Yeah, she said she'd call Julie and ask her what size Trey wears. They're about the same size."

"How long am I going to be here?" Alberto asked.

I knelt down and looked him in the eye. "Here on our island?"

He nodded.

"Just tonight, for now. In the morning, we're going for a boat ride."

"Like in the police boat? They let me turn the lights on."

"My boat's a lot bigger," I said. "And Savannah's boat is even bigger than mine."

His eyebrows shot up. "Really?"

I grinned. "Yeah, really. And both boats even have two bedrooms, a kitchen, and everything like a house."

I could see in his eyes that he was struggling to comprehend. I didn't know much of anything about amnesia. I often wondered why a person afflicted with it could talk, since that was something learned over time. I assumed all memory wasn't lost.

Did Alberto even know what a bedroom and kitchen were?

"Want to go see them?" I pointed toward the stairs. "My

boat's just down there."

"You boys go ahead," Savannah said. "It'll just take me a few minutes to finish up here." She scraped all the shells into a small pot and handed it to me. "You can dump these while you're down there."

I rose and went with Alberto to the steps, where I flicked on the lights for the dock area below the house.

Alberto scooted down ahead of me but stopped halfway.

"Whoa!" he exclaimed again, gazing at all the polished fiberglass and chrome rails.

He hurried to the bottom of the steps and stood alongside the *Revenge*, looking up at her high bow flare. "*Maravillosa*," he breathed, scanning the length of the forty-five-foot hull.

I dumped the shells from the pot and left it at the foot of the stairs. Then I led him to the stern and helped him over the gunwale into the cockpit.

"This is my fishing boat," I said, then pointed at the fighting chair in the middle of the cockpit. "And that's called a fighting chair. It's where the fisherman sits to catch the really big fish."

He looked up at me, quizzically. "How big?"

"Bigger than you," I replied. "Sometimes bigger than me."

I opened the door to the salon, and we went inside.

Alberto stood just inside the hatch, looking around. The interior of the *Revenge* often left visitors speechless. It was done in light maple and holly, with tons of natural lighting.

Even though Alberto didn't have anything to reference the experience to, I could see that he was awestruck.

"This room is called a salon," I said. "Sort of like a living room in a house. And what we call a kitchen in the house is a galley on a boat." I went past him to the refrigerator and opened

it. "Care for a juice?"

"Yes, please," he replied.

Good manners, too.

I gave him one of Jimmy's mango juice bottles. He thanked me and struggled to open it. Finally, he looked up to me for help. I twisted the cap off and handed both back to him.

"Always recap a drink when you're on a boat," I said. "They'll spill pretty easy."

He took a swallow and licked his lips, then recapped his juice.

"Come on down here," I said, flicking on the lights to the passageway and leading the way.

Opening the first hatch on the right, I turned on the light. "Up in the house, you'd say this is a bathroom."

He looked up at me with recognition in his eyes. "What's it called on a boat?"

I smiled. He was a bright kid. "It's called the head."

Turning, he opened the hatch on the opposite side and looked in. The guest stateroom had three single beds. The two lower ones could slide together to create a double, with a pull-down, Pullman-style berth above.

"What's this room called?" he asked, stepping inside.

"When you're aboard, we'll call this Alberto's stateroom."

His face turned up, glee in his eyes. "Really?"

"Really," I replied with a grin.

His face fell slightly. "When I was in the hospital, they asked me my name and I couldn't remember. Then they started calling me Alberto."

"That was the name that was carved into the wood on the boat we found you on. They said you had a pocketknife, so we guessed you'd put the name there—Alberto Mar."

His face contorted, as if trying to force a memory.

"Don't worry," I said. "It'll come back to you. Did the hospital give you your knife back?"

He shook his head.

"Follow me," I said, moving forward and opening the door to the master stateroom.

"Wow!" he exclaimed again. then looked up at me and smiled. "This is Jesse's stateroom?"

"And Savannah's," I replied, moving toward the small dresser below the washer and dryer combo.

I opened the drawer and dug through my clothes until I found what I was looking for.

"Here," I said, extending it to him. "A man should always have a knife. You never know when you'll need one."

The Schrade Old Timer had been Pap's and he'd given it to my dad. When Dad died, Pap gave it to me.

"Take very good care of that until we get yours back, okay?"

"I will," he said, turning the knife over in his hands. "I have a question."

"What is it?"

He looked aft through the open hatch. "I didn't see a steering wheel up there. How do you drive this boat?"

Steering wheel?

I wondered if Andersen had told him what that was while allowing Alberto to turn on the lights. Or did amnesia only affect personal memories? Could his knowledge of what a steering wheel was, have come from a memory of riding in a car with his parents?

I made a mental note to find out more about what memories amnesia erases.

"You're a very observant young man," I said. "Follow me."

He put the knife in his pocket, and we retraced our steps through the salon. Once out in the cockpit, I pointed up the ladder just to port.

"Up there's the bridge," I said. "That's where you drive from."

"Can we go up there?"

"Sure. Just be careful on the ladder. Whenever you're on a boat, especially when it's underway, you should always maintain three points of contact. If you're lifting a foot to climb a ladder, both hands should hold onto something. When you move a hand, both feet should be standing on something."

He went up the ladder awkwardly, consciously keeping three points of contact with it.

When we reached the bridge, he went straight to the helm.

"What's that?" he asked, pointing at the cover over the large chart plotter.

I removed it and turned the unit on. "This is like a map. Do you know what a map is?"

"To show you where you're going?"

So, it seemed that not all memory was lost when a person developed amnesia. Basic things were retained. He'd seen a map before, maybe in school.

Or maybe Andersen had explained what the chart plotter on the patrol boat was, as well as the steering wheel.

"Exactly," I replied. "But instead of street names and towns, this one shows how deep the water is and where land is."

I turned on the other electronics and even turned on the ignition, but didn't fire the engines up. He asked a lot of questions. Smart ones.

Footsteps could be heard on the stairs.

"Sounds like the admiral is coming down for an inspection," I said.

"The admiral?"

"I'm the captain of the boat, but Savannah's the admiral. She outranks me. That means she's my boss."

"How come?"

Another good question.

"You'll understand later," I said.

"When I get my memory back?"

I laughed. "No, probably not until you're a few years older—when you have a girlfriend."

"Ahoy," Savannah called out.

I looked over the side. "Up here."

I felt the boat move and knew that Finn or Woden, or more likely both, had jumped over the gunwale into the cockpit. The boat moved again as Savannah came aboard.

"Y'all get back," I heard her say as she started up the ladder.

Alberto looked up at me, standing next to him at the helm. "Who's she talking to?"

"The dogs," I replied, as Savannah joined us.

"Can they come up here?"

"No," I replied. "They're not very good at going up a ladder and even worse going down."

"Teaching him to dive next?" Savannah asked, parroting my earlier question when I saw the fish ID book on the nightstand.

I grinned down at the kid. "No, we haven't gotten to that yet."

CHAPTER THIRTEEN

We spent the rest of the day showing our new guest around. We waded the shallows at low tide and visited some nearby sandbars and tidal pools, where he got to see small fish and crabs trapped by the receding tide.

In the distance to the west, a group of boats were gathered in Content Passage, a shallow, natural channel between the two largest of the Content Keys.

"What are those boats doing?" Alberto asked.

It being a weekday, I told him that I wasn't sure. "Sometimes people just like to come up here and hang out."

Later, we cooked fish over an open driftwood fire and ate with our fingers, using banana leaves for plates. As the sun set, we went out onto the north pier to watch it slip below the horizon.

I told Alberto about the green flash you could occasionally see, though I didn't think conditions were right on that particular night. He still made a silent wish.

We stayed out there until it got fully dark—or at least as dark as the first quarter moon, directly over our heads, would allow. Living on an island with few lights, far from the light pollution of the more inhabited keys, allowed a person's eyes to adjust. The

moon illuminated everything around us and the stars were like a million little diamonds scattered across a black velvet blanket.

I pointed out some of the clusters of stars that could be seen close to the horizon and told Alberto the stories of what early man thought he saw in the night sky; pictures to describe the different constellations.

"How long have you lived here?" he asked, as we gathered up our things to head back to the house.

"Oh, a little over twenty years," I said.

"I like it here," he offered. "That's what I wished for when the sun went down. That I could stay here."

"Aw, that's sweet," Savannah said, as we crossed the dark clearing toward the house.

"Who lives in those other houses?" Alberto asked.

"That one," I said, pointing to Jimmy's place on the west side, "is where my first mate lives. A first mate works for the captain."

He looked up at Savannah and smiled in the moonlight. "And the captain works for the admiral."

Savannah laughed.

"What about the two by the pier?" he asked.

"Our daughter, Flo, lives in one," Savannah said. "And the other one is going to be Jesse's workshop."

"You have a daughter?"

"She's away at college," I said.

"What's that?"

"College?" I asked. "It's the school you go to after high school."

Alberto stopped dead in his tracks, turned and looked back at the bunkhouses. Even in the dim light of the moon, I could see fear etched on his young face.

I knelt beside him. "What's wrong?"

He looked at me, concentration replacing some of the fear I'd seen in his eyes. "I don't like school."

I looked up at Savannah; she quickly knelt in the sand beside me. "Do you remember something?" she asked. "Even if it's something you don't like, it will help to try to remember it."

He seemed to study her face for a moment as he thought. Then a tear came to the corner of his eye and slowly trailed down his cheek.

"I can't remember," he said.

She took the boy in her arms and held him. "Don't worry," she said. "You're safe with us and your memory will come back. Remembering might be scary at first, but soon you'll remember happy things too."

That night, after Alberto had gone to sleep, I checked the provisions on the *Revenge* and did a complete systems analysis, except for starting the engines. We didn't have enough groceries aboard to sustain five men for more than a day, but there was a small grocery store near the marina in Fort Myers.

When I returned to the living room, Woden and Finn lay sleeping on either side of Alberto's bed, and Savannah was sitting in one of the recliners, reading.

When she looked up, I nodded my head toward the open bedroom door.

I woke early, well before sunrise, and slipped quietly out of our bedroom without disturbing Savannah. Woden raised his head as I walked past Alberto's bed, but I held a halting hand up to him

and he remained where he was.

The coffee, set on a timer, was ready. It was the smell that had awakened me. Better than any noisy alarm clock. I poured a cup, then headed downstairs, flicking on the dock area lights.

Once aboard the *Revenge*, I powered up my laptop, which connected wirelessly to the onboard modem. That device could connect to WiFi, but it could also connect to a second encrypted modem, which was hard-wired to an antenna, mounted to the roof of the house. While the boat was under the house, that was the only way to connect to a satellite in geosynchronous orbit, thousands of miles up in space.

I sent a message to Billy, asking what his status was, then started searching the news outlets for anything of note in the Fort Myers area.

I found three news stories dated within the last week about gang activity.

One was about a shooting between rival gangs, in which more than a dozen shots were fired, resulting in one person being slightly injured. It was no wonder gangs were on the rise—they couldn't shoot for shit.

The other two stories revolved around drug arrests in the area. Primarily methamphetamine and crack, the current drug of choice in American cities.

But none of the three stories mentioned MS-13. It made me wonder.

How many gangs could there be in a small town?

Fort Myers wasn't Miami or Orlando. I remembered as a kid, I'd learned that the population was under forty thousand. Even today, I doubted it had grown to more than eighty thousand. By comparison, Cape Coral, just across the Caloosahatchee River,

had grown from being smaller than Fort Myers to almost two hundred thousand people today.

There were also quite a few news articles about the discovery of the bodies of two known prostitutes in the area—Shaniqua Raines and Carmel Marco—though all of them were short, page-two reports from different news outlets. One of them mentioned that other prostitutes in the area were missing.

I looked at public police reports going back ten years, noting an alarming rise in drug-related and violent crimes over the last few years.

Fort Myers had changed since I'd first left there for Parris Island so long ago. In the years since then, I'd only returned maybe six or eight times. Most of those had been taking leave with Rusty during my first enlistment. Since my grandparents' funerals, I'd hardly been back at all. I just hadn't had a reason to return. The Keys were my home.

But in the last couple of years, I'd been to Fort Myers three times. All with violent outcomes.

The laptop pinged an incoming message. It was a reply from Billy.

First night. Nice ride. All quiet.

I heard footsteps above. Savannah was up.

Closing the laptop, I returned it to its cabinet and left the boat.

"Oh, there you are," Savannah said, as I started up the steps.

"Just running one last check," I said.

"Alberto's up. And guess what?"

"He's hungry." I looked at my watch. "We can leave now and y'all can eat at the Anchor if you want."

"That would be faster," she said, then turned to Alberto.

"Would you like a banana to hold you over until we get there?"

Alberto nodded, sitting cross-legged on the rug, and petting the dogs, one on either side of him.

He was wearing the same clothes he'd worn the previous day.

"We have some new clothes waiting at a friend's place," I told him. "If we leave now, you can eat all the breakfast you want there. Old Rufus makes the best breakfast burritos you've ever tried."

He got to his feet and looked down at the dogs. "Will they be coming with us?"

Finn and Woden looked up at me, as if waiting for an answer, too.

"Yes," Savannah replied. "But if we're going to eat soon, we'd better get going. It's about thirty minutes in the boat to Tank and Chyrel's, then a short car ride to get to the Rusty Anchor."

Both dogs rose and with tail and nub wagging, headed for the stairs.

"They understood you," Alberto said.

"They're pretty smart," Savannah agreed, as we followed the dogs down to the dock area below the house.

Ten minutes later, we were idling into Harbor Channel. Alberto sat up on his knees in the second seat so he could see all the gauges and over the helm. He didn't want to miss a thing.

Savannah had opted for the forward-facing seat in front of the helm. Her hair was pulled back with three bands holding it in place and she wore a light sweater against the morning chill. The sun, just beginning to peek over the horizon, gave her skin a rich glow.

I increased speed to a high idle.

"Is this as fast as your boat will go?" Alberto asked.

"Oh, no," I said, then pointed to the island at the entrance to Harbor Channel. "A friend lives there and we don't want to wake his boat."

"His boat sleeps?"

Savannah and I both laughed. "He means the wave that a boat makes," Savannah explained, turning back to face us. "It's called a wake, and if we go too fast, our wake will rock Mac's boat."

Once clear of Mac's place, I brought the *Revenge* up on plane, much to Alberto's delight. I turned the wheel slightly to starboard and the big boat leaned into the wide turn like a Thoroughbred at the end of the back stretch.

Setting a course that would take us toward Tank's house on Grassy Key, I checked the chart plotter and explained to Alberto how it worked.

"I don't cross these waters in this boat often, so we need to know where the deep water is."

"How come?"

"It's a big boat," I replied. "If we try to go in water that's too shallow, we'll run aground and be stuck."

"No. How come you don't take this boat here?"

I glanced down at the boy. I knew that kids that age were always asking questions. Pap used to tell me the only dumb question was the one I *didn't* ask.

"You saw the smaller boats under the house, right?" I asked.

He nodded.

"Those boats are better suited for shallower water," I explained. "Like here on the Gulf side. We call this kind of boat a blue water boat, and we usually only use it offshore, where the

water's very deep."

On the chart plotter, I pointed to Bluefish Bank and Bamboo Bank, just beyond it. Both were close to our course, so I turned slightly, ensuring that we'd pass well to the north of them. The course line on the chart plotter moved to the left of the shallows.

Alberto craned his neck and looked out over the bow. "I don't see anything."

"They're still several miles ahead," I said. "And we'll pass them a mile to the north. From a distance, it's hard to tell shallow water from deep."

Alberto looked back and I followed his gaze. The wake we left in the water could be seen far astern.

"That's a big wake," he said. "Good thing we didn't go fast when we passed Mac's island."

I looked at him and grinned, remembering my first ride in a big, offshore boat. I was about the same age as Alberto when I went with Pap and a couple of his friends on an offshore fishing trip. We slept on the boat, miles from shore, and I remember catching a wahoo. From that point on, I was hooked.

CHAPTER FOURTEEN

In no time at all, I slowed and turned toward the dock extending out from Tank and Chyrel's house. Tony and Paul were standing at the end of the T-head, behind Tank's boat, waiting to catch lines.

Right after buying furniture for his new house, Tank had bought a slightly used twenty-six-foot Proline with a walk-around cuddy cabin. It'd only had sixty hours on the twin 200-horse Mercs. Over the months that followed, he'd tripled that, making daily runs out from the dock, fishing and exploring, sometimes overnight.

"Who are those men?" Alberto asked, as Savannah went down to toss lines.

"A couple of friends of mine," I replied. "You and Savannah will go with another lady named Chyrel to get breakfast. Then the three of you and the dogs will follow me in Savannah's boat."

"How come?"

"Me and my friends are going to take this boat," I said. "We'll all meet up in a few hours, probably about lunch time."

I laid the *Revenge* against the dock, and Tony and Paul quickly made her fast. Then they picked up three black, tactical bags and

came aboard, stashing their gear inside.

"You must be Alberto," Chyrel said, as she and Tank approached the T-head.

Savannah made the introductions and each of them greeted the boy with big smiles.

"Later, there's gonna be a test on everyone's name," I said to Alberto.

He looked over at the dock and rattled off each person's name.

"Okay, maybe there's no need," I offered, as I helped him up to the dock.

I kissed Savannah goodbye, then she and Chyrel led Alberto toward the house.

Tank heaved a cooler from the dock, passing it over to Tony. "We made some food for the trip."

"Then let's get going," I said. "DJ Martin is going to meet us in Fort Myers."

"He one of your Armstrong spooks?" Tank asked, as he stepped aboard.

Tony laughed. "DJ's not a spook, man. With just one leg, he's lucky to sneak up on a glass of water."

"You'll like DJ," I said. "He was a snake eater in Afghanistan."

"That where he lost a leg?"

"And received the silver star in doing so," Tony replied.

Paul stayed below to untie the lines as the rest of us went up to the bridge. Once I had the engines running, he tossed the lines off and stepped down into the cockpit. I put the engines in gear and idled away from the dock as he coiled and stowed the lines.

"So, what's the plan?" Paul asked, once he joined us.

"Recon," I said. "Billy has a house staked out. A girl who lives there busted up an attempted kidnapping and MS-13 wants to get back at her."

"That's it?"

I looked back toward shore and saw Chyrel's car pulling out of the driveway. "Alberto's involved somehow."

"The kid?" Tony asked. "How could he possibly be connected?"

"I have no idea," I replied honestly. "He was found on a homemade Cuban boat, covered with a tarp made in Fort Myers."

Tony grinned, his brilliant white teeth in sharp contrast to his ebony skin. "And of course, you don't believe in coincidences."

I nodded.

"And Billy is?" Tank asked.

"Billy Rainwater," I replied. "Chieftain of the Calusa people."

"The Indian kid you were buddies with, in 3/9?"

Tank and I were with Weapons Company, Third Battalion, Ninth Marine Regiment, when we deployed to Lebanon the first time. When we rotated back to Camp Lejeune in early '83, I was nearing the end of my first enlistment and Billy had just transferred in, fresh out of Infantry School. Tank was reassigned as a marksmanship instructor shortly afterward, so he'd hardly met Billy. Yet nearly four decades and thousands of Marines later, he remembered him.

"We were only back for a week before you got orders to the range," I said, bringing the *Revenge* up on plane. "You were the company gunny and Billy just a boot PFC. How could you possibly remember him?"

Tank glanced over at me from the port bench. "I served fifty-one years in the Corps. Guess how many Native Americans I served with."

He was right. The Corps reflected the demographics of the nation very closely, though skewed slightly in favor of minorities. But in my twenty years, I'd only served with one other Indian.

"Probably close to the number of black guys I served with," Tony quipped from the second seat. "Not a lot of brothers among the SEAL teams."

"Three," Tank said. "Besides, I always made it a point to know my troops."

I set a course of 320° magnetic and engaged the autopilot. We were making thirty-five knots and it'd take four hours to get there, with one course correction in about three hours. I checked my watch.

"It'll be close to noon when we arrive," I said to Tank. "What's in the cooler?"

He grinned. "We went for a run this morning. Five miles in just over forty-five minutes. When we got back, you were probably just waking up, but we were hungry. So, Chyrel made a dozen biscuits and cooked up a whole package of lean sausage."

Tony was up like his seat had voltage running through it. "I'll get it."

A moment later, he came back up the ladder with a brown paper bag in his hand. "I thought you said she made a dozen."

Tank shrugged. "Like I said, we were hungry."

Tony opened the bag and passed out three tightly wrapped packages that were still warm. Tank waved him off.

"Is sausage the right thing to eat in your condition?" Paul asked.

Usually quiet and observant, Paul rarely offered an opinion, except from a psychological point of view. Tank was dying of cancer. It wasn't bad in any one particular part of his body yet, but by the time it was discovered, it'd spread throughout his abdomen and bones.

"I only had one," Tank said. "Along with some sliced melon, strawberries, wheat toast, and OJ."

Tony looked down into the bag again. "There's only five left."

Tank grinned at him. "What can I say? Living with an old Devil Dog gives a woman an appetite."

I'd never pried into his and Chyrel's relationship. At first, their marriage sounded like a business deal. Chyrel wasn't a kid, but she *was* twenty-five years younger than Tank. She'd agreed to care for him when the time came that he couldn't take care of himself. In exchange, she'd get the house he'd bought and a survivor's pension. Knowing her as I did, and how much she simply liked the man, I knew she'd have done it anyway. She'd already confided to me that when the time came, she'd sell the house and put the proceeds into Tank's charity fund.

Tank figured that since he'd been a Marine from the age of seventeen and had retired less than three years ago at sixty-eight, he wouldn't receive a fair pension for all his years of service. By marrying Chyrel, though, she would be eligible for a survivor's pension when he was gone.

But over the months since they'd married, they seemed a lot more like a couple than business partners. I'd never been one to judge. Hell, Savannah was ten years younger than me. Tank and Chyrel were more than old enough to make life choices on their own. Chyrel had never wanted a husband and to Tank, that was

perfect—by not remarrying when he was gone, she'd collect his pension for a long time.

As we headed away from the Keys and into the deeper waters of the Gulf, there was a moderate chop. But the *Revenge* was a blue water boat, so the waves were barely noticeable.

I told the men about what I'd learned online, about the gang wars, missing and dead hookers, and the drug connection.

"You think MS-13 filled the void after the Blanc cartel was dismantled?" Tony asked.

"That's possible," I replied. "Where there's a demand, someone else will eventually come in to fill the gap."

Paul had been quietly taking everything in, digesting it all in that analytical mind of his. He turned his head and looked back at me. "How were the two prostitutes murdered?" he asked.

"A bullet to the back of their heads," I replied. "Execution style."

"And others have been reported missing, you said?"

"Yeah," I replied. "Maybe half a dozen or more."

"They're dead," Paul said flatly. "The gangbangers just did a better job of disposing of the bodies."

"What makes you think that?" Tank asked. "Some psychological profile or something?"

"Simple economics," Paul replied. "If there's a turf war between rival gangs, ultimately it's going to be about money. Whether that money comes from drugs, prostitution, or a bake sale doesn't matter. Each gang will try to cut off the revenue flow of their rivals."

I thought about that a moment. From what I'd learned about MS-13, they were ruthless and used murder and intimidation as tools. I didn't think it would be beyond them to just kill off

prostitutes who worked for a rival gang.

"If you can't raise the bridge," I said. "Lower the river."

Tony looked over at me, swallowing a bite from his biscuit. "You mean take the hookers out of the equation?"

I nodded. "And the drugs, too, if we can figure out how."

"And just how do you figure on doing all this?"

"Cash," I said.

I saw the light flicker in Tony's eyes. "You mean we go into these seedy neighborhoods and proposition hookers?"

"Most of these women are drug addicts," Paul said. "Many come from broken homes and abusive relationships. And most addicts don't want to be one. They can't stop using on their own and just don't have the wherewithal to get treatment."

"Call Chyrel," I said to Tony. "While they're at the Anchor, she can use Rusty's Wi-Fi to find the nearest drug rehab center around Fort Myers. We'll grab the hookers and take them there. Even if they don't complete the treatment, they'll be safe for a few days."

"Do you really think they'll go willingly?" Tank asked.

I thought about that a moment. "While you have her, tell her to send two hundred thousand dollars from my account to me at the BB&T on McGregor in Fort Myers."

They all looked at me, surprised.

"We'll give each one an incentive," I said. "Five grand when they complete the treatment and relocation to another town."

CHAPTER FIFTEEN

In a squalid, abandoned apartment building, Maria Gonzalez huddled in a corner of what had once been a second story unit's small living room. She was done, spent, used up for the night. But she had cash in her pocket. Just what that meant to her these days, she really couldn't comprehend.

Across from her, a black woman named Shanice sat cross-legged on the floor. Both were high on meth, but it was from the night before and they were starting to come down—tweaking.

The initial rush of methamphetamine produced a feeling of euphoria that lasted for hours, sometimes all night. After that, the high slowly subsided as the user's body began to shut down, unable to handle the continuous rush. It was during this post-euphoric high stage that a meth user was most lucid, but usually argumentative. Once the high was gone, nothing else mattered except finding more meth.

Both women knew of the missing and dead hookers and both had taken precautions, as best they could, to not be picked up by someone in the rival gang. Yet, there they were, sitting across from one another in the same room—a Hispanic MS-13 prostitute and a black one who worked for the Lake Boyz gang.

Maria drew her knees up and pulled her sweatshirt down over her legs. It wasn't terribly cold, but there was a chill in the early morning air.

"I don't think my people can protect me anymore," Maria said.

Shanice looked over at her. How the two had ended up in the same room, neither of them knew. It had just started to get light outside, and like vampires hiding from the daylight, they'd wandered into the same hiding place.

"Your people started this," Shanice argued.

"My friend was killed a week ago," Maria said. "And her son kidnapped. Your people ransacked Razor's place and took the boy. So, Razor hit back."

Shanice looked down at her ankles. She'd heard Bumpy bragging about killing several Hispanic working girls. "Bumpy killed her."

"Huh?"

"He's Lake Boyz," Shanice said. "I heard him bragging about killing a few *chicas* and trashing that Razor guy's place.

Maria was horrified. "Why would he do that?"

Shanice lifted her head and glared at the other woman. "You don't belong here," she spat vehemently. "Before your posse came, Lake Boyz ruled and everything was good."

Maria didn't want to argue with her. She was right. The Hispanic population in the area had slowly grown over time. It wasn't her fault that her parents had brought her to Florida. It was where her dad could find work. Up until he was killed in a drive-by shooting several years earlier.

"Look around," Maria said. "You call this good? Neither of us is safe. What can we do?"

"I started turning tricks to get out of this hellhole," Shanice said. "I didn't have no job and got evicted from my shithole apartment. I thought I could do it for a few weeks and save up, ya know. I never wanted to smoke it."

"Me neither," Maria said, a tear trailing down her cheek. "But it made things easier. Now I can't stop."

"So, what's left?"

"I don't know," Maria said. "Just die, I guess."

"Nobody gets out alive."

"My mom's forty," Maria said. "I used to think she was young. But I know I'll never get to be her age."

Shanice rose and went to the window. It was boarded up, but there was a small crack between the two sheets of warped plywood.

"It's getting lighter," she said, peering through the crack.

"You got someplace to go?" Maria asked.

"No. Do you?"

"I was staying with a friend," Maria replied. "But he kicked me out two days ago. Said it was too dangerous."

The location of the abandoned apartment building was between the two neighborhoods controlled by Lake Boyz and MS-13—neutral turf. But since this latest war had started, working girls weren't safe anywhere.

"There's a Popeye's across the street," Shanice said, angling her head to the right for a better view. "You got any money?"

"A little," Maria said. "But I don't feel like going out there."

"Gimme five dollars," Shanice said. "I'll go get us something."

Maria eyed her suspiciously.

"Fuck it," Shanice said. "I'll buy and you can pay me when I

get back. Deal?"

"Sure," Maria replied.

The black girl pulled the door open and left. Maria could hear her footsteps on the stairs for a moment, and then it fell quiet. Alone with her jumbled thoughts, the silence was oppressive.

She stood and moved over to the window. She had to stand on her toes to see through the crack. Her knees shook.

After a moment, she saw Shanice on the sidewalk below. She walked down the street a little way, then turned to cross over to the fast-food restaurant.

Suddenly, a Chevy lowrider came careening around the corner. It stopped and several Hispanic men jumped out and grabbed Shanice before she could take two more steps.

The men wrestled her toward the car. When she screamed for help, they started to beat her. Finally, they threw her into the backseat and climbed in on either side of her.

The car's engine roared and rattled as the Chevy sped off down the street.

Maria collapsed to the floor, sobbing.

CHAPTER SIXTEEN

Once we reached the marina and got the *Revenge* tied up in her slip, I told the others to stay aboard while I walked to the bank. I carried a well-worn backpack on one shoulder.

It was only a mile and the walk allowed my mind to decompress from the run up from the Keys. When I arrived at the bank, I stood in line for the teller windows and when it was my turn, I asked to speak to the manager.

I'd done this kind of financial transaction before and knew it was a waste of time to tell the window clerk what I wanted. She asked me to have a seat in the lobby and Miss Thompson would be right with me.

I sat and watched the news on a TV with the sound turned down. After a few minutes, a middle-aged woman approached. She wore a business suit and skirt, and her hair was cut short.

"I'm Noreen Thompson," she said. "What can I help you with?"

I stood and extended a hand. "Jesse McDermitt."

She shook my hand and invited me to her office.

I dropped my empty backpack in one of the chairs in front of her desk and sat down in the other one.

"I received a wire transfer for you," she said. "But I'll need to see some identification."

After showing her my license, she asked how I'd like the funds.

"Twenty straps," I replied.

She picked up her phone and talked to someone for a moment, then after hanging up, turned to her computer. After a few seconds, the printer started, and she produced a receipt and asked me to look it over.

She seemed reserved and slightly put off, and I knew why. Bankers encounter all kinds of businesspeople. But a rough-looking customer picking up a ton of cash usually meant only one thing in South Florida. What she thought I was doing with the money or what kind of person she thought I was didn't matter, and I offered no explanation.

The receipt seemed in order and I only nodded.

An armed security guard came in with a metal briefcase. He placed it on her desk and left, closing the door behind him.

Miss Thompson pulled the blinds, then turned and opened the briefcase. Inside were neatly stacked bundles of one hundred-dollar bills. She removed them one by one, counting them out as she placed them on her desk.

"Please sign here, if everything's okay," she said, moving the receipt closer and pointing to an X.

I signed for the cash, then put it all into my backpack.

Ten minutes after walking in, I was back out on the street, headed toward the marina, with nearly a quarter million dollars in my backpack. I wasn't armed, but I also didn't look like a target.

Muggers and thieves usually worked in darkness, anyway.

And they preferred victims who wouldn't fight back. Though there were some gray hairs around my temples, at six-three and over two hundred pounds, any would-be thief would think twice. So, I wasn't worried.

Still, as was my habit all the time, my head was on a swivel and I walked with a confident stride.

The sidewalk was busy, but not crowded, as I made my way back to the marina. Most of the people I encountered were office workers, probably going to or from lunch.

When I got back to the boat, DJ had arrived. They were all sitting around the cockpit coaming, talking.

"Hey, Jesse," DJ said, as I stepped down into the boat. "The guys were just filling me in."

"Let's go inside," I suggested.

In the galley, I slid behind the counter and put the pack on top of it, unzipping it. I took out one of the bundles, tore off the strap and counted out five stacks with five bills in each.

"Go out and buy something," I said. "Anything small—a coffee or something. Pay for it with a hundred-dollar bill."

"What gives?" DJ asked.

Tony stepped forward and picked up a stack of bills. "Hookers don't make change."

"That's right," I said. "And the type we're looking for will be suspicious of a hundred-dollar proposition."

"You sound like you've done this before," DJ said, stroking his long goatee.

"Saw it on TV," I lied.

The truth was, I don't watch a lot of television, and aside from the one on the *Revenge*, we didn't have one on the island.

It just made common sense. Streetwalkers weren't the same as

high-dollar Las Vegas call girls. Those who turned tricks in a filthy alley to get drug money probably wouldn't spend more than ten minutes with a client. I had no idea what the going rate was but would be surprised if it was more than twenty bucks.

"Paul, there's a Publix a couple of miles from here. Get an Uber and head over there. Stock up with enough to last us a few days, okay?"

He nodded, scooping up a stack. "About $101 worth of groceries?"

I grinned. "Probably three times that, but yeah, break as many bills as you can."

"We could probably use a car," Tank suggested.

"Billy's tied up," I said. "But why don't you go with Paul and have the Uber driver take you to the nearest car rental after dropping him off at the Publix. You can pick him up on the way back."

Tank and DJ picked up a stack of bills and we exited the boat, each heading in different directions. I went to the marina office and paid cash for three nights. It came to a little over $400. Then I stopped at the fuel dock on the way back and asked if the hose could reach the *Revenge* at the end. The dockmaster said it would reach the whole face dock.

"I'll need about three hundred gallons," I told him.

After that, I went back to the boat and powered up the laptop while I waited for him to unroll the hose.

I had an email from Chyrel and one from Jack Armstrong. I opened his first. In it, he explained that work was going well on the ship, but the cabin renovation might take a little longer. He said to not plan on arriving until the following Monday.

I wondered at the necessity of it. Odds were that whatever

happened with Alberto, he'd be gone from us in a short time, and there was little that Savannah or I could do about it.

In the email from Chyrel, she said that they were at the Rusty Anchor but would be underway shortly. The time stamp was several hours ago, so they were likely halfway to Fort Myers already.

She went on to list nearly a dozen rehab centers in the Fort Myers area, which surprised me. Looking at the addresses, I immediately dismissed half of them—they were too close. Then I noticed one that was in Fort Myers Beach, well out of town, out on Estero Island.

"Ahoy *Gaspar's Revenge*," a voice called from outside.

I stepped out into the cockpit and saw the dockmaster there with the fuel pump hose. I opened the access hatch and removed the cap, then took the hose from him.

"About three hundred gallons?" he asked.

"No more than that," I replied. "We're at about half a tank now."

"Roger that, Captain," he said. "I'll start the pump and set it to shut off at three hundred. It'll probably take a good ten minutes. How do you plan to pay?"

"No hurry," I replied. "I'll pay with cash."

He disappeared back toward the little shack in the center of the dock. I squeezed the trigger on the nozzle and wedged the cap under the trigger to keep it open.

When the pump stopped, I removed the nozzle, closed the fuel cap and door, and set the nozzle up on the dock. I could see the dockmaster was busy bringing in another boat, so I went.

I searched for the facility on Estero and called them. I gave the woman my name, then lied and said I had a friend who

needed their help and asked how I could go about setting up and paying for her treatment.

"You'll need to bring your friend in for an assessment," the pleasant-sounding woman named Audrey said. "We have plenty of room just now, but the doctors only take new patients on a case-by-case basis."

"Can I come in and meet with the doctors before I bring her in?"

"Well,"—she paused—"that's a little out of the ordinary. We usually prefer to meet with the patient."

I wasn't going to be dissuaded that easily. "I think when the doctors meet with me, they'll understand why this is necessary."

"Let's see," she said. "I can probably schedule it for next Wednesday."

"I was thinking more like this afternoon," I said.

"That's out of the..."

"I'll pay two thousand dollars for ten minutes of their time."

"Huh?"

"Look," I said. "This is very important. Can you arrange for the doctors to meet me at fifteen hund...er, three o'clock? Whether they take my friend as a client or not, I'll make a two-thousand-dollar donation on the spot, before we talk."

"This is very unorthodox, Mr. McDermitt."

"What can I say? I'm an unorthodox sort of guy. Can you do it?"

There was a short pause. "Not at three," she said. "But all three doctors will be in a conference at three-thirty. Can you come then? They'll only be able to give you ten minutes."

"That's perfect, Audrey. I'll see you then."

I ended the call and went back out to the cockpit just as the

dockmaster was walking up to the boat.

"Three hundred gallons, Captain," he said, moving the nozzle to the center of the dock.

"What's the damage?" I asked.

"That'll be $947.70," he replied.

I grinned. "Perfect. Hang on a sec."

I went back inside and took another eleven bills from the open bundle. I handed the dockmaster ten of them and told him he could keep the change if he'd break the other bill into tens for me.

"Can do, sir," he replied, then hurried away.

He was back before I finished wiping down the insides of the access hatch.

"Does the marina have a loaner car?" I asked, taking the bills from him.

"Two, actually," he replied. "Need to get some groceries?"

"Something like that," I said. "Is it available twenty-four hours?"

"No," he replied. "Just while the marina's open."

I studied his features. He was average height and slim. Though he was probably only in his thirties, his face was lined from squinting in the sun and the short hairs at his neck were darker than on top. The patch on the front of his shirt said his name was Mark.

"You live aboard, Mark?" I asked.

"Yes, sir," he replied. "A Hunter 27."

"One of the guys I'm with has one," I said. "He named it *Whole Nine Yards*. Yours a twin keel?"

He grinned. Boaters liked to talk about their boats. "Cool name. Yeah, the twins make her a pig pointing to windward, but

the shallower draft lets me get into gunkholes where a lot of monohull sailboats can't. She's not real big, and she doesn't go fast, but she's comfortable and gets me where I want to go. Plus, when the tide goes out, she sits upright on the sandy bottom."

"How'd you like to make a hundred bucks a night for the next couple of nights?"

He eyed me suspiciously.

"Nothing illegal," I assured him. "I just need a car and driver to ferry people over to Estero."

"What time?" he asked.

"Come aboard," I said. "If you have a minute."

He dropped down and leaned against the coaming.

"Are you aware of the gang war that's going on here?" I asked point blank, to gauge his reaction.

He nodded somberly; a sour look on his face. "Hard to ignore," he said. "This marina's just a stone's throw from some pretty seedy neighborhoods."

I dug into my pocket and took out a little metal card holder that had the seal of the Marine Corps engraved on it.

I took a card out and handed it to him. "I'm a private investigator. My associates and I need someone we can trust locally."

He nodded at the metal card holder. "You a Marine?"

I saw the look in his eyes. A fire born of more than two hundred years of history. I'd met another Jarhead.

"Retired twenty years ago," I replied. "Infantry."

"Oh-four to oh-eight," he said. "Arty."

I grinned. Cannon-cockers were a tight bunch. "There are few problems that liberal doses of high explosive artillery can't resolve."

"I have my own car," he said. "But I can't get involved in

anything that would jeopardize my job."

"I understand completely. We're here to try to put an end to the problems those neighborhoods are having. And hopefully find out what happened to a little boy."

"What do I have to do?" he asked.

CHAPTER SEVENTEEN

On the flybridge, I watched boat traffic out on the Caloosahatchee while I waited. It was hard to believe that just a few blocks away, rival gangs were fighting over territory, people were being killed, and drug addiction was being fed by the almighty dollar.

I'd grown up here. Dad had taken me and Mom with him whenever he was stationed somewhere that allowed it. I'd lived a short time up at Camp Lejeune and out at Twenty-Nine Palms. But Dad always thought a stable home was important, and he'd bought a house not far from Mam and Pap's place. They'd lived out on Highway 80 in the Fort Myers Shores neighborhood.

Pap had bought land on the Caloosahatchee soon after he returned from the war in the South Pacific. He'd built a modest home on it, mostly by himself. He'd gone to college under the old GI Bill and earned a degree in architecture and design.

When Dad followed in Pap's footsteps as a Marine, Pap had given him the down payment to buy a house in the neighborhood that had sprung up around his home. Dad married soon after and began to put down roots.

Mam and Pap's old place stood just sixteen miles upriver, and

the house Dad had bought was just a few blocks away from it. The dark water flowing past was no different now than it had been then. I'd played along the river's bank, swum in its water, and later, as a teen, explored every inch of shoreline from here to Labelle by canoe.

I pulled my phone out and called Billy.

"I was just thinking about you, Kemosabe," he said, without greeting.

Billy and I had always had a deep connection. We'd grown up together in this area, and even though our homes were separated by several miles, we were of different cultural backgrounds, and two years apart in age, we'd been awfully close friends.

"I'm sitting on the flybridge watching the Caloosahatchee flow by," I said.

"That explains it."

"How are things there?"

"A bit of excitement last night," he replied. "But quiet today."

"What happened?"

"A van loaded with gangbangers stopped by for a visit," he said, his voice subdued. "A couple of them needed help walking back to their van and one will have a little trouble hearing."

I grinned. Billy wasn't prone to bragging, so I took what he was saying to mean he'd hurt several MS-13 members pretty badly. I knew it was a waste of time to ask if he was okay, but I did anyway.

"Nothing a few ibuprofen can't fix," was his reply. "Why are you here?"

"We're coming at the problem from a different angle," I replied. "MS-13 is having problems with a rival gang. I have a few

snake eaters with me, and we plan to make life miserable for both sides."

He chuckled softly. "Playing both ends against the middle, huh?"

"Keep your head on a swivel," I told him, as Tony and DJ came walking down the dock.

"And my *ear* to the ground," he said. He laughed at some inside joke, then ended the call.

"Come on up," I called down to Tony and DJ. "Everything go okay?"

"No problem," Tony said, pulling a wad of small bills from his pocket.

"Just hang onto that," I told them both. "Tonight, we're going shopping. I have a second car and a driver."

"Who?" DJ asked.

"One of the dockmasters," I replied. "A guy named Mark. He's a former Marine gun bunny who offered to carry our guests down to a treatment center on Estero Island."

"Where's that?" Tony asked.

"Ten miles south of here," I replied. "Across San Carlos Bay from Sanibel Island."

"Ya know," DJ began, "rousting the gang's hookers won't amount to much of a disruption."

I grinned at him. "Which is why I'm glad you're with us, DJ."

His features turned wary. "What's that supposed to mean?"

"Drug dealers would be pretty suspicious of me, just based on my looks," I said. "Same with Paul and Tank."

"That's an understatement," Tony said. "All three of you look as straight as the proverbial arrow. But I can pull it off in certain neighborhoods."

I nodded and clapped DJ on the shoulder. "But DJ here, he looks the part better than any of us."

"Oh, gee, thanks," he grumbled. "Um..." He paused.

"You have a question?" I asked.

"Don't take this the wrong way," he said. "I don't mean anything personal by it. But Tank? How old is he?"

Tony looked over at DJ. "You don't know who he is, do you?"

"Just met him a little while ago."

"In 1970, that old guy saved the lives of more than a dozen men in Vietnam," Tony said. "They were pinned down in a minefield and Tank brought them back to the helo. Those who could walk followed in his footsteps through the minefield. Those who couldn't walk, he carried. He was later awarded the Medal of Honor."

DJ's eyes went wide. "You mean I've been sittin' here talkin' to this guy and none of y'all thought to tell me that?"

"You don't have to worry about Tank," I said. "If the shit hits the fan, there's nobody I'd rather have with me."

"You have an idea?" Tony asked. "About how to drop the feces into the oscillator?"

I nodded. "Tonight, while Tank and I are busy rounding up prostitutes, you and DJ are gonna rip off as many drug dealers as you can."

"Simple as that, huh?" DJ asked, rhetorically.

"It won't be simple," I replied. "We'll only have one car."

"No, we won't," I heard Tank say from the dock.

I looked down to see him climbing aboard alone. "Where's Paul?"

Tank came up the ladder and leaned on the rail. "I got to

thinking," he said. "I couldn't see how we could hit them hard enough with just one set of wheels. As it turned out, the nearest car rental was Enterprise. You know their slogan?"

Tony grinned. "We'll pick you up?"

"Yep," Tank said. "I rented three cars and had one dropped off at Publix and the other delivered here. The agent on duty sent a fourth car to pick up the other two drivers."

"I should have suggested that myself," I said.

"You were just a gunny. Master gunnery sergeants get shit done."

DJ laughed somewhat nervously.

"So, what'd I miss?" Tank asked, sitting next to DJ.

"DJ and Tony are gonna use two of the cars to drive around and rip off as many drug dealers as they can find."

"Finding them might not be easy," Tank said. "I doubt they'll have a neon sign over their businesses."

"Not as difficult as you'd think," DJ said. "I've been offered all kinds of drugs just sitting in a bar or walking down the street."

Tank looked at him. "Is that right? Never happened to me before."

"Understandable, sir," DJ said. "You don't look like a user. I do."

"What's this sir crap?" Tank asked. "You on drugs now, son?"

"I don't do drugs," DJ said. "Well, maybe a joint now and then."

"Then you can shitcan the sir," Tank ordered. "I was an enlisted man, just like you. Or was that *sir* crap a reference to my age?"

"I think DJ's a little hero-struck," Tony said. "He didn't know

who you were."

Tank's eyes bored into DJ's. "Wanna know what I think?" he asked, then continued without waiting for an answer. "In the last couple of decades, I started hearing about World War II guys being the greatest generation. They did, in fact, save the world. But if you ask them, and I served with a bunch of 'em, they'll all tell you what I'm about to say. That's hogwash. Those guys did what needed to be done, when it was required, short and simple.

"What makes a man stand up against overwhelming odds isn't generational. We're all born with a sense of right and wrong. I was just in the right place at the right time to make a difference. If I hadn't been there, someone else woulda done it. Look at you. I understand you got a Silver Star in exchange for that peg leg. You think you were any different than the guys you saved?

"No," DJ replied.

"I'm no more or less a man than you, son. You read me?"

"Yes, sir," DJ said, with a grin. "And that one was in deference to your wisdom."

"Let it be the last," Tank said. "Now tell me about that gimp leg."

DJ told his story, short and sweet. He'd been part of a team that was clearing houses in Fallujah when a grenade landed in their midst. Without thinking, he'd knocked the rest of his four-man team to the ground and tried to kick the grenade out the door.

"I was only partly successful," he said.

"When this is over," Tank offered, "I'll drink to your leg."

DJ grinned. "And I'll drink to your knowing where the mines were."

Tank roared with laughter, then started coughing. Finally, he

slapped DJ on the shoulder. "I didn't have any idea where those mines were."

The VHF crackled and I thought I recognized Savannah's voice. I reached over and turned it up.

"Go to one-seven, *Sea Biscuit*," the dockmaster said.

I switched channels with them, and Mark told Savannah he had her on the inside of the same dock we were on.

"Will you need assistance?" he asked.

I keyed the mic before Savannah could answer. "Negative, Landings Marina. She's expected. We'll get down there and tie her off."

A few minutes later, *Sea Biscuit* turned around the end of the face dock and Savannah maneuvered her boat into place. Chyrel was on the foredeck and Alberto was up on the flybridge with Savannah. He was beaming from ear to ear.

CHAPTER EIGHTEEN

Later that afternoon, Savannah and I took one of the rental cars and drove the short distance to Fort Myers Beach. It had grown up a little over the years; newer businesses here and there and a lot more homes, but it was still basically the same.

"I've been here a couple of times," Savannah said, looking around. "Flo and I anchored in Matanzas Pass for a week once. Quiet area."

"Yeah, it is," I said, turning into the parking lot of the treatment center. "I've probably been to the beach here a thousand times as a kid."

I checked my watch. It was 1525. We were five minutes early.

When we walked in, a pretty receptionist greeted us. I recognized her voice.

"Hi, Audrey," I said. "I'm Jesse McDermitt, and this is my wife, Savannah."

She smiled warmly. "I thought you said you were seeking treatment for a friend."

"Not me," Savannah said. "Someone else."

"Oh, I'm sorry. Hold on just a sec and let me buzz the doctors. They're in the conference room now, going over the case

load."

She made a call and announced that we were there, then hung up the phone, and came out from behind the counter.

"Follow me, please," she said, then went down a hallway.

Audrey ushered us into a room, where two men and a woman were seated at a conference table. One of the men rose and extended a hand.

"I'm Dr. Porter," he said. "And these are my associates, Doctors Wilson and Lopez."

I introduced Savannah and we shook hands all around. Then I took a small roll of bills from my pocket and placed it on the table.

"This is just for agreeing to see us on short notice," I said. "My wife and I would like to make you a proposition."

Dr. Porter ignored the wad of cash. "Audrey said you have a friend who needs treatment."

"More than one, I'm afraid."

"How many?" Dr. Wilson asked.

I'd told Savannah and Chyrel our plans while DJ had taken Alberto for a walk around the docks to show him the boats.

"We don't know for sure," Savannah said. "Maybe quite a few."

"You don't know how many friends?" Dr. Wilson asked.

"Can we sit down?" I asked.

"Yes, of course," Porter said.

He was a few years older than the other two, slightly built, with dark hair starting to go gray around his ears.

Once seated, I laid out what we were planning to do, including giving each woman we brought in $5000 and a chance at a new life somewhere else if they completed the treatment pro-

gram. The doctors listened attentively.

"In short," I said, "we need your help to curtail the prostitution problem in Fort Myers."

"Quite an endeavor," Porter said, tenting his fingers under his chin.

"And very philanthropic," Wilson added. "But what makes you think you can do this? And where will the money for treatment come from?"

"My husband can do anything he sets his mind to," Savannah said. "And our organization is made up of some very wealthy people."

Dr. Lopez had sat quietly through the whole discussion, taking in everything. She was an attractive woman in her mid-thirties, with dark hair, brown eyes, and light brown skin.

"We'll do it," Lopez said, her voice firm.

Porter turned to her. "But we don't have—"

"Then we'll get it," she said, cutting him off. "This center was created to help exactly the type of people the McDermitts are talking about. If I could bring them in myself, I would. So, if the McDermitts can do what they say, we will treat these girls."

The two men were silent. I'd assumed Porter was the head of the organization.

Dr. Lopez turned to Savannah. "My sister, Ariana, was one of those streetwalkers," she said. "She died of a heroin overdose ten years ago."

Savannah offered her a sad smile, reached across the table, and put her hand on the other woman's. "I also lost my sister to drugs," she said.

"Ariana died just before I completed my bachelor's in psychology. It was because of her that I went on to med school. I

never wanted to be a psychologist. I planned to use my degree in the marketing world. After residency, I worked and saved and eventually created this facility. We are at your disposal and if we run out of room, we can put these women into other facilities."

"Thank you, Doctor," Savannah said.

"My friends call me Cat," she said. "It's short for Catalina." She picked up the roll of hundred-dollar bills and extended it to me. "This isn't necessary."

"A deal's a deal, Cat," I said, making no effort to accept the money.

"Very well," she said, with a smile. "We will consider it a deposit on the first case. When should we expect the patient?"

"Tonight," I said. "Probably late. And with any luck at all, more than just one."

Cat rose from the table. "I will be here all night."

With the meeting over, Savannah and I left.

"I thought the older guy was the boss," I said, once we got into the rental car.

Savannah smiled as she buckled her seatbelt. "I knew it was her all along, just by the way she didn't talk much."

"Much? She didn't say a word until she agreed to help."

As I drove across Matanzas Pass Bridge, I asked, "Are you sure you're okay with me doing this tonight?"

"What?"

"Picking up prostitutes."

She turned in her seat, facing me. "What you and your friends plan to do is a noble thing, Jesse. If you can help get just one girl out of that situation, it will all be worth it."

We drove across San Carlos Island in silence, passing Doc Ford's Rum Bar, and onto the mainland. When we arrived back

at the marina, the others were sitting around the expansive bridge deck on *Sea Biscuit.*

"What's going on?" I asked, following Savannah up the ladder.

Tony was sitting opposite Alberto at the small table. There was a checkerboard game between them.

"We're losing our shirts to this kid," DJ said.

Tony reluctantly moved one of only two remaining black checkers and Alberto made a double jump, picking them both up.

He looked up at Tony and grinned, extending his hand. "One dollar."

Tony stood and pulled a dollar bill out of his wallet and handed it to the boy. "How can you have amnesia and know how to play checkers?"

Alberto shrugged. "I dunno."

"You're teaching him to gamble?" Savannah asked.

DJ took Tony's seat. "It was the kid's idea," he said. "And it's hardly gambling, when he wins every game."

"How'd it go?" Paul asked, watching DJ and Alberto rearrange the checkers.

I moved over closer to him and spoke in a low voice. "We have a place to take the girls." I nodded toward the kid. "What do you make of this?"

"The checkers?" Paul asked.

I nodded.

"There are many kinds of memory loss," Paul said. "What Alberto is experiencing is likely dissociative amnesia, brought on by a traumatic experience. It could be permanent, or he could regain his earlier memories. Whatever happened to him, it's caused his subconscious mind to block out everything personal about himself. People with this type of amnesia will retain motor

skills, language, and usually some learned behavior, like how to play simple games. He's a remarkably intelligent young man. I've been watching him play. He's always thinking several moves ahead, with alternate moves dependent on what his opponent does. He doesn't have to wait, but makes his move instantly after his opponent. So, he's actually thinking several moves ahead in several different scenarios. I wonder if he plays chess?"

"You think he'll be okay?" I asked.

"Hard to say," Paul replied. "Some patients recover fully and are then faced with the memories of what happened to them. Others never regain the memory of what caused the disassociation, yet go on to live a normal, productive life."

"I'm glad you're here with us," I said. "Is there anything we can do to help him remember?"

Paul looked up at me. "He's had a hard life up to now. Chyrel got into the hospital records so I could look at his file. The physician who treated him wrote in his notes that he guessed he might be as old as eight or nine, but a lifetime of malnourishment had stunted his growth."

Paul paused and looked over at Alberto again. "It's probably best not to push it. If his memory returns, it returns. If it doesn't, he may be better off for it."

"King me," Alberto said.

The game was progressing swiftly.

"How?" DJ asked. "I don't have any more of your checkers."

Alberto took one of the checkers he'd already captured from DJ and put it under his piece on the back row. His hand, in midair, began to shake. He sat back suddenly, clasping his hands together between his knees, and tightly closing his eyes.

DJ quickly moved around the table and sat beside him, pulling him close. "It's okay, little man. You're safe here."

Savannah went to his other side and wrapped her arms around both of them. "DJ's right," she whispered. "Nobody can hurt you here."

"He's just had a flash of memory," Paul whispered to me, watching the boy closely. "He's frightened—terrified."

DJ Martin was usually a boisterous, fun-loving guy, but being a former Army spec-ops soldier, he could turn instantly dangerous. To see him gently holding Alberto and stroking his hair was so out of character. It was something I'd have expected from his partner, Jerry Snyder, but not DJ.

After a moment, Alberto looked up at him with a pitiful expression and tears in his eyes. He looked down at DJ's prosthetic, festooned with stickers from bars, dive boats, and military organizations. I could see a bond between them. What it was, I didn't know.

"Did you remember something?" Savannah asked. Then she looked up at Paul. "It's okay if he talks about it, right?"

"If he wants to," Paul said.

The rest of us knelt on the deck around Alberto.

"You can think of me as your grandpa," Tank said, chucking the boy on the shoulder. "And the rest of us are your aunts and uncles. We're all family and we take care of each other."

Alberto looked around at each of us, wiping his eyes. Then they fell on Tony. "You too?"

"Me too, kiddo," Tony said. "Me, Tank, DJ, Paul, and Jesse are all just like real brothers."

He looked at Savannah. "I remembered someone," he said, then pointed to Tony. "Someone like him."

"Someone black?" I asked.

"Yeah," he replied. "I think he was my dad."

CHAPTER NINETEEN

After a late dinner aboard the *Revenge*, Savannah and I took Alberto down to *Sea Biscuit's* forward stateroom. He either wasn't able to or didn't want to recall anything more about the black man in his memory.

We sat with him for a while, Savannah reading from one of Flo's books, until he fell asleep.

We'd changed our plans up a little, since we had three cars. Tank and Paul would stand watch on *Sea Biscuit*, just as an added measure of security, while DJ and Tony took separate cars to hit the drug dealers and I'd take the third car to pick up prostitutes.

Chyrel had her laptop set up in the large salon and was going to sleep on the couch. "How's he doing?" she asked when we came back to the salon.

"He's sleeping," Savannah replied. "It's been a long day."

"It's going to be a long night, too," I said.

Savannah kissed me and then I headed over to where the guys were waiting on the *Revenge*. I opened the cabinet where my laptop was located, removed a small box, then passed out communication devices. I only had four, but Tank and Paul could share as they relieved one another on *Sea Biscuit*'s flybridge.

I doubted there would be any trouble, but with Alberto aboard, I didn't want to take any chances. Chyrel could monitor all the comms from her laptop.

We waited until 2200, then went over to Mark Ramsey's 27-foot Hunter. There was a light on, so I called out quietly. Mark's head popped up out of the companionway.

"We're heading out," I said. "I'll take the first girl I can find to the center myself, but I'd like it if you'd come with me, so I can introduce you to Dr. Lopez."

"No problem," he said. "I usually sleep in the salon anyway. I'll be ready."

"Give me your number," I said. "I'll call you and you can meet me out by the road."

He gave it to me, and I punched it into my phone, then hit the *Talk* button. When I heard his ring tone down below, I ended the call, storing his number in my recent call log.

The three of us set off for the parking lot where the three rentals were located. We were all well-armed.

"Don't take any chances," I told Tony and DJ. "As soon as someone produces drugs, pull your weapons. Make sure they don't have a knife or anything, and flex cuff their legs. Just leave them where you find them but get all their drugs and cash."

Tony nodded. "We'll hit hard and fast. As soon as someone finds one of them, word will spread and the rest will be ready."

I got in the car and started the engine. I had a good idea where I'd begin. I remembered a day when I was a kid, driving down Anderson Avenue through town with Pap. At a stop light, a woman wearing a short skirt and tank top had leaned in the car's open window. Pap hit the button to put the window up before she could say anything, causing her to jump back and then start

swearing at him. When I asked who she was, he told me to never talk to the girls on that street, which later became Dr. Martin Luther King Junior Boulevard.

As I got older, Pap told me about other parts of town I should avoid, one of them being Pine Manor, which wasn't far from the marina.

Ten minutes later, I turned onto US 41, known locally as Cleveland Avenue, and headed north. In downtown Fort Myers, Cleveland intersected MLK, just before crossing the Caloosahatchee to North Fort Myers.

The stretch of 41 I was on was rundown, with many of the businesses closed and boarded up. Those still in business had bars on the windows.

I drove slowly, with the windows down. I don't know why, but whenever I was driving and looking for something—a street sign or address—I always put the windows down, as if it allowed me to see better.

Approaching a green light, I saw movement behind the big concrete power pole that supported the traffic lights. A woman stepped out of the shadows and I slowed, then came to a stop.

"Wanna date?" she asked, stepping closer.

A date? I suddenly realized I had no idea how to pick up a hooker.

"How much?" I asked, deciding that would be the correct response.

"Are you a cop?" she asked, stepping closer still. "Cuz if you are, you gotta say so."

I doubted that was the case.

"No, I'm not a cop," I replied. "Just a lonely guy, new in town."

She pulled on the door handle, but it was locked. I clicked the button, and she opened the door and got in.

"Start drivin'," she said, her voice a little slurred. "A cop jes' went by, and I think he seen me."

I started driving, still heading north.

The girl was Hispanic, with dark hair and eyes. She was young, probably early twenties.

"It's ten bucks for a hummer," she said. "Twenty if you wanna screw."

I looked over at her as we approached a streetlight. She looked emaciated and frail. Her face appeared droopy, like an Andy Warhol portrait. She was obviously a meth user—probably an addict.

"I didn't actually pick you up for a date," I said. "Will you listen to a different kind of proposition?"

"You some kind of sicko or something?" she asked, shrinking back away from me.

"No," I replied. "I want to help you."

"What the fuck's that supposed to mean, *pendejo*?"

"If someone offered you a way to get off the meth and enough money to start a new life, would you take it and stop what you're doing?"

"Huh?"

"You have to know how dangerous it is for you with the war going on between MS-13 and Lake Boyz."

"Whadda you care?" she slurred.

"Why doesn't matter," I said. "I just want to help get you and as many other working girls as I can off the streets. I will pay for your treatment down in Fort Myers Beach and give you enough money to start over somewhere else."

She looked at me with weary eyes. "Why you wanna do that?"

The light ahead turned red and I was worried she might just jump out of the car if I didn't win her over quickly.

"A few friends and I intend to stop this gang war," I said. "And the fastest way to do that is get the victims out of harm's way. Will you let me help you?"

"You don' even know me."

"My name's Jesse," I said, then pointed to the earwig in my right ear. "Believe it or not, my wife is listening to our conversation."

"Yeah, right," she said.

I pulled the earwig out and extended it to her. "Talk to her yourself," I said, as I slowed for the light.

"Huh?"

"Just put it in your ear, like an ear bud."

She took the earwig and fumbled with it as the car came to a stop. A look of surprise came to her face, and then she asked, "Who is this?"

I watched as the girl listened for a moment. The light turned green and I took a chance, turning into the parking lot of a closed convenience store.

When I looked over, I saw a tear roll down the girl's cheek. "*Esto es en serio?*" Her voice cracked a little, as she asked Savannah if this was for real.

I pulled back out onto Cleveland Avenue, headed south, and hoped that whatever Savannah was telling her from Chyrel's comm center would work.

"*No hay cuerdas?*" the girl asked.

She listened a moment, then started nodding her head.

"Okay, but this better not be some kinda setup."

She handed the earwig back to me and I put it in my ear.

"Where are you taking me?" she asked, resignedly.

"To a nice lady named Dr. Catalina Lopez."

I saw the look of recognition slowly come to her eyes. "Isle of Palms?"

"You know the place?" I asked.

"Yeah," she said. "Okay, I'll go with you, but you gotta pay me a hundred right now."

I reached into my pocket and pulled out two $100 bills and handed them to her. "Do you know any other girls who might need help?"

She took the bills and stuffed them in her pocket. "There aren't many of us left," she said.

"I know. That's why we want to help. What's your name?"

"Bella," she whispered, slumping down in her seat. "Bella Tomas."

Suddenly, she became agitated. "Pull over," she shouted. "There's Maria."

I slowed, and noticed another dark-haired girl walking down the street.

Bella fumbled with the button and finally got the window down. "Maria! *Ven aquí, chica.*"

The girl approached cautiously. "Bella? What's going on?"

"Get in back," Bella said.

The girl named Maria did as her friend told her, then Bella climbed over the seat, kicking me in the shoulder.

The two talked in rapid-fire Spanish.

"She's telling the other girl what I told her," I heard Savannah say over the earwig.

After a moment, the second girl leaned over the seat. "Let me talk to her," she said.

I removed the earwig and handed it back to her.

There was more Spanish. I can speak and understand a few words and phrases, but not when it's spoken fast. Savannah spoke fluent Spanish.

Finally, Maria handed the earwig back. "I am Maria Gonzalez."

"I'm Jesse McDermitt," I said. "That was my wife you were just talking to. Her name's Savannah."

"She is not Hispanic," Maria said. "Her Spanish is good, but with an accent."

I looked back at the two in the rearview mirror and grinned. "No, she's not Hispanic. She's from South Carolina."

We drove a few more blocks, and then I told the girls I needed to stop to pick up a friend who was going to be helping us. That made them seem a little nervous.

"He's okay," I said. "We trust him and I'm asking you to trust him, too. I can just have him follow us if you'd rather."

"Yes," Maria said.

I pulled out my phone and called Mark. "Get to your car," I said. "Meet me at McGregor and follow us to Fort Myers Beach. I'm in a white Nissan."

"On my way," he said. "I'm in a blue Dodge Ram."

I looked back at the two of them and asked, "Do either of you know a little boy named Alberto Mar?"

Maria's head snapped up, her face suddenly more lucid. "Alberto Marco?"

"He's about eight," I said. "But small for his age. Half black and half Hispanic, maybe."

"How do you know him? What happened to him?"

I nearly slammed on the brakes. The odds were so high against it, yet she seemed to know who Alberto was.

"My wife and I found him three days ago, drifting in a boat. He was hurt, but he's okay now. He doesn't remember anything, not even his name."

"*Madre Dios*," Maria said, making the sign of the cross on herself. "I was so sure he was dead. I knew his mother."

Knew? Past tense?

"He's all right," I said again. "He's with my wife, asleep on our boat."

"His mama's name was Carmel Marco," Maria said. "She was my friend, but now she is dead—murdered by a man named Bumpy who is with Lake Boyz."

"Tony," I said quietly, "did you and DJ get that?"

They both replied that they had.

"If you encounter anyone by that name," I said. "I want to see him."

CHAPTER TWENTY

A dark-colored Dodge pickup was sitting at the entrance to the marina. It didn't move, though there was no traffic, and I was still a block away. When I flashed my headlights, the lights on the truck went off and came back on.

Fifteen minutes later, we were on Estero Island and I pulled into the clinic, Mark right behind me. There were only four cars in the parking lot—the night shift.

Before I even got out of the car, the door opened and Dr. Lopez came out, her white lab coat billowing behind her, exposing her street clothes—a light blue blouse and dark blue skirt. She walked quickly toward the car.

"Mr. McDermitt," she said. "I was in doubt that you would return."

I nodded to her, went around to meet her on the passenger side of the car, and opened the door.

"This is Maria and Bella," I said. "Ladies, this is Dr. Cat Lopez. She runs this place."

The girls slid out of the backseat. They stood side by side, faces cast down, hair shrouding their features.

"*Estoy aquí para ayudarte a recuperarte,*" Cat said softly.

"We speak English," Maria said.

She seemed to be the stronger of the two.

"Please come inside," Cat said. "We have food and drink."

"Can I speak to Maria?" I asked, as Mark's truck pulled up on the other side of my car.

"What for?" Maria asked.

"I want to know more about Alberto," I replied. "Anything that you can tell me will help him."

"Can I help you?" Cat asked, as Mark got out. "We are closed for visitors."

"He's with me," I said. "Mark Ramsey, meet Dr. Lopez. He might be dropping off more patients. I just wanted you to meet him first."

"Come inside, Bella," Cat said. "Are you hungry?"

Bella nodded and Cat put an arm around her shoulders, guiding her toward the door.

"What else can you tell me about Alberto?" I asked Maria.

"He's smart," Maria said, her legs starting to shake a little. "I used to sit for Carmel."

"You said a man named Bumpy killed her? How do you know that?"

"I met a girl who worked for Lake Boyz who told me that Bumpy killed Carmel and some others. That same night, a week ago maybe, they trashed Razor's place and took Alberto. He was staying there while Carmel worked."

"Did you know his father?"

"I never met him," she replied, as Cat came back out. "She told me once that his name was LeBron Green. He was killed in an accident when Alberto was five."

"Did he have a hand in raising Alberto?"

She nodded. "They lived together. Carmel said he was a good man."

"I need to get her inside," Cat said.

"Okay," I said, then lifted Maria's chin. I smiled at her. "There are a lot of people working tonight to make things better. This facility is open to your friends. Do you know anyone else who Cat can help?"

She nodded and her eyes searched mine, not breaking contact. I was probably the first man she'd met in a long time who didn't want anything from her.

"I know a couple," she said.

"That's good," I whispered softly. "Go with Cat now and if you can contact any of them, tell them to come here." I dug into my pocket and produced a wad of ten-dollar bills. I pressed them into Maria's hand. "Tell them you have cab fare covered and the driver can call here to confirm, okay?"

She nodded and then Cat escorted her inside.

"Whoa," Mark said, after the two women went inside. "That was intense. I didn't know all this was going on."

"Murdered hookers isn't exactly front page news," I said. "Not good for tourism."

"Do you really think you can make a difference?"

"We already have, brother. Maybe the difference isn't big in the grand scheme of things." I paused and looked at the door. "But it's huge to those two girls. They have a chance at a path to recovery and to start a new life."

Mark headed back to the marina and I drove back to the Pine Manor area. I cruised up and down Cleveland a few more times with no luck, so I moved on northward toward the bridge to North Fort Myers.

Turning right onto MLK, I came to a red light. A black girl stepped out of the shadow of a magnolia tree. My window was down.

The proposition was made, money was offered, and she got in.

It went on like that for several more hours. In all, I picked up eight more prostitutes, five of whom took me up on my offer. Two were black, one Hispanic, and two white girls. Savannah talked to each one and I took them to where Mark waited at the marina entrance.

Finally, just after 0200, I drove the last girl to the clinic. Cat got her checked in and I went with her to her office.

"I can't believe you're doing this," she said with a yawn, taking a seat behind her desk. "Three more girls came in from the Pine Manor neighborhood. That's ten altogether."

I opened the go-bag I'd retrieved from the trunk of the rental car and counted out ten bundles of hundred-dollar bills. "Will this be enough for their treatment and to give each one who completes it five grand for a new start in life?"

She stared at the pile of banded Benjamins a moment, slightly aghast. "I don't think I've ever seen that much cash at one time." She looked at me, and I could see suspicion in her eyes.

"I assure you, it's not from anything illegal."

"Nobody does this kind of thing for nothing, Mr. McDermitt."

I gave her a half grin. "I thought we were friends, Cat."

She looked down at the money and back up at me. "Okay, Jesse, then. Why are you doing this?"

"I grew up here," I said. "As did my late father and his father before him. Dad was killed in Vietnam and Mom took her own

life a few days later. I lived with my grandparents from the age of eight until I joined the Marine Corps. Pap left me a sizable fortune and I've been fortunate to find some lost treasure over the years. This is just my way of giving back to the community, I guess."

"You guess? That's more than I take home in a year."

I reached into the bag and took out two more bundles and added them to the stack. "Consider this a donation. What you're doing here is important work, Cat."

"How did you ever convince so many to come in?"

I smiled. "I didn't. To be honest, I had no idea how to even proposition a hooker to get in the car when I started." I pointed to my earwig, which was still on. "It was Savannah. She talked to each girl and convinced them to come."

"What'd she tell them?"

"I don't know," I replied, then touched my ear. "Are you still there, Savvy?"

"She's gone to bed," I heard Chyrel reply over the comm. "She was emotionally drained."

"Okay," I said. "If she wakes up, tell her I'm headed back."

I shrugged. "She's gone to sleep," I said to Cat.

"You should, as well. You look exhausted."

I rose and extended my hand. "The word is out. If any more girls come in, just let me know and I'll send you more."

She rose and shook my hand. "I wish there were more people like you in this world, Jesse."

"There are," I said, with a grin. "You, Dr. Porter, Dr. Wilson; the world is full of people who are willing to help others."

I left then, feeling good about what we'd accomplished. Chyrel had DJ and Tony on a different comm channel and had

given me updates throughout the night. As I got in the car, I asked her to switch me over to their channel.

"Tony, DJ, how's it going?"

"There's three dealers lying under bushes up here in the north end of town," Tony replied. "I have about a pound of meth and a couple thousand in cash. Left enough on each one to put them away for a while."

"Roughly the same here in the south end," DJ reported. "Maybe a bit more cash. These idiots walk around with way too much money and confidence."

"Let's call it a night," I said. "We put a big dent in both gangs' ability to make money. You recorded the GPS locations of all of them, like we planned?"

"Yeah," Tony replied. "Chyrel has them all."

"Go ahead and make your call, Chyrel," I said.

"Hang on," Tony interrupted. "I think I might have one more."

"Hold on, Chyrel," I said. "Let's see if Tony can't bag and tag another one."

I got in the car and started the engine while I listened on the comm.

"Hey, man," Tony said. "You know where I can score some party supplies?"

I heard someone in the background say something but couldn't make out anything other than it sounded like a man.

"No, man, nothing like that," Tony said. "A brother told me I might find a guy named Bumpy around here and he could hook me up."

"I'm Bumpy," I heard the man say clearly.

CHAPTER TWENTY-ONE

My mind raced. I didn't want Tony to bring the guy back to the boats. Too many potential witnesses, and there was no way I wanted Savannah to know anything about this guy.

"Make the call, Chyrel," I said, backing out, and turning around. "Tony won't be leaving this one behind."

Our plan was for Chyrel to contact Fort Myers PD's Gang Suppression Unit and give them the GPS coordinates of the dealers Tony and DJ had taken down. She'd make the call via her computer and would route it through hundreds of bogus landlines, so the call couldn't be traced. Tony and DJ had left each dealer with enough drugs to ensure that they would go to jail for distribution.

I heard Tony talking to the guy who called himself Bumpy as I started north, and then I heard a loud thump.

"As you would say, Jesse," Tony said over the comm, "one more turd fondler down."

"Get him in your car, Tony," I said. "Cuff his hands and feet, then head east on Highway 82." At a light, I pulled up a map on Google. "DJ, you start heading that way, too. I know a place we can take him."

"Roger that," they both replied.

It took me a while to find the spot on Google maps. The light turned green, but there wasn't anyone behind me. When I found it, I could tell from the aerial photo that it was still the same.

Decades earlier, a developer had built roads in part of the Corkscrew Swamp, near Immokalee. But nothing had ever happened with it and the roads were abandoned. I got the GPS coordinates and relayed them to both men.

"What do you want me to tell Savannah if she wakes up?" Chyrel asked.

"Don't tell her anything," I said, accelerating northward. "In fact, after you make the call to the DSU, unplug and go to bed. We'll see you in the morning."

I headed north on 6-Mile Cypress Parkway, driving a little over the speed limit, but not enough to attract attention. It was late and there were few cars on the road.

Tony was the closest, but only about ten minutes ahead of me and five ahead of DJ. When I reached County Road 876, I hung a right and, not seeing any traffic, floored it for the half-mile crossing of 6-Mile Slough, slowing before I got to the other side. From there, I kept it at a sedate speed for the next eight miles, then made another right onto State Road 82.

"I'm on 82 now," I said. "Y'all are probably a little ahead of me."

"Do you know a place called Wild Turkey Strand?" DJ asked. "I'm just passing it now."

"You're a mile or two ahead of me," I said.

"I'm in the middle of East Jesus, Nowhere," Tony said. "Wait a sec…just passing CR 850."

"That's Corkscrew Road," I said. "DJ and I are about fifteen

minutes behind you."

"Where exactly are we going?" DJ said. "And who the hell made up these names?"

I ignored the second question. "We're going deep into Corkscrew Swamp near Immokalee," I replied. "As remote and wild as any part of Florida gets."

Tony chuckled. "Sounds like a scary place."

"It is," I agreed. "Follow your GPS, and once you turn off of Lake Trafford Road onto Pepper Road, you'll wind your way back into the swamp, taking a series of rights and lefts for a good five miles to stay on Pepper. When your GPS tells you to turn right where there doesn't look like there's a road, just trust it. That trail won't have a name and it'll be rough going. Go about an eighth of a mile and wait for me."

"This guy's starting to wake up," Tony said. "I have him flex-cuffed in the backseat."

"Let him wake up," I said. "Don't talk to him at all. Let the drive put the fear of God into him."

Forty minutes passed and the only voice I heard was Bumpy asking Tony what he thought he was doing and where he was taking him. Each time he spoke, he became more and more agitated and demanding. Then he finally started to sound a little scared. I figured Tony had turned onto Pepper Road.

"Drive it like you stole it, Tony," I said. "If you're on Pepper Road, there's nothing out there except swamp and gators. The road is straight as an arrow to each right and left turn. Just slow when you approach a wall of saw palmetto, so you can tell if it's a right or a left."

Bumpy's voice sounded panicked and then he became silent for a second.

"Why you stoppin', man?" I heard Bumpy say. "C'mon, man! What'd I ever do to you?"

I heard the door open, and the dinging sound of the car's warning that the keys were still in the ignition. Then the door slammed, and I heard nothing for a moment.

"Man, you weren't kiddin'," Tony said, as DJ and I turned onto Pepper. 'It's spooky as all hell out here."

I stayed right behind DJ, driving with my lights off, so as not to blind him, and to keep the glow down. It was flat ground and swamp all around, with occasional cypress hammocks and live oak trees dripping with Spanish moss. I doubted anyone was within a mile, but if they were outside, they could likely see the glow from two sets of headlights.

Finally, DJ slowed and turned off of Pepper onto an overgrown track that threaded between overhanging water oaks and live oaks that grew up along the banks of abandoned canals. Saw palmetto had taken over much of the area where the oaks allowed light.

It was slow going. There was no way to tell that the road had ever been maintained, let alone paved. The asphalt had been broken up and choked with weeds when I was a kid. Bigger trees and the saw palmetto, so common to the area, didn't take root in the cracks, maybe due to the presence of the petroleum in the asphalt.

"Just stay between the palmettos," I told DJ.

"That would've been nice to know when I pulled in," Tony quipped. "But being a Navy man, I knew to stay in the middle of the channel."

Just ahead, I could see the reflection of Tony's taillights. He stood off to the side of his car as DJ came up behind it.

"Leave your lights on, DJ," I said. "And angle park so they're on the side and back of his car."

I did the same thing on the other side and turned my lights back on, bathing the rear and both sides with light. Then I shut off the engine. I could see the effect our arrival had on Bumpy. His face looked panicked, as he peered out the back window, struggling against his bonds.

"Okay," I said, "he knows we're here. Kill the lights."

Tony and DJ came over to my car as I climbed out. "What's the plan?" Tony asked in a low voice.

"I want names and addresses," I said. "And I want to know how many girls this guy has personally killed."

"Here's his cellphone," Tony said, handing it over. "He got three calls while we were coming out here. Caller ID showed just a number for one of them. The other two were from someone named Malik. Be sure to check his texts."

I took the phone and scrolled through the recent call log first. Bumpy had called or been called by Malik ten times in the last two days. The guy got a lot of incoming calls late at night. Many of them were just numbers, not in his contact list. I guess that was to be expected for a drug dealer, though.

Next, I checked recent text messages. He and Malik had an ongoing conversation going back more than a month. The most recent was from Malik, asking him where he was.

Security didn't seem paramount to these guys. In a text conversation from a week ago, Malik told Bumpy to "round up every *puta* in town and kill them all." Bumpy then asked if he and the Boyz could have fun with them first, to which Malik replied, "As long as they end up floating out to sea, I don't give a fuck."

The text messages went on to describe what Bumpy and his

crew had done to at least eight women. Scrolling back farther, I found where Malik told Bumpy to "take a few brothers over to Razor's and kill him, then tear his place apart."

Razor was the name of the guy whose place Alberto had been staying at while his mother was out turning tricks.

The next two exchanges turned my heart cold.

There's a kid here.

Send the little shit for a boat ride.

"Malik must be the head honcho," I said. "And this Bumpy seems to be the one who takes care of his wet work. At the very least, he's responsible for killing eight women. One of them was Alberto's mother."

DJ turned suddenly and lunged for the car door. I grabbed him by the arm and held him back.

"Easy, man," I said. "This guy's not leaving here. But I want to know what he knows first."

DJ looked at me with fierce conviction in his eyes. "He was probably the one who beat Alberto up."

I handed him Bumpy's phone. "Those texts were the night Alberto was taken. Malik ordered him to send Alberto down the river in a little boat to die in the heat out on the Gulf of Mexico."

"I'll kill this fuck with my bare hands," DJ growled.

I nodded somberly. "He meets Satan tonight," I said, my words as cold as ice. "But we do this slow and methodical."

"What's your plan?" Tony asked again.

I looked from DJ to Tony. "Bumpy is going to die here tonight," I stated flatly. "Whether that's from extreme pain or a bullet in his brain depends on how tough he is."

Both men looked me in the eyes and nodded. Having read the texts, we were all in agreement.

"Get him out of the car," I said to Tony.

Tony wasn't real big, but he was wiry and powerfully built. When he opened the door, Bumpy kicked out his cuffed-together feet at him, so Tony grabbed his ankles and yanked him out hard. Bumpy's head hit the door sill before he was dumped unceremoniously onto the dirt.

Bumpy looked around, dazed. "Whatta you guys want, man?"

"Pick him up," I growled. "And open the trunk."

Tony opened the car door and reached inside. The trunk lid popped open. Then he and DJ dragged the gangbanger to the back of the car.

"Cut the cuffs off his wrists," I instructed. "And hold his arms tight."

Bumpy struggled after the plastic strap was severed, but DJ and Tony were too strong.

"I can get you anything you want, man," Bumpy pleaded. "Money, meth, women, guns, *anything*! Just let me go."

"Is that right?" I asked, grabbing him by the hair and straightening him up. "Can you get Carmel Marco back? Or any of the other girls you killed this week?"

"They was nuttin' but hoes, man. Those MS-13 punks been killin' ours, too."

I punched him squarely in the face—a big haymaker from way in back. Blood spurted from his nose as his head rocked back.

"Where does Malik live?" I roared at him.

The blow stunned him, but he just shook his head and spat blood on the ground. "That the best you got?"

I wrestled his right hand away from DJ and folded all his

fingers except the pinky. Then I looked him in the eyes. "You're going to tell me everything I want to know, Bumpy. Every time you refuse or give me the wrong answer, you lose part of a finger. That simple. We have the rest of the night and I'll work my way all the way up to your shoulders if you don't give me what I want to know. By the way, that was your first wrong response."

I pressed his little finger into the gap between the car's body and the trunk lid, then slammed the trunk closed. He screamed in pain as blood spurted from the stump of his finger.

"Got a lighter?" I asked DJ.

He produced one, a mini-butane torch, for lighting campfires. In seconds, with Bumpy screaming in pain, DJ cauterized the stub of his pinky to stop the bleeding.

It took two more fingers before Bumpy started spilling his guts about everything and everyone. Tony jotted down names and locations on his phone's notepad.

I had no qualms about what I was doing, nor about what Bumpy's final end would be. Back in Marathon, a sheriff's investigator once accused me of being judge, jury, and executioner. He was right. For some low-life turd fondlers, prison and trials were a complete waste of taxpayers' money.

When we had all the information we were going to get from Bumpy, I personally dragged him through the saw palmettos and oaks to the water's edge and shot him in the back of the head.

We left him for the alligators.

CHAPTER TWENTY-TWO

"We hit three locations simultaneously," I said, as we drove back toward the north end of Fort Myers. Before we'd left, Tony sent me and DJ the list of names and locations. "All three of Malik's lieutenants first. If you guys have any problem with what we're gonna do, say so now."

"Let the bodies hit the floor," came DJ's growled response.

Tony replied, "One! Nothing wrong with me."

I'd heard the Drowning Pool song before, though I'd never been a fan of heavy metal.

"DJ, you take the second address on the list," I said. "Tony can take the third, and I'll hit the fourth. Then we'll converge on Malik's place. It'll likely be better guarded and they may be on alert."

As we reached town, we split up, each going to an assigned place. I wasn't worried about me or the other two guys getting hurt. We were trained professionals. We were going against punks who grabbed their crotches and held their weapons sideways when engaging. If any of us came up on more gang-bangers than rounds in a single magazine, we'd have to rethink things.

Tony arrived at his location first and circled the block until DJ and I were in position. Both reported few cars and no activity outside.

"No prisoners," I said.

"And no survivors," DJ replied.

"Don't hurt any non-coms," I warned. "We want this to look like what it is—retribution. Combatants only."

I got out of the car and walked toward the house identified as belonging to Bumpy's friend Roshaun, who he said had been part of the gang rapes and killings. The lights were on inside but there weren't any lights on outside of the house.

As I approached the front door, I pulled my Sig Sauer 9mm from the holster at my back. I tested the door. It was locked, with only the standard deadbolt above the doorknob. I could either knock politely, putting anyone inside on alert, or do a forced entry.

I stepped back, then lunged forward, planting my boot heel just above the doorknob. The frame splintered as the door flung inward.

Three black men were sitting on a couch and recliner as I entered, leading with the Sig. I shot all three in the center of the chest.

At the same time, I heard gunfire erupt over the comm. Tony and DJ had made their entries, too.

Movement caught my eye from beyond the living room. I wheeled and found a fourth man rounding the kitchen counter with a big Colt .45 coming up in his right hand.

I fired twice, dropping him back behind the counter.

The house became deathly quiet.

One of the men on the couch moved, so I shot all four in the

head for good measure.

Then I collected my brass and left.

Outside, it was still dark—no lights coming on in the neighbors' houses. I got in the car and took off. The whole engagement had lasted less than a minute and I'd left four men dead.

"You guys okay?" I asked.

"All good," Tony said. "Lake Boyz lost three soldiers."

"Make that five," DJ added.

"Nine," I said. "Head toward Malik's place. Tony, you're closest. Find a public place that's open and we'll meet you there and all go in my car."

Five minutes later, I pulled into a 24-hour Winn-Dixie and found the others parked in the middle of the lot. DJ got in front and Tony climbed in the backseat.

I drove three blocks to where Malik lived. This house had lights on outside and there was a guy sitting in a chair on the front porch.

"It doesn't look like they're ready for us," DJ said. "Just the one guy outside.

"Drop me half a block down," Tony said. "Then time your arrival for when I get to the porch."

DJ and I, being white, would never get close to Malik's yard, let alone the covered porch where the guard sat.

I dropped him off at the corner then circled the block. As DJ and I approached the house again, Tony was starting up the sidewalk. I stopped at the curb and DJ and I bailed out of the car, moving quickly.

The guard rose. Tony pulled his Beretta and shot him twice. The man slumped back in his chair, blood spreading across his chest.

DJ and I were already at a run coming up on either side of

Tony as the door flew open and two men stepped out, handguns raised. We opened fire before either man got a shot off.

Automatic weapons fire erupted from inside, blowing the window out. All three of us took it for what it was—a show of superior firepower.

But being able to shoot a gun was a lot different than shooting with accuracy. The gunman did nothing more than break glass.

We returned fire instantly, advancing toward the house. On the porch, we got low, taking positions around the open door and shattered window.

I heard a thump as something or someone slammed against the wall just inside the door. I stepped back and fired through the wall, spacing four rounds between the door and window.

A shirtless black man fell just inside the door. I nodded at Tony and he went in first, diving over the three corpses and barrel-rolling to the right. I went in behind him, moving to the left. DJ was right on my heels, weapon raised and covering the center of the room.

A tall, black man stood naked at the head of a hallway, holding a terrified Hispanic-looking woman, also naked, with an arm around her neck and the muzzle of a gun against her temple.

"Who the fuck you think you are, bustin' inna my crib?" the man said, shielding himself with the girl.

I'd seen this scenario play out many times. Human shields were only effective against poor marksmen. The bad guys always seemed to leave their head vulnerable when doing it.

My and DJ's weapons fired at the same time. Our bullets found their marks, less than an inch apart, on Malik's forehead. His brain ceased to function before the sound even reached his ears, as two nine-millimeter hollow points ripped through the

cerebrum, the front part of the brain, which initiates movement, among other things. His head flung back, and he dropped his weapon as his body collapsed to the floor.

The girl screamed and fell to her knees.

Tony and DJ swept the room as I went to the girl and knelt before her. "Is anyone else in the house?" I asked urgently, picking up Malik's handgun.

She was gasping for air, unable to form words. I took her by the shoulders and shook her a little.

"Is there anyone else?" I asked more forcefully.

"No!" she shouted.

"Get your clothes," I told her. "Hurry!"

She disappeared down the hall, then returned quickly, pulling a tank top over her head, but still naked below the waist.

"Let's get out of here!" DJ shouted.

I took the girl by the elbow and guided her past the dead men at the doorway, down the steps, and out to my car. Tony got her in the backseat and slid her over roughly as he got in beside her. DJ and I got in front and as soon as I put the still-idling car in gear, I stomped the accelerator.

Three minutes and five more dead. Fifteen men dead in all. I didn't know how big the Lake Boyz gang was, but losing their leader, his second, his three lieutenants, and ten foot soldiers in one night was going to put a serious hurt on their ability and will to do much of anything. Not to mention the drop in income from losing their drug dealers and prostitutes.

"Who are you guys?" the woman asked, struggling to get her shorts on in the backseat.

DJ turned in his seat. "I'm the judge," he said. "That guy beside you is the jury."

"And I'm the executioner," I said, as I turned south on Cleve-

land.

I slowed the car and took stock of what we'd done. Fifteen of the Lake Boyz gang were now dead, three of their street dealers were probably in jail by now, and half a dozen of their hookers were off the streets and safe.

"Where are you taking me?" the girl asked, fear rising in her voice.

"I can take you to the Pine Manor area," I replied. "Or out to Isle of Palms…Maria, Bella, and several others are there."

"You're him," she said.

I glanced back at her in the mirror.

"*El gran hombre blanco,*" she breathed. "Maria called me, just before one of those *cabrons* picked me up. She said to go to Isle of Palms."

"Would you like to go there?" Tony asked her softly. "It's a rehab center. You'll be safe and the people there can help you."

In the mirror, I saw her look at each of us in turn. Then she caught my eyes in the mirror and slowly nodded. "*Si, por favor.*"

I handed my cellphone to DJ. "Pull up the number to the clinic and make the call."

He did and handed me the phone. Cat answered after several rings.

"It's Jesse," I said. "We have one more for you tonight."

"I thought you'd stopped," she replied.

Two police cars flew past, headed north with their lights on. I glanced in the mirror. The Hispanic girl worked for MS-13—the other half of this gang war. They were still alive and well, minus a few street dealers and prostitutes. That is, unless they'd gone after Callie while Billy was watching over her. That would definitely result in a change in the balance of power.

"No, Cat," I said. "Our job is only halfway complete."

CHAPTER TWENTY-THREE

After retrieving the other cars, we went back to the marina. Dawn wasn't far off. Shutting off the car's engine, I suddenly felt very tired.

I got out and saw Mark, leaning against his pickup, smoking a cigarette.

"Is that it?" he asked when I approached.

"For tonight," I said. "There may be more tomorrow night."

There was a click from inside Mark's car, and then a staticky voice announced, "Juliet four, multiple one-eighty-seven. Five dead, including Malik Taylor."

Mark reached inside for a moment. "That's a police scanner," he said, straightening and looking me in the eye. "Am I a conspirator to multiple murders? That's the fourth one in the last hour. All up in the Harlem Lakes area."

"No, brother," I said, shaking my head. "The only thing you're guilty of is taking a bunch of women who needed help to a place where they can get it."

"That was you three," he said, jerking a thumb toward his truck's open door. "Tell me I'm wrong."

I didn't say anything. Tony and DJ stood behind me, on ei-

ther side.

Mark looked at them and then back at me. “You just wiped out the Lake Boyz gang.”

“I have no idea what you’re talking about,” I said. “I’m tired and going to bed.”

The three of us moved toward the docks.

“Jesse, wait.”

I turned back to face Mark.

“Semper Fi,” he said. “If you need help tomorrow, you know how to reach me.”

I nodded. Then we went down the dock to where the boats were tied up on opposite sides of the T-head.

“Tomorrow night?” Tony asked. “We hit MS-13?”

“We only have one full name to go on,” I said. “Diego Alturaz is the head of the gang here. His top lieutenant is someone named Esteban. And I’m sure Razor wasn’t given that name by his parents.”

“It’s a start,” DJ offered.

“Billy’s been watching over a girl here,” I said. “She’s been targeted by Alturaz and his MS-13 posse. He’s already put a few of their gang out of commission. I’ll call him and get a status report and we can talk about what’s next in the morning.”

Tank and Paul were standing on the dock between the two boats as we approached.

“How’d it go?” Tank asked.

“Lake Boyz are out of commission,” DJ said. “And MS-13 has lost a bunch of their prostitutes and drug dealers.”

“What about the gang itself?” Paul asked.

Since the subject didn’t seem to want to rest until morning, I pulled out my phone. “Let’s find out.”

Billy answered on the first ring.

"As always, Kemosabe," he whispered, "your timing sucks."

My instincts went on alert. "What's wrong, Billy?"

"Reader's Digest version," he said. "I only have a minute. Callie and two other girls, plus a young boy, were taken captive. Callie's Krav Maga instructor, Eva, who is a fine lady and exceptionally good with a gun, helped me get them out. MS-13's leaders are all dead. The police arrested us, then let us go. I have some cuts and bruises, which Eva has patched up. She's in the head getting into something more comfortable and I am resting in her bed."

"Jesus, Billy. You had me worried."

"You should be," he said, and I visualized his grin from the tone of his voice. "Eva is an extremely energetic woman."

"So, MS-13 is out of commission?"

"Not completely," he replied. "They're new in town, and the whole organization could fall apart without their leaders. Then again, more might come from Miami tomorrow to take their place."

"Did any of the tangos go by the name Razor?"

"Not that I know of," he said. Then I heard a woman's voice in the background but couldn't make out her words. "Gotta go, Kemosabe. You owe me, heap big."

I looked down at my phone to find the call had ended.

I relayed to the others what Billy had told me, leaving out the part about him being with a woman named Eva.

"In short," I summarized, "MS-13 in Fort Myers is like a small boat without a rudder and no way to make money to buy a new one."

"Think that's enough?" Tony asked.

I thought about it for a moment. Billy and Eva had taken out MS-13's leadership. The gang had only recently become active in the area and that might be enough. But I didn't think so.

"It's a Band-Aid at best," I said. "Others will join, and new leaders will rise up."

"So, what *was* the point of what we did?" Paul asked, his question a leading one.

I looked over at *Sea Biscuit.* Through the hull porthole, I could see into the forward cabin. A nightlight was on and I could just make out Alberto's form under the covers.

"We slowed the advance of evil," I replied, paraphrasing Jack Armstrong's unwritten mission statement for his organization. "And we protected the innocent, even if only for a little while, and in only one small place."

"Think global," DJ said. "And act local."

"Y'all get some sleep," I said, checking my watch and noting the sun would be up in a couple of hours.

Tank and I climbed aboard *Sea Biscuit* and the others headed over to the *Revenge.* He went up to the bridge for his watch while I stepped below.

The dinette in the salon had been lowered into a bed on which Chyrel was asleep, the blankets thrown back on the half she wasn't occupying. Her laptop sat open on the shelf next to the spare bunk, her headphones beside it. And on the screen, a black background with a wall of text was visible.

I stepped closer. At the bottom of the screen, I read my last words to the group outside: *Y'all get some sleep.*

Chyrel hadn't shut down like I'd told her to. What had happened earlier were events I didn't want certain others to know about. Savannah, definitely. Chyrel was a team player all the

way, but still…

Reaching across her, I moved my finger on the mouse pad so the menu bar would appear, clicked the *Disconnect All* icon, then closed the laptop.

Down the companionway in the aft cabin, I found Savannah asleep in the big queen bed.

After a quick shower, I got under the covers with my wife. She stirred and put a hand on my chest, nestling her head against my shoulder.

"We could keep him if we wanted to," she mumbled sleepily.

Her eyes were closed and at first, I thought she was talking in her sleep.

"We qualify as adoptive parents," she said, her voice clear and fully awake.

I nuzzled her hair. It smelled like flowers. "Adopt Alberto?"

"He doesn't have a mom and dad anymore, Jesse. He needs us."

A son?

I hadn't been around to raise Eve and Kim, my oldest daughters. And I didn't even know about Flo until she was a teenager. My grandson, Fred, filled part of the void I felt, but his visits were few and far between.

A son…

"We could," I said, more to myself than Savannah. "But we'll have to wait and see."

She wriggled closer, as if satisfied with my reply. After a minute or two, her breathing became shallow and steady.

"I wasn't worried about you," she mumbled. "Rest now."

CHAPTER TWENTY-FOUR

Light was streaming through the overhead portlights at an angle when I woke up. I blinked my eyes and sniffed coffee in the air.

The other half of the bed was empty. I got up and pulled on my pants from the previous night, then padded barefoot up the companionway.

"Look who's finally up," Savannah whispered to Alberto. "But don't say anything to him yet. *El Gran Hombre Blanco* needs his coffee."

Damn, I thought. She'd been privy to nearly all that went on last night.

Alberto looked at her, puzzled. "*Porque le llamas asi?*"

We both turned and looked at Alberto in surprise. He and Savannah were sitting at the dinette that had been Chyrel and Tank's bed the previous night.

"*Tu hablas español, Alberto?*" Savannah asked.

He spoke Spanish far too fast for me to keep up, but I caught my name at the end. I looked at Savannah questioningly.

"He said some of his memory returned during the night. Nothing personal about him, though. And he asked when you

can be talked to."

I went straight to the galley and got a mug from the cabinet, filling it with the dark brown brew from the coffeepot. "Some people think I'm unable to speak without coffee, Alberto. But as you can see, that isn't quite true."

The first sip was good—the second one better.

"It's not that he *can't* speak," Savannah said. "He's just a little grumpy without his java."

"Are we going for another boat ride today?" Alberto asked.

"Do you like boats?" Savannah asked him.

"Yes," he replied. "This one is like a big house."

I wondered what he was comparing it to. How had he lived before being set adrift by Bumpy? Had Carmel Marco and Alberto's father been good parents? Had they lived in a house?

Savannah ruffled his thick black hair. "*Sea Biscuit* was my home for a long time."

"Really?" he asked.

"Since before Flo was born," she replied.

I sat down at the dinette with them. "We might be going on a really big boat this weekend."

"How big?"

"Bigger than all of my and Savannah's boats put together."

He pointed out the starboard hatch, where a small, coastal cruise ship was tied up. "Bigger than that boat?"

I looked across the river. The cruise ship had three decks. It wasn't like the mega cruise ships that hit all the big tourist ports like Miami, Key West, and Nassau. It ran up and down the Florida coast, visiting smaller towns.

I nodded emphatically. "Almost exactly that size."

He smiled broadly.

Savannah got up. "I'll get lunch going. Tank and Chyrel are up on the bridge, and I saw DJ stretching over in the cockpit of *Gaspar's Revenge*."

"Have you seen Paul yet this morning?" I asked.

"He and Tony went for a run," she said. "They should be back any time."

I followed her into the galley and spoke low. "How much Spanish do you think he remembers?"

She smiled at me. "He's as fluent as a native speaker would be. Remember? Paul said most amnesia sufferers retain language skills. Alberto is bilingual."

Just then, I saw Tony and Paul running along the sea wall, headed toward the ramp down to the dock.

"I'll be right back."

"You don't even have a shirt on," Savannah called after me as I went up to the side deck.

"Hey, Jesse," Tony said, as he and Paul walked the last few yards to the boats.

I dropped down to the dock. "How was the run?"

"Rough," he replied. "Paul sets a grueling pace and he got more sleep than I did last night."

"Paul, Alberto is suddenly speaking Spanish…like fluently."

"He hadn't before?"

I shook my head. "No. And I mean rapid-fire Spanish."

"That's probably normal," he said. "Being bilingual, I would think it would be, anyway."

"We know his name now," I said. "It's Alberto Marco, not Mar. And we know who his mother was. Both his parents are dead."

"And you want to know if it's safe to divulge that information

to him?"

"Yeah."

Paul rubbed his chin in thought for a moment. "Hard to say. But like I told you yesterday, he's an intelligent child. Why don't you ask him if he feels like he's ready to hear some bad news?"

"That's it?" I asked. "Just ask him?"

"Preface it by telling him you've learned something of his past that isn't good. He'll know if he can take it or not."

"Thanks," I said and turned back toward *Sea Biscuit.*

Paul grabbed my arm. "Jesse, wait."

I turned back around to face him.

"How about waiting a bit? Let me get a shower and allow everyone to eat lunch first. I'd like to be there in case he says yes."

"Savannah's making lunch now," I said. "Why don't we all meet up on her flybridge. It has the biggest table."

I went back aboard *Sea Biscuit* and told Savannah everything that Paul had told me.

"I'll put together a bunch more sandwiches," she offered.

"Fifteen minutes," I said. "Up on the bridge?"

"That's the only place we can seat all eight of us. But we'll need to break out a couple of deck chairs. You go get a shower and get dressed. I'll handle it."

I kissed her on the cheek and hurried down to the aft cabin. It only took me ten minutes to take a quick shower and put on a pair of cargo shorts and a faded Rusty Anchor T-shirt.

When I got up to the bridge, everyone but Paul was lounging around the big table, eating deli sandwiches. I got two deck chairs out of the storage locker at the back of the bridge deck next to the dinghy and set them up at the empty front end of the table.

Paul came up the ladder carrying a box. I recognized the custom chess set Pap had made and given to me years ago. It was a hinged wooden box with dark mahogany and white oak squares. When opened, it created a chess board. The pieces inside were all hand carved teak.

Without a word, Paul opened the box and scattered the chess pieces on the table, then placed the box, velvet side down, next to them.

He looked at Alberto. "Checkers is such a simple game."

Alberto looked up at him, then back down at the pieces scattered on the table. He put his sandwich down on his plate and picked up one of the pieces—a black rook. He placed it at the corner of the board nearest him.

While it was the correct piece and he'd put it in the right place, it was also the nearest corner to him. So, I didn't read a lot into it. Paul sat down and picked up the white queen, placing it on the center black square on his back row.

"That's not right," Alberto said, and moved the piece over one. "The queen takes her color."

"Oh yeah," Paul said, with a grin. "I forgot."

They played fast as everyone else ate and watched. Paul opened with a queen's gambit, which Alberto foiled before Paul's third move—queen to king's bishop three.

Paul looked up at me and nodded. "Quite a talented chess player we have here."

Alberto smiled and took another bite of his sandwich.

The game continued until finally, Alberto laid his king over on its side. "You will checkmate in two moves," he said with a cunning smile. "Can we play again?"

"Perhaps in a while," Paul said. "Jesse has something to tell

you."

Alberto looked at me and I guess the expression on my face erased his smile.

"We learned some things last night," I began. "Things about you and your past. I'm afraid some of it might be upsetting for you to hear." His dark eyes shifted from one of mine to the other, looking for advice in my demeanor. "Do you think you're ready for me to tell you these things?"

He subconsciously scooted closer to Savannah; she put an arm around his shoulders. Then his eyes sought DJ's, but his new friend looked solemn and said nothing.

Alberto looked back at me and nodded somberly. "Yes. I want to know."

"Your last name is Marco," I began, judging his reaction.

He nodded again but showed no outward sign that it jarred a memory.

"Your mother's name was Carmel Marco and your father was LaBron Green."

He stared into my eyes. "Was?" he croaked.

"Yes," I replied. "I am terribly sorry, Alberto. They are both dead."

Tears welled in his eyes, but he wiped them away before they could fall. "My mom and dad are dead?"

I looked over at Savannah and saw tears in her eyes, as well. She gazed at me, imploringly.

I knew what she wanted. I wanted it too.

I nodded.

"Your mother and father are no longer with us," she said softly. "But Jesse and I can be your dad and mom. If you want us to be."

Alberto looked up at her, then at all the others sitting around the table, finally resting on DJ.

"You won't find a better substitute," DJ said. "Jesse and Savannah can teach you things and show you stuff nobody else in the world can."

Alberto looked back up to me.

"There's probably a lot of red tape," I warned him. "The cops will determine if you have any family. They'd be first in line to adopt."

"How did my mom and dad die?"

Behind him, I could see Paul shake his head no. He didn't think the boy was ready to hear all the details. I decided to be honest but not to tell him everything.

"Your father was killed in an accident when you were five," I said. "And your mother died the night you were put on that little boat."

The tears flowed and Alberto made no effort to hide them. His lip quivered as he fought for control. Savannah pulled him close and cried with him. The whole group moved nearer, leaning over him. He sobbed for several minutes. I worried that my telling him might bring back bad memories.

After a moment, he looked up at Paul. "Dad taught me how to play checkers and chess." Then he looked up at me, sadness etched in his dark brown eyes. "Did the drugs kill my mom?"

I couldn't hold it back any longer: the strain caused a great amount of sweat to run down my cheeks from my eyes.

I took his hand in both of mine. "Yes, Alberto," I lied. "It was the drugs."

CHAPTER TWENTY-FIVE

An hour after we told Alberto what had happened to his parents, we said goodbye to DJ on the docks.

"I'll come down and visit you soon," DJ told Alberto.

"We're going on a big boat this weekend. It's called *Ambrosia*."

"Better still," DJ said, kneeling on his good knee. "You'll love *Ambrosia* and I visit there pretty regularly."

DJ helped untie the lines and we were soon idling out into the Caloosahatchee. Savannah, Alberto, and I remained aboard *Sea Biscuit*; Alberto seemed to like it better, and we both wanted to stay close to the boy, so it was just the three of us.

Tony, Paul, Tank, and Chyrel took the *Revenge*. They'd go back to the Rusty Anchor, where Chyrel's car was.

Once we cleared the high bridge going over to Sanibel Island, we headed out to open water. Tony accelerated a little and the *Revenge* started to pull away. Then Savannah pushed the throttles forward and the big Grand Banks accelerated, matching Tony's speed. Alberto sat next to Savannah at the helm, with me across from them on the port bench.

"Can it go faster?" Alberto asked her.

"A little," she replied and pushed the throttles to the stops.

The boat gathered more speed, and we were soon overtaking the much faster *Gaspar's Revenge.*

"What about that boat?" he asked me, leaning forward, and looking around Savannah.

Tony was on the Gulf side of us, so I reached over and took the mic, switching the VHF over to the channel I knew the standby radio on the *Revenge* was tuned to.

"Hey, Tony," I said. "Alberto wants to know if that's all you've got. How about making a big circle to starboard? Wide-open throttle."

Even from a hundred yards away, I could see Tony's big, toothy grin. The *Revenge* had twin MTU 10V2000 M96 engines, manufactured by Rolls Royce for larger yachts. But we had the room and shoehorned them in there a couple of years ago to replace the original 1300 horsepower Caterpillars. The MTUs produced 1500 each.

The *Revenge* began accelerating, pulling ahead of us. When she was a quarter mile ahead, Tony turned the wheel, heading out to sea at full speed.

"Wow!" shouted Alberto.

Tony kept the wheel over as the distance between us increased. He made a full circle nearly a mile wide, then straightened her up a half mile behind us.

Alberto turned around in his seat, getting up on his knees.

"Now watch this," I said, as the *Revenge* neared *Sea Biscuit's* wake.

He looked over at me, grinning, then looked back aft, just as the *Revenge* hit our inside wake. The big Carolina bow flares shot a stream of spray to both sides as the *Revenge* plowed through. Then she encountered the larger, more tightly packed bow waves. She

was traveling at nearly double our speed and huge fountains of white water shot up and out from both sides in rapid succession till she found the calmer waters ahead of our wake.

The *Revenge* came up fast and close, then Tony pulled back on the throttles and settled in beside us at twenty-five knots.

"How fast does it go?" Alberto asked.

"She," I corrected him. "You call a boat she, not it. She goes a little over fifty knots, almost sixty miles per hour."

"Is *Ambrosia* fast?"

I smiled at him. Apparently, the kid was a speed demon, like me.

"*Ambrosia* is even faster," I replied. "But she doesn't go real fast very often."

His eyes grew wide. I figured he was trying to imagine that coastal cruise ship we'd seen earlier going faster than the *Revenge.*

It took nearly three more hours before we picked up Harbor Key Light off to starboard. I texted Detective Andersen, giving him Alberto's full name and those of his parents, and asked him to meet us at the Rusty Anchor.

By the time we arrived, it was mid-afternoon. Savannah had let Alberto drive a good bit of the way but took the helm as we approached the shallower waters nearer the Keys. She slowed and Tony let us go ahead of him.

Savannah kept us right in the middle of East Bahia Honda Channel at twenty knots, until we neared Moser Channel and the Seven Mile Bridge. There, she slowed to trawler speed.

Alberto studied the chart plotter and then looked up at me. "Isn't your island over there?" he asked, pointing off to starboard and aft.

"Yes, it is," I replied. "But we keep *Sea Biscuit* at the Rusty

Anchor. It's too big to fit under the house."

"Why do you call her *Sea Biscuit?*"

"Seabiscuit," Savannah said. "Just one word—was a champion racehorse from long ago. When I bought her, my dad had her completely rebuilt with brand new, more powerful engines. She was fast then, but even faster now."

Twenty minutes later, before entering Rusty's canal, Savannah turned the boat around, then backed her into the end slip, across from *Salty Dog.*

"Whose big sailboat is that?" Alberto asked. "And whose airplane?"

"Both are ours," I replied. "Would you like to go flying in it?"

"Can we?"

"Definitely," I replied. "That's how we're going to get to *Ambrosia.*"

Jimmy met us at the dock, and I tossed him a line, then jumped over with the stern line in hand and we quickly made her fast.

"There's room for the *Revenge* next to the barge," Jimmy said.

"Let's go help Tony," I called up to Alberto.

He came quickly down to the gunwale and jumped over to the dock, just as the *Revenge* idled past. Alberto ran ahead of me and Jimmy.

"How'd it go up in Fort Misery, man?" Jimmy asked.

"We learned who Alberto is and he's regained much of his memory. That's all that's important."

"So, you know who his parents are?"

"Were," I replied. "Alberto's an orphan."

"Aw, man. That sucks."

"Savannah and I talked about it last night," I said. "If it

comes to pass, we're going to petition for adoption."

"What?" he exclaimed, as we reached the barge where Alberto was waiting.

"I'll tell you all about it later," I promised. Then to Alberto, I said, "Go ahead on over onto Rusty's barge. Paul will throw you a line."

We joined him, and Alberto caught his first line, not really sure what to do with it.

"Let Tony maneuver closer," I told him, catching another line from Tank. "She's too big to pull in. When the boat bumps the fender, loop the line twice around that cleat."

He looked around and, seeing the deck cleat, positioned himself near it. I tied off the spring line, while Jimmy took care of the bow, and then I went over to Alberto and showed him how to make a proper cleat hitch.

"No need to get fancy and wrap it a million times," I said. "One full loop around both ends, then over the top, and under the end." I showed him as I explained. "Then make a loop so the bitter end is on the bottom and put it over the other end of the cleat and pull it tight. Extra loops and knots won't make it any more secure."

I then untied it and let him do it. He struggled with the loop at the end, but finally twisted it the right way and pulled on the bitter end, making it fast.

"Now, what would you do with the rest of the dock line?" I asked him.

He looked at the ten feet of bitter end and shrugged. "I dunno."

I straightened the line out and brought the end back to the cleat, where I knelt beside him.

"Do like this," I said, pinching the end of the line and turning it half a turn. I released it and did it again. Then again, until the line started to coil around itself.

"When the coil gets big, use your palm, like this, and keep turning it till it's snug and coiled tightly beside the cleat."

We left the others and went back to *Sea Biscuit.* Savannah had added more spring lines.

"Can I make the coils?" Alberto asked.

She looked down at him and said, "Sure, honey. You just knock yourself out."

He followed my instructions and soon had all the lines coiled and shipshape.

"He learns fast," Chyrel said, as she and Tank approached.

"Yeah," I replied. "I think he'll make a good waterman."

Alberto beamed.

Tank knelt in front of him. "Chyrel and I are going to head back up island now. I'm a little old for all this. You'll come and visit us, won't you?"

"I'd like to," Alberto said, looking up at me.

I shook Tank's hand and looked down at Alberto. "Sure, we can. We don't have to leave for a few days. We'll pick Tank up and go fishing."

They left then, collecting Paul and Tony on the way, who both shouted goodbye.

"You hungry?" I asked Alberto.

"Uh-huh. Are we going to eat here?"

"Sure," Savannah said. "I could use some time off from cooking for you hungry men."

We went inside and Rusty greeted us from behind the bar. "Y'all stayin' for supper?"

"What's fresh?" I asked.

"Dink just dropped off some cobia a little while ago. They were swimming this morning."

"Three plates," I said, and we went over to a table in the corner.

Dink was a local fishing guide who always brought fresh fish to Rufus's kitchen. By his own admission, Dink wasn't much of a cook, often saying he could burn Kool-Aid. So, since he brought Rufus two or three nice fish every day, Rusty let him eat for free. Rusty had the same arrangement with a few other guides and often let them eat free, even on days when they got skunked on the water. Having local guides meet their clients at the Anchor increased Rusty's revenue. And it probably cut the kitchen's fish budget in half.

A moment later, Rusty brought us a water pitcher and glasses. "Want a beer with your food?"

"No, thanks," I replied. "We're gonna head back up to the island before it gets dark."

While we waited, I sent another text to Andersen, to see how long he'd be. He came through the door reading it.

"Got time for dinner?" I asked, as he approached our table.

"Ha, I just ate lunch. Dinner for a cop is usually around midnight. How are you doing, Alberto?"

"Good," the boy replied. "I remember some things."

"Like what?" Andersen asked, settling into a chair.

"My name's Alberto Marco," he replied. "I'll be nine in June. My dad was LaBron Green. He was a mechanic and could fix anything. He taught me how to play chess, but he died in a car wreck when I was five. That's when Mom started using drugs." He paused for a moment and his eyes shifted to mine.

I nodded.

He looked somberly at the detective. "Mom died from the drugs."

Andersen glanced over at me. "I did the check, as you asked. It's confirmed."

"We want to adopt Alberto," Savannah said. "We'll give him a good home."

Andersen smiled at the kid. "If it was up to me, I'd say yes." Then he turned his gaze to me and Savannah. "But it's not up to me. Lee County is investigating. If there are no relatives who can take him, he'll be able to be adopted." Then he grinned. "But I have good news. Your application to foster was fast-tracked and approved. Alberto can stay with you until a relative comes forward, or he's adopted. If you want to do that, you need to file paperwork with the Department of Children and Families, then hire an adoption attorney. Foster parents are almost always approved to adopt their foster kids if no relatives can."

"How long will that take?" I asked.

"Who knows? I would guess it'd be several weeks at least, maybe months. And that's only after Lee County finishes their investigation."

"I don't think I have any other family," Alberto said. "Mom didn't have any brothers or sisters, and I've only seen pictures of my grandma. She's in one of those homes."

"A nursing home," Andersen said to me. "That much, they've already reported. Her name's Regina Marco, forty-nine, suffered a stroke five years ago and is an invalid. Probably not a candidate to be an adoptive parent."

"My dad used to talk about his brother who lived in Detroit," Alberto said. "But he told me he got shot. I don't think he had

anyone else."

"Can I talk to you outside?" Andersen asked me.

"I'll be right back," I said to Savannah, then followed Andersen out to the back deck. It was early and there wasn't anyone there yet.

"I didn't want to say anything in front of the kid," he said. "But there's been a lot of gang activity up in Fort Myers. A sudden escalation this week ended up with a lot of dead gangbangers and hookers, so they're a little back-logged up there."

"Alberto's mother was one of them," I said. "Raped and shot in the head by one of the Lake Boyz gang. I only told him it was the drugs that killed her because he asked if that was what it was. She was murdered."

He eyed me suspiciously. "I don't even have the coroner's report on manner or even *cause* of death yet. How do you know this?"

"I have ways," I said. "Remember the driver's seat in Cobie Murphy's car?"

He nodded. That seemed to satisfy him.

"I do have one question," I said. "We're planning to leave on Monday to go to Bimini and don't know when we'll be back. Is that okay with DCF?"

"Probably, but how did you get him a passport so quickly?"

"Still working on that," I said. "But we should get it by the end of the week."

"Can you delay your trip if it doesn't?"

"I can't," I said. "I'll be taking command of a research vessel. But we'd originally planned on Savannah joining me after a two-week shakedown cruise."

"You're a commercial captain?" he asked.

"Unlimited tonnage," I replied. "*Ambrosia* is a 199-foot former superyacht, converted for oil exploration. If Alberto's passport doesn't arrive in time, they can join us at sea, as we'd originally planned."

"It sounds like you've got things all planned out." He paused a moment. "Are you sure you want to adopt this kid?"

"We're sure," I replied. "We didn't have to discuss it at length—it's something we both wanted. The truth is, I always wanted a son and have three daughters. And Savannah isn't ready to stop being a mom just because our kid is grown and gone."

"I have two," he said. "Girls that is. Even our dog's female."

"Keep me posted on anything you find out from Lee County?"

"I will," he replied, pulling a pair of wrap-around Costas from his pocket, and putting them on. "Best of luck to you and the wife."

I stood there a moment as he walked toward the parking lot and climbed in his car. Then I turned and headed back inside. The food had arrived, and Alberto wasn't waiting.

"What's cobia?" he asked, as I sat back down. "It's good."

"It's a pelagic fish," I replied. "That means it swims freely in the ocean, but they do come close to reefs and even into the mangroves to feed on crab and smaller fish sometimes. They look a little like sharks."

"I've never seen a shark in real life."

I reached over and ruffled his hair. "Well, we'll have to remedy that real soon."

CHAPTER TWENTY-SIX

That evening, after we'd returned to the island, we sat by the firepit and snacked on fresh pineapple, while I pretended to play guitar. I wasn't particularly good—my fingers were too fat for the strings. But I'd been trying for a few years. Lately, I'd been learning some songs by female artists. Simple ballads, like most I knew. Savannah had a beautiful singing voice, whereas I sounded more like a cat and a bufo toad fighting.

I set the guitar down and looked at Alberto, licking his fingers. We grew several dozen pineapple plants on the little island nearly connected to our main one.

We also had two large solar units on that part of our property. In the morning, the panels opened up like flowers, tracked the sun across the sky all day, charging the battery shack, then folded themselves up at night.

The dogs lay with their backs to the fire and their heads away from it. I often thought they did it to maintain night vision, but it was probably just to keep their sensitive noses away from the heat and smoke.

"This is good," Alberto said. "What is it?"

Savannah gave him a shocked look. "You've never had pine-

apple before?"

"I like apples. But this doesn't taste anything like an apple."

"Europeans weren't the best at naming things," I offered. "Apples were common in Europe, and the pineapple has a tough, gnarly hide." I showed him the top, which I'd saved to replant. "Kinda like the bark of a pine tree. So maybe that's how they got the idea to name it. Columbus, or more likely, one of his crewmen, was the first European to see a pineapple. By the time he arrived, they'd been farmed by Indians across South and Central America and the Caribbean."

Alberto yawned.

"Are you ready for bed?" Savannah asked. "Or are Jesse's drawn-out stories that boring?"

"They're not boring," he said. "I guess I'm sleepy. But I don't know what time it is."

I laughed and he gave me a curious look.

"Out here, there's no need for a clock," I told him. "We sleep when we're tired and eat when we're hungry."

"What do you do the rest of the time?"

"We work, little man," I replied. "But work here is fun. Tomorrow, me and you will go pick up Tank and catch some fish. The freezer is running low."

"That's fishing, not work."

"Didn't I say that work here is fun?"

He yawned again.

"Come on," Savannah said, rising from her chair. "Let's get you to bed."

"What time will we wake up?"

"When the sun comes up," I told him. "That's our clock. Maybe a little before if you want to catch the sunrise."

"Yeah," he said. "Will it be like the sunset?"

"Different," I replied. "But just as magical. Sunset is a time to look back on your day, what you accomplished, and what steps you might have taken to do better. Sunrise is a new beginning. You wipe the slate clean and have the opportunity to fix anything from the previous day."

I started to get up too, but Savannah patted my shoulder and smiled down at me. "Stay put, Socrates. Contemplate the stars. I'll be back in a few minutes. I'm going to get a glass of wine. Would you like a beer?"

"Thanks, but make it two fingers of rum, please."

They left, with Woden trotting ahead.

Finn rose and came over to me, sniffing around on the ground, looking for a place to sit. He finally plopped down on my left foot and leaned against my leg, watching them go.

"You like Alberto?" I asked him, while gently stroking his head.

He whined and licked his chops.

"It's gonna be a lot different having a little boy around full-time. I hope you and Woden can keep up with him."

Savannah returned, carrying a wine glass and a pewter mug with the *Gaspar's Revenge Fishing Charter* logo on it. She handed my grog ration to me, then pulled her chair closer and sat down.

I sniffed the rum. The mixture of Caribbean spices and a slight scent of orange peel told me what it was.

"I thought we were saving the Appleton Estate for a special occasion."

"Nothing wrong with your nose," she said, clinking her glass to my pewter. "This is a big step in our lives. We're going to be parents again. Together."

"Maybe," I cautioned her, taking a sip. "Just because he didn't know of any other family doesn't mean there aren't any."

"Have faith, Jesse. God put us on that bridge for a reason."

I wasn't about to argue theism with her. I believed in God, but they took things to a whole different level in South Carolina, where she was from. The fact that we were entered in the Seven Mile Bridge Run was because of her desire to be more social in the community. Had we run up in the front with the leaders, we might never have even seen the boat.

"We'll do the best we can," I assured her.

"I know. You never do anything halfway."

"Where's Woden?"

"Sleeping beside Alberto's bed," she replied. "They were both very tired."

"Yeah, this one's making my foot go to sleep," I said, looking down at Finn, now snoozing with his rump still on my foot.

She was silent for a moment. Then she looked me squarely in the eye. "Are you going to tell me what happened last night?"

I knew that she already knew.

"Chyrel's laptop was still open when I came to bed this morning," I said by way of a reply.

"Is that all there is to it?"

"You know everything that happened. What more is there for me to tell you?"

She looked down at her glass, swirled the wine a moment, then took a sip before replying. "I knew what you did when I married you, Jesse. I knew the kind of man you were when I first met you and you rescued me and Char from those men at Dockside. Those men last night got what they deserved if you ask me." She paused and looked up at me. "I want to know what you

felt when you pulled the trigger."

I couldn't help it and grinned over at her. "I felt recoil."

She punched me in the shoulder. "You know what I mean."

I gazed into her eyes. "How did you feel on Hoffman's Cay?"

"It made me physically ill," she replied. "Not at the moment, but later."

"Me too," I admitted, gazing into the flames. "The first time was on my second deployment to Lebanon. I killed a terrorist from five hundred yards away. That night in the barracks, I threw up thinking about it."

"Did it get easier?"

I thought about it for a moment. Taking a life was something that should never become easy. At least not for a person with morals. I considered what we'd done the previous night as saving innocent lives more than the taking of lives.

"Some," I said, searching for words. "But not a whole lot. People like those we killed last night aren't like you and me. Yes, I feel some remorse for what we did, but I'd do it all over again. People like them kill without remorse and there's only one way to stop them."

"I don't fault you," she said softly. "Or DJ and Tony. I just worry how it will affect you."

"Well, you won't have to worry about that after next week. This old cowboy's hanging up his guns."

"Somehow, I don't think so," she said.

"Being captain of a ship like *Ambrosia* will be a full-time job and then some."

"Well, I know you, Jesse McDermitt. You're a hands-on kind of man."

"I promise I'll—"

"Please don't make a promise you can't keep," she interrupted.

"I'll do my best," I said, realizing she was probably right.

She looked up at the sky. "It's a beautiful night. Let's go down to the pier."

"I like that idea," I said with a grin, knowing her penchant for making love under the stars.

We walked hand-in-hand toward the pier extending past our house on the south side of the island. After grabbing a couple of big beach towels from the locker under the stairs, I spread them at the end of the pier, and we sat with our feet dangling in the water, then lay back to look up at the stars. By then, our night vision had returned, and we could see millions of them.

Savannah sighed contentedly. "Every time I look up at the night sky, I'm reminded how small and insignificant we are."

"Two people, out of more than seven billion Earth inhabitants," I said. "And it's just one planet in a vast solar system that's a miniscule part of a galaxy twirling through infinite space with millions of other galaxies."

She turned her head toward me. "Does anything we do really make a difference?"

I thought back to an event that had happened right before my parents died and I'd gone to live with Mam and Pap.

"When I was little," I began, looking up at the stars, "Mom and Dad took me sailing in a boat he and Pap had built. It was Christmas and Dad was leaving for Vietnam shortly after that. We'd gone ashore at Cape Sable to walk the beach, and we came across thousands of sand dollars. Some were alive and piled up at the water's edge, but the tide was going out and many were dying on the beach. Mom used her shirt as a basket and carried dozens

at a time out to deeper water. Me and Dad helped, though he'd said it was impossible to save them all. I'll never forget what Mom told him. She stood facing Dad, in water up to her waist, picked one sand dollar out of her shirt and held it up to us, saying, 'What we do can't save the world. But it means the world to this one sand dollar.' Then she put it in the water, along with dozens more in her shirt."

"I would have loved knowing them," Savannah said, then rolled onto her side and kissed me.

CHAPTER TWENTY-SEVEN

Carlos Santiago leaned back in his recliner, holding a cell phone to his ear. Another man sat across from him on a luxurious sofa. The atmosphere was tense.

"Bring her here," Santiago told the man on the phone.

"To Miami?" he asked.

"Yes," Santiago replied. "Do you know the warehouse on the river?"

"*Si, Jefe,*" the man said. "But why?"

Santiago sat forward and glared at the man sitting on his couch. He wasn't the object of his ire, but being the only one in the room, he was the recipient. The man on the couch was used to it.

"Because I said to, *cabron*!" he shouted into the phone. "I personally sent Enrique—the Razor—over there. Now you tell me he is dead, along with those he has recruited. It makes me wonder how you are still alive."

"Just lucky, *jefe*. Besides the dead, three other *camellos* are in jail and our *putas* have disappeared."

"Bring the *piruja negra* to me," Santiago growled. "I will find out who did this."

"*Si, Jefe.* I will be there by morning."

"No," Santiago said, suddenly anxious. "Take her to the air-strip where we bring the *coca.* I will alert the pilot."

He ended the call and turned toward his friend and the number two man in their organization. "Take Gabriel. Go out to Opa-locka field and bring the girl to the warehouse."

"*Si*, Santiago," Manuel Ortolano replied. "Would you like me to call the pilot there and alert him?"

"*Si*, Manuel. *Gracias.* I will be at the warehouse at midnight."

Ortolano left without another word.

At the bar, Santiago poured a double shot of Corralejo, a sipping tequila, and tossed it down, grimacing as the clear liquid burned his throat.

An hour later, he had one of his men drive him to the warehouse on the Miami River. The flight from Fort Myers should only have taken thirty minutes, but when they arrived, Manuel's car wasn't parked outside.

The two men walked toward the door, where Santiago ordered the driver to stand guard outside.

As they entered the outer office, a squat little man rose quickly from a chair behind a small desk. "*Jefe*, I didn't know you were coming."

"I'm not here to check anything," Santiago said. "When Manuel and Gabriel arrive, they will have a woman with them. Tell Manuel to bring her to my office."

Without waiting for a response, Santiago strode down a hallway and unlocked the last door.

His office wasn't as opulent as his home, but it surpassed the average business office in the warehouse district. The walls were done in a rich, dark wood, with ornate trim. Leather and wood

furnishings decorated the space. The floor was brown Ecuadoran tile.

Being the leader of the largest and most notorious gang in South Florida had its advantages. Need was a relative thing for Carlos Santiago; it bordered on what he wanted.

Santiago seated himself in the custom leather chair behind his desk. After opening his laptop, which was connected to a private network, he quickly checked the status of MS-13's vast drug importation business while he waited.

Ten minutes later, there was a knock on the door.

"*Entra*," he said, and closed the laptop.

Manuel opened the door and came in. Gabriel was behind him, shoving a bound, gagged, and blindfolded black woman ahead of him.

"Go outside and bring me three strong men," Santiago told Gabriel.

As he left, the big man closed the door behind him.

Santiago pointed to a chair in front of his desk and Ortolano pushed the woman down into it.

"Remove the gag and blindfold," Santiago ordered, as he leaned back in his chair.

Ortolano did as he was told and the woman looked around, obviously frightened.

"Do you know who I am, *puta*?"

The woman's clothes were disheveled. She had an open cut on her cheek, and dried blood smeared her skin.

"No," she replied nervously.

"My name is Carlos Santiago," he said. "I run MS-13 here in Miami."

Her eyes locked on his. "What do you want with me?"

"Do you know what happened in Fort Myers last night?"

She looked up at Manuel, standing next to her with his arms folded across his chest, then turned panicked eyes back to Santiago. "I heard there were some shootings," she said.

Santiago could see in her eyes that she knew about all the black prostitutes he'd ordered Razor to kill in retaliation for the murders of MS-13 hookers.

"Where were you when last night's shootings happened?"

"I was in a rehab center," she replied. "Please…I had nothing to do with what happened."

"What were you doing in rehab?" Santiago asked, as he opened his desk drawer and took out a small bag of crystal meth.

She eyed the bag with a look that bordered on voraciousness.

Santiago produced a small meth pipe and butane lighter, placing them beside the drugs.

"Me and a b-bunch of other working girls went there," she replied. "I left this morning. I couldn't take being there anymore."

"Just *puta negras* like you?" he asked, unworried that he might be insulting her. "Or were there *Chicanas*, as well?"

"Both," she replied. "Even a coupla white girls. More than a dozen altogether."

There was a knock on the door.

"*Un minuto*," Santiago said, as he dropped a large rock into the pipe and pushed it and the lighter across the desk. "Go ahead," he told the woman. "Ride the cloud."

With her hands tied, she fumbled with the pipe.

"Untie her, Manuel," Santiago said. "I think she is being very cooperative, don't you?"

Manuel flicked a big knife open. "*Si, jefe*."

The blade parted the nylon rope binding her wrists.

"What is your name?" Santiago asked.

"Aliyah," she replied, flicking the lighter and holding the flame to the bottom of the bowl. "Aliyah Wilkins."

As smoke started to swirl in the pipe, she put it to her lips and inhaled deeply until it was all gone. Then she blew out a gray-blue plume and slumped back in the chair.

"Is that better?" Santiago asked.

"Oh yeah, man."

"Open the door, Manuel."

Ortolano turned and opened the office door. Gabriel entered, followed by three gang members—warehouse workers—stripped down to their jeans. Each had numerous gang tattoos covering their sweaty torsos. The three men looked at Santiago, then at the woman.

"Take this *puta* out to the warehouse and fuck her up good," he told the biggest of the three men. "Let the others join in if they want. Just don't kill her."

Aliyah looked confused.

Two men lifted her by the arms and the third man grabbed her knees, bringing her legs up until her butt smacked his groin. She struggled, but not much, as the three men easily carried her out of the office.

"Do you think she knows anything?" Ortolano asked.

"Maybe," Santiago said. "Go out there and question her while the men gangbang her. I want to know why so many were in rehab and I want to know who was responsible."

CHAPTER TWENTY-EIGHT

I woke early, before dawn's first light. Looking out the east-facing bedroom window, I could still see stars, which was all the weather forecast I needed. The old idiom of red sky in morning, sailor take warning was true—at least in spring, when weather patterns typically came out of the east.

It was going to be a nice day.

Savannah stirred as I rose from our bed. "What time are you leaving?" she mumbled, rolling onto her side.

"After sunrise. I texted Tank last night that we'd pick him up by zero eight hundred. He chastised me for being a late riser."

"You'll be back in time for dinner?"

"By mid-afternoon, at the latest," I replied, pulling on my boxers. "Dink said he was getting cobia off Channel Key Bank."

"Channel Key Bank?"

"A few miles northeast of Grassy Key."

She sat up and the sheet fell down to her waist. We typically slept in the nude when it was warm. I was tempted to stay but knew Alberto would be rising soon.

"I'll make some breakfast," she said. "And some sandwiches to take with you on the boat."

"Thanks. I'm gonna get Alberto up, get the boat ready, and go out to the dock to watch the sunrise."

She looked at her watch, the only thing she had on. "It's an hour before dawn. I'll make some sausage biscuits and bring them down there."

Pulling on a clean pair of shorts and a T-shirt, I left the bedroom. Finn and Woden lifted their heads, one lying on either side of Alberto's makeshift bed.

I went to the little galley and poured two cups of coffee. I'd set the machine up the night before. The aroma of fresh-brewed Costa Rican Tarazzu caused my nostrils to flare.

The dogs rose and went to the door, so I opened it to let them out. The closing of the door woke Alberto.

He sat up and looked around. "Is it daytime yet?"

"It will be in a little while," I replied. "Savannah is going to make breakfast and bring it out to the dock for us, so we can get the boat ready and watch the sun come up."

Alberto's new clothes were in a suitcase beside his bed. He got up, picked out a pair of shorts and a T-shirt and was dressed before Savannah came out.

"We'll have to do something about that suitcase," I told him. "But since we're leaving in just a few days, that'll have to do for now. Once we get to *Ambrosia*, you'll have your own bedroom and dresser."

"Really? I never had my own room," he said, as Savannah entered.

I wondered just how much of his memory he'd regained.

"Not even before your dad's accident?" Savannah asked. Then she turned quickly and faced him. "Oh, I'm so sorry. You probably don't like talking about that."

"It's okay," he said. "It was a long time ago. I don't remember a whole lot from when I was little."

He'd been five when his father was killed. I couldn't recall a lot from when I was that age either. Yet, he'd retained the ability to play chess, and play it well. He must have continued playing someone after his father was killed.

"I mostly slept on the couch after Dad died," he explained. "Me and mom lived with her friends sometimes and sometimes in the car."

Savannah covered her mouth with her hand to stifle a gasp.

"Well, this is just temporary," I said. "On *Ambrosia,* you'll have a whole suite to yourself."

"What's a suite?"

I chuckled. "It's a small room with a separate bedroom and bathroom. You'll even have your own TV."

"You mean it? I can't wait."

"Y'all go on," Savannah said, shooing us toward the door. "I'll bring breakfast down in a few minutes."

"Come on," I told Alberto. "You can help me get the boat ready."

I flicked on the light below the house as I started down the steps, illuminating the dock area.

"Are we taking the big boat?" Alberto asked.

"Not for this job. The *Revenge* is for the ocean." I walked around to my Mirage Maverick in the far bay. "We'll take this one."

I stepped down into the flats skiff and used the key fob hanging in the ignition to open the big outer doors.

"What's this one's name?" he asked, looking down from the dock.

"It doesn't have a name," I replied. "It's just a work boat. Good for shallow water, but not for offshore."

"You sure have a lot of boats," he said, looking around the docks.

"Each has a different job," I explained. "That other Maverick belongs to my daughter, Kim. The big center console, *El Cazador*, is for small groups fishing the Gulf."

"That means *The Hunter*," he said.

I nodded as I went to the end of the middle dock and opened the storage closet. "For hunting grouper and snapper on reefs."

I chose three light rods with spin-casting reels and handed one to Alberto. "Think you can handle this?"

He took the rod and held it horizontally in both hands. "I think so," he replied. "Dad took me fishing some when I was little."

"Let's stow these onboard," I said, stepping down into the boat.

I eased the tip of one rod into a holder under the starboard gunwale, then settled the handle into place. I did the same with the second rod, leaving the upper holder for Alberto.

"Right there?" he asked, pointing.

I nodded and he carefully slid the tip into the hole and placed the handle into its cradle. Then he stood up, grinning, and looked around again.

"What's that one for?" he asked pointing to my little eighteen-foot Grady-White center console.

"That one's kind of an all-purpose boat," I replied. "We use it mostly for bringing groceries from Marathon and reef fishing with just two people."

"Does it have a name?"

"*Pescador*," I replied.

"That means fisherman," he said. "How come they have Spanish names but you don't speak it very well?"

"How do you know I don't speak it?"

"Because Savannah had to tell you what I told her."

"Ah, yes," I said. "Well, I understand more than I speak, but I know enough to get by."

"And that one?" he asked, pointing toward the homemade boat tied up behind the Grady. "What's it for?"

"That one's called *Knot Late*," I said, sounding out the name on the transom. "She only has one purpose."

"What?" he asked walking around behind her and looking at the woodwork and the spelling of the name, *Knot L-8* on the transom.

"She's for going real fast," I replied. "Nothing else."

He smiled, staring down at the sleek runabout. "Can we take it?"

"She doesn't make much of a fishing boat," I said. "And we have work to do. She's just for fun and showing off. But we can take her out one day this weekend."

I started the Maverick's outboard and Alberto came back over to the boat. I helped him in, then untied the lines. A couple of minutes later, I tied her off to the south dock and killed the engine.

"What do we do now?" he asked, looking around in the dark.

"Now we wait," I replied, pointing toward the east-northeast, where it was starting to get light. "The sun is going to come up over there. Just to the right of that island in the distance."

"And we're just going to wait for it?"

I moved over to the gunwale and leaned against the dock

where, just a few hours earlier, Savannah and I had made love. Then I put my feet up on the little center console.

"That's what you wanted to see, right?" I asked. "The sky's already getting light over that way. It shouldn't be long."

Alberto stepped up onto the aft deck and put a hand on the aluminum framework around the engine. "What's this for?"

"It's called a poling platform." I pointed toward a push pole mounted on the port gunwale. "See that long pole? In real shallow water, you stand up on the platform and use the pole for pushing the boat and looking for fish."

"It's a little boat," he said, standing on the other side of the console. "Is it fast?"

I grinned at him. The kid had a one-track mind.

"Yes, she is," I replied. "Clients like to get to where the fish are as quickly as possible."

"What's a client?"

"A lot of people like to fish, but not all of them have a boat or know where the fish are. Some of those people will hire people like me—a fishing guide—to take them out and find the fish. Those people are clients."

As the sky to the east continued to brighten, Alberto looked around the boat some more. I turned on the aerator on the live well and grabbed the cast net from below the aft deck.

"What are you doing?" he asked.

"We'll need bait," I said. "As soon as the sky starts to get light, pinfish come out from under the dock to forage."

I made two casts, right alongside the dock, and put several dozen baitfish into the live well.

"Look," I said, pointing toward the sun, as the first sliver began to appear.

I sat back down, and he came over beside me and sat cross-legged on the aft deck.

"You two look comfortable," Savannah said, walking toward us with the dogs following behind her. "Is there room for one more?"

"Sure," I replied, standing, and taking a small cooler from her.

I placed it on the aft deck and opened it. The aroma of fried sausage hit my nostrils, reminding me how hungry I was. Savannah sat next to Alberto and I handed them both a biscuit, half wrapped in a paper towel.

"What is it?" he asked.

"Mana from Heaven," I replied, taking a big bite.

"Mana?" he asked, looking up at me puzzled. "That's not Spanish or English."

I laughed. "No, it's not. It's Polynesian."

"You speak Polynesian?"

"No, but I've been to the South Pacific. Mana means the life force that permeates all things in the universe."

"He means mana with one N," Savannah said. "But he referenced the Biblical story of manna from Heaven with two Ns."

Alberto looked at her with revelation in his eyes. "When Moses fed the people?"

She smiled at him. "Exactly. But Jesse's version probably sounds more adventurous."

We sat on the gunwale and ate the biscuits as the sun rose slowly.

"Mmm," Alberto hummed, as he chewed and swallowed a bite. "Mana is good."

We were silent for a few minutes, as the sun gradually re-

vealed itself from beyond the horizon. As we ate, the sky changed from inky purple to a cobalt blue in just a matter of minutes. Twilight was shorter on the water.

"There are two more in the cooler," Savannah said. "Plus, a half dozen sandwiches, some tortilla chips, salsa, sliced pineapple, and bottled water. That should hold the three of you over until you get back."

"What's for dinner?" Alberto asked.

"That depends on what you catch," she replied, then wiped her mouth on a cloth napkin. "Don't you boys let me down."

She patted Alberto on the back, then rose and gave me a kiss before stepping up to the dock.

I started the engine and untied the stern line while Savannah got the bow line.

"Bye," she said. "Good luck."

"Thanks," I replied, putting the boat into gear. "Love you."

"Love you, too," she called out, as we idled away.

At the end of my channel, I turned left into Harbor Channel, bumping the speed up a little.

"What did she mean when she said, 'don't let her down'?" Alberto asked.

"Remember I said that work was fun here?"

He nodded.

"You and I are going to work," I said.

"Fishing is work?"

"It is for us, little man," I said as we neared Mac Travis's island. "And work is fun out here on our own. We don't buy much food from stores. We catch or grow just about everything we eat."

Mac Travis was our only neighbor. At least the only one with-

in about five miles. He tended to keep pretty much to himself, working his lobster traps throughout the season and looking for treasure during the off-season. His girlfriend, Mel Woodson, actually owned the island, having inherited it from her dad. I never knew his first name; everyone just called him Wood. She was a lawyer and stayed on the island with Mac off and on.

Seeing Mac wading toward his boat, I turned and angled toward him. I killed the engine ten feet away.

"Hi, Jesse," he said, as he caught the gunwale. "Who's that you have with you?"

Mac held us in place against the incoming tide. It didn't take a lot of effort to hold the Maverick into the current.

"This is my friend, Alberto Marco," I replied. "Alberto, meet our neighbor, Mac Travis."

Mac extended a hand, and the boy shook it.

"Alberto's staying with us for a while," I said. "We're heading out to catch some fish."

Mac looked at the boy curiously. "Are you the kid Jesse found in a drifting boat?"

Alberto nodded. "Him and Savannah both. They jumped in the water and took me to shore."

"How'd you know that?" I asked Mac.

"You know how it is," he replied, nodding sagely. "Coconut telegraph."

It was hard to keep anything a secret on a small island. Though we'd tried to keep everything under wraps, I knew word would get around. But islanders were tight and I doubted if many knew what had happened.

"Figured you'd be packing," Mac said. "Aren't you leaving tomorrow?"

"There's been a delay," I replied. "We're not leaving until Monday—all three of us."

"Jimmy'll be staying at your place while you're gone?"

"Yeah," I replied. "He and Naomi will be out later this morning and staying on permanently."

"I'd heard she was moving out of her apartment."

"Hope they don't get too wild," I said with a half grin.

"Jimmy could never be as much a pain as Tru," he said with a laugh.

Trufant was Mac's first mate. He was a lanky Louisiana Cajun with a mouthful of pearly whites you could see from a mile away. The man had a penchant for finding trouble. And crazy women.

"Where is Tru?" I asked. "Not like him to miss work."

"He called and said he was running late," Mac replied. "After an hour, I figured it'd be faster for me to go to him."

"Ah, one of those situations."

"Some girl he and Pamela met at Burdines last night."

"Well, be careful out there," I said, starting the engine.

"You do the same," he replied, pushing the bow toward the channel.

I put the engine in gear and idled toward the flats south of the channel until we were far enough away.

"Hang on," I told Alberto. "We need to be moving fast to get across the sandbar."

He leaned forward and grabbed the rail on the starboard side of the console as I pushed the throttle forward.

The little boat leapt up onto the surface of the water and we skimmed across the shallow sandbar with no more than eight inches of the lower unit in the water. I glanced over at Alberto.

The grin on his face said it all.

CHAPTER TWENTY-NINE

An old Chevy crunched across the gravel and came to a stop beside its modern cousin. It was still dark but would be light soon. The white, 1964 Bel Air sat incredibly low on hydraulic suspension—a lowrider. The system had a leak and during the drive from Fort Myers, the car had settled lower and lower, until finally, it was almost scraping the gravel in the parking lot.

Manuel "Bones" Bonilla had been to the warehouse only once before, just over a year earlier, but he was certain he was in the right place. By the door, a beefy-looking Hispanic man leaned back in a chair on two legs. That was a good indication. As was the SUV Bones had parked next to.

As Bones got out of the car, the man in the chair rocked forward onto all four legs and stood. "We heard you was dead, Bones."

Lifting his shirt, Bonilla revealed a large bandage on his lower left shoulder, as well as many gang tattoos. "An inch lower and I would have been." He glanced over at the Cadillac Escalade beside his old Chevy. "Is the *jefe* here?"

"Yeah, man, yeah." The guard opened the door and nodded to another man sitting behind a desk just inside the outer office.

"Bones is here, Julio," he announced. "Wants to see the boss."

Bones stepped past the guard and entered the warehouse's reception area. Julio Mendoza rose from behind the desk and stared, slack-jawed.

"I need to talk to Carlos," Bones said.

"We heard you got shot."

"I did," Bones replied. "But I ain't dead."

"Hang on," Julio said, picking up the desk phone's handset and pushing a button. "Bones is here, *jefe*." After a moment he said, "*Si*," and hung up the phone.

"Go on back," Julio said. "He's questioning a *puta negra* we had brought here from Fort Myers."

Bones walked down the corridor to the last door and knocked.

"*Entra*," he heard Santiago say from inside.

He turned the knob and stepped into the private office. Santiago was standing over a black woman who was practically naked and bleeding from several wounds to her torso—razor cuts—one of MS-13's favored methods for extracting information from rival gang members or police informants. Her face was a swollen mess from a beating.

"They said you were killed in the shootings," Santiago said, coming toward him.

Once more, Bones lifted his shirt. "Shot twice, *jefe*." He puffed his chest up. "But it wasn't enough."

The two men shook hands and Santiago waved him toward a chair beside the injured woman. Santiago's personal bodyguard stood on the other side of her.

Bones sat down, ignoring the woman in the next chair. He'd seen, and *done*, much worse. The woman was alive, but he knew she wouldn't be for much longer. She wouldn't die from the

injuries she'd received; Santiago could keep someone alive and experiencing more pain for a long time.

Santiago went around his desk and sat down. "Tell me what happened."

"I was with Razor," Bones said. "This crazy Indian and a woman, with probably three others with them, busted in. Diego and Esteban are both dead. So is Razor. I barely got out alive."

"Yes, we heard." He nodded toward the woman. "And now we know the name of one of the people who was a part of it."

"The woman who rounded up all the *putas*?" Bones asked, amazed that Santiago had found out so fast.

"Woman?" His eyes cut to the bloody girl sitting next to Bones. "She said it was a white man named Jesse McDermitt."

Bones nodded, putting what he'd learned on his own together with what Santiago had just told him.

"I learned from two sources that a white man picked them up, but it was a woman named Savannah, talking to them with one of those Bluetooth things." He twirled a finger around his ear. "She was the one who talked them into checking into rehab. The Lake Boyz shootings happened later that night. I found one of them still alive, just before the cops got there, and he described the same man who'd picked up the girls."

Santiago sat back in his chair and thought for a moment.

"They were a team, this McDermitt and the woman," he finally said. "And they had others."

"*Si, jefe*," Bones said. "From what I learned, they hit three Lake Boyz locations at once, not long after they hit Diego."

"So, this crazy Indian was a part of their gang? Someone new trying to take over both us and Lake Boyz?"

"*No lo creo*," Bones said. "Whoever they were, they wiped out both gangs' leaders, took *prostitutas* and *narcotraficantes* from both

sides, and then just left."

"That makes no sense," Santiago said. "I would have continued the attack and taken over everything. Something I should have done from the start, instead of trying to play nice with Lake Boyz."

"I learned that the man who picked up the *putas* left on a boat," Bones offered. "With another boat following it. Each boat had a blond woman aboard."

"Did you see the name of this boat?"

"Better than that, *jefe*." Bones smiled, revealing a gold-capped tooth. "More than that. I know where the man who owns the boat lives."

"The w-woman," the black girl croaked between split lips. "She was his w-wife."

Santiago cocked his head and stared at her for a moment, as if seeing her for the first time. Manuel moved away from her slightly.

Bones looked over at the side of her battered face.

Of course, he thought. Husband and wife, do-gooder vigilantes. That would explain why they'd just left when all the girls were rounded up and both gangs all shot to shit.

Santiago pulled open a desk drawer to his right, drew a silenced handgun and pointed it at the woman's face. "You should have told me that before. It would have saved me time and you, much pain."

The gun bucked in his hand, emitting no more sound than punching a heavy bag. A pink mist from the back of the woman's head sprayed across the floor.

Santiago looked up at his bodyguard and spoke calmly. "Manuel, roll that thing out of here, get rid of it, and have the chair cleaned and returned."

CHAPTER THIRTY

Reaching deeper water, I turned southeast, searching for the microwave tower on Grassy Key. There was no need of a chart plotter or depth finder; we'd just crossed the shallowest water we were going to encounter.

I finally spotted the tower and turned toward it, pointing. "See that tower sticking up way out in front of us?"

Alberto craned his neck and looked over the console. "That one?" he asked, pointing toward it.

"That's close to Tank and Chyrel's place," I said, then opened the throttle a little more. "We'll be there in fifteen minutes."

The two of us sat slightly hunched to absorb what little bounce there was and enjoyed the ride.

Finally, I slowed as we neared shore, angling toward the dock behind Tank's place. He and Chyrel were waiting.

"Wasting daylight, Gunny," Tank said, as I came alongside the dock. "I thought fishermen got up early."

"I wanted to see the sunrise," Alberto said in my defense.

Tank sat on the edge of the dock, holding the boat in place with his feet. "Was it worth the wait?" he asked, tousling Alber-

to's hair.

"It sure was," he replied. "And we had sausage biscuits."

Chyrel handed me a small cooler. "There's a few sandwiches and water in there, plus his meds."

"Thanks," I said, placing it with Savannah's cooler.

How we were going to eat three sandwiches each, I wasn't sure.

She leaned over and kissed Tank on the cheek. "You be careful and don't forget when to take them."

"We'll be back in a few hours," Tank said, scooting down to the gunwale and shoving off.

Tank took the little seat in front of the console and a minute later, we were up on plane, heading north. After several minutes, we passed Marker 9 and I angled toward the northeast. Channel Bank wasn't all that far—within sight of Grassy Key and the bridge—but you still had a sense that you were in another world there.

I slowed as we approached the bank. "Dink was out here yesterday," I called forward to Tank. "He said he was getting cobia at the north end of the bank."

"Cobia?" Alberto asked. "Like we had yesterday?"

"That's right," I replied. "If we can catch one or two, we won't have to worry about food for the rest of the weekend."

"I like cobia," he said.

I took the boat out of gear and shut off the engine. We drifted along the shoal in the current as I got the rods out. I hooked a pinfish through the meat just ahead of its tail and passed the rod forward to Tank, who moved up to the forward casting deck. Baiting another, I handed it to Alberto.

"Let's see what you can do," I said, as I prepped the third

rod. "Try to get it close to the bank, but not too close."

He gripped the upper part of the handle, getting the line between his thumb and forefinger, then flipped the bail arm over on the spinning reel. His cast wasn't far, and the bait hit the water pretty hard, rather than arcing high. But he obviously knew at least the basics of what he was doing.

"You *have* done this before," I said. "Not too bad. Give him some slack, and when he wakes up from that wallop you gave him, he'll swim toward the shoal."

I cast mine close to what looked like a ledge that ran along the bank for thirty or forty feet, then reeled in the slack so the pinfish couldn't get to it.

"Fish on!" Tank yelled. "Looks like a red snapper."

He quickly wrestled the fish close to the boat, then knelt down and grabbed the short leader, looping it around his hand and lifting the snapper aboard.

"Definitely a keeper," I said. "You don't even have to measure that one, even if we were over on the Atlantic side."

Tank quickly unhooked the fish and put it in the fish box.

Alberto's rod bent and he nearly lost it, but he quickly leaned back, raising the tip. "I got one!"

He moved closer to the gunwale, bracing his little body against the side for leverage. He worked the fish with some difficulty, as it dove and moved left and right.

"Keep your line tight, son!" I coached. "That's right. Move your rod in the opposite direction the fish goes."

Alberto looked over at me and grinned.

I suddenly realized I'd called him son. It's a normal thing for a man to call a boy, like kiddo or young man. But I suddenly felt something different deep in the pit of my stomach. If Savannah

and I were successful in our application to adopt Alberto, he *would* be my son.

"It's a cobia!" Tank shouted from the bow, where he had a better view down into the water.

Alberto continued to fight the fish, reeling as he lowered the rod, and the fish taking some of it back from the drag as he raised it. But Alberto was slowly winning the fight.

He was also beginning to tire. It'd only been five days ago that he was pulled from a drifting boat, nearly dead from dehydration.

I stood beside him, ready to catch him if he wore himself out too much or catch the rod if it slipped from his grasp. I could see the fish—a big cobia—well over the thirty-three-inch limit.

"Do you want me to boat him for you?" I asked, concerned.

He looked up at me, determination etched in his little face. "I can do it. I can catch him by myself."

Tank moved back with the net ready. I pulled a long gaff from under the port gunwale.

"No need for the net," I told Tank. "That's definitely legal-sized."

I thought Alberto was on the verge of collapsing when he finally got the fish close to the boat. With a quick, fluid movement, I gaffed it and lifted it over the side.

The sudden lessening of the tension on his line caused Alberto to stumble back. He landed on the deck, sitting up with the rod still in his hands.

I dropped the cobia to the deck, where it flopped feebly, and then I knelt beside the boy. "Are you okay?"

He nodded, breathing hard. "Yeah, but he got away."

"He didn't get away," I said, moving so Alberto could see his

catch.

"Holy cow!" he exclaimed. "That's the biggest fish I ever caught."

I took the rod from him and helped him onto the little seat in front of the console. "Take it easy," I told him. "You caught him all right. No man could have done a better job; that is one big cobia."

Tank went aft and held the fish alongside the ruler stuck to the inside of the hull. "It's forty-four inches," he said.

"Can we keep it?" Alberto asked, looking back.

"Anything over thirty-three at the fork is good," Tank said. "This fish is well past that."

I got a small scale from the console, hooked it in the fish's gill, and lifted it. "Just over forty pounds!"

I carried it forward. "Stand up, young waterman. Check out your catch."

With the tail almost touching the deck, the fish and Alberto were practically eye to eye.

"That's a big fish," he breathed, looking it up and down. "We didn't let Savannah down."

"You sure didn't," I agreed, smiling broadly. "They don't get much bigger than this on the Gulf side."

"Can we have it for dinner?"

"Absolutely, little man."

Tank sat down on the gunwale and I noticed his face was flushed and he was breathing heavy.

"You okay, Master Guns?" I asked, dropping the fish in the box.

"Just a little winded," he replied. "There's an inhaler in the cooler."

I quickly retrieved it and handed it to him. He pushed the button and took a deep breath from the mouthpiece.

"What's wrong?" Alberto asked, moving over beside Tank, and putting a hand on the man's knee.

Tank squinted up at me and I nodded.

He smiled at Alberto and ruffled his hair. "I'm sick, kid."

"Huh?"

"I have a disease," Tank said. "It's called cancer and I don't have much longer to live."

"Then you'll be dead? Like my mom and dad?"

"Yeah, son," he said, pulling Alberto to his side. "Everyone dies sooner or later. It's the only thing in life that's guaranteed. But if a man's lucky, he can *choose* how he spends his last days. I chose to spend mine down here, where the air is warm, and the fish are biting."

Tank smiled down at him. Alberto seemed to accept and understand Tank's wisdom, and smiled back.

We drifted along the bank, fishing. Alberto caught another cobia that was too small, but he made up for that with his next cast, boating a near thirty-pound black grouper.

By the time the current carried us to the north end of the shoal, the fish box was half full. I started the engine and moved around to the opposite side. At the south end of Channel Bank, I shut off the engine and we drifted north again.

"You called him Master Guns," Alberto said, leaning against the gunwale, rod in hand. "And he called you Gunny. What's that mean?"

"Tank and I used to be in the military—the Marine Corps. Do you know what that is?"

He shook his head. "Like a soldier?"

"Soldiers are Army," Tank told him. "Marines are soldiers of the sea. The smallest, fastest, and most deadly branch of America's military."

"When I retired, my rank was gunnery sergeant," I explained. "And Tank was a master gunnery sergeant. Gunny and Master Guns are sort of short for those."

My cell phone chirped, resting on its charging pad. It was Savannah.

"Alberto didn't let you down," I said, grinning at him. "He's caught the biggest so far—a forty-pound cobia."

"Really?" she asked. "That's amazing. How is he?"

"The fight wore him out a little," I said. "But he was fine after a few minutes rest, and he's caught a grouper and a couple of snapper."

"Are you sure he's okay?" she asked, the concern clearly evident in her voice.

"He's fine, babe. Want to talk to him?"

"That's okay," she replied. "Just make sure he doesn't overexert himself. And be sure to put sunscreen on him."

"I will," I assured her. "Was there a reason you called or just checking up on us?"

"Jimmy called me," she said. "He knew you were fishing. The boat wouldn't start, and he asked if I'd go pick him and Naomi up at the Rusty Anchor. We're leaving in just a minute."

"We?" I asked.

"The dogs haven't been off the island in days," she said. "I thought I'd take them and let them run while I had lunch with Sidney and Rusty to catch up on things."

"Sounds like a plan," I said, glancing at my watch, and seeing it was almost noon. "We'll be home in a few hours."

We ended the call and I put the phone back on the charger.

"You told her about my cobia?" Alberto asked.

"I did, and she was amazed."

He grinned, just as his rod tip bent again. "I got another one!"

Alberto worked the fish away from the ledge. He was still a little clumsy but getting used to the tackle. I could tell by the bend in the rod it was something large.

"Shark!" Tank shouted. "A three-foot lemon."

"A shark?" Alberto asked, lowering his rod, and reeling as fast as he could.

"Work him alongside the boat," I instructed. "Get him in close."

"So you can get him with that big hook?"

"Lemon sharks aren't the most edible fish in the world," I replied. "I want to get the hook out if I can and let him go. Tank, grab your phone and we'll get a picture."

When Alberto got the little lemon shark alongside, I put a glove on my right hand and grabbed it by the tail, hoisting it aboard. Sharks have denticles on their skin, which can tear the skin right off your palm.

"Stay back," I warned Alberto, as the fish tried to twist its mouth up to my hand. "He can still bite."

With the shark on the deck, I pulled a pair of needle-nose pliers from my pocket and quickly removed the hook. There was a second hook, which I removed also. Then I lifted it by the tail again and stood on the forward casting deck, making sure my shadow wouldn't be in the shot.

"Step over here, Alberto," I said, as Tank got his phone ready. "Pretend like you're holding it up, but don't grab too tight.

The skin's real rough."

He stepped over to the other side of the shark and looked it up and down. "I never saw a shark in real life."

"And the first one you saw, you caught!" Tank said, as he knelt to take the picture.

I stepped down and lowered the shark into the water, moving him back and forth to get water across his gills.

"What are you doing?" Alberto asked.

"You've seen how fish open and close their mouths to breath, right?"

He nodded.

"That moves water across their gills, which gives them oxygen, like when we breathe air."

"Even when they sleep?"

"Some sharks never sleep," I replied. "At least not like we do. They don't have eyelids and they're visually aware of everything around them, even those that can breathe at rest like other fish. Some sharks, like the great white, have to swim to move water across their gills. They start swimming when they're born and don't stop until they die. I'm just helping this guy breathe."

I felt movement in the tail and let the shark go. It swam to the bottom and headed back toward the shoal.

"Take a look at this," Tank said, holding his phone out.

I knelt beside Alberto. Tank got the shot perfectly, with my hand above Alberto's and completely out of frame.

"Whoa!" he exclaimed. "I can't wait to show that to Savannah."

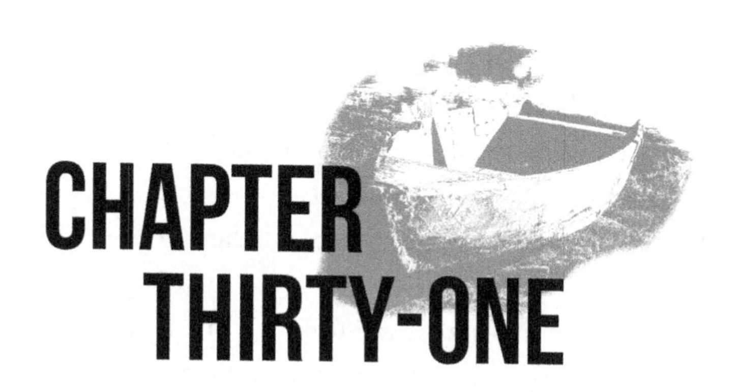

CHAPTER THIRTY-ONE

Several hours after the murder in the warehouse, Santiago's white Escalade crossed the bridge onto Grassy Key. He and Manuel Ortolano were in the back, while Julio Mendoza drove. Bones rode up front, giving directions from his cell phone.

Bones turned in his seat. "It's just a few more miles, *jefe*. Just past the airport."

"Remember what I told you," Santiago said. "It's almost noon. If the man isn't home for lunch, we hold the woman until he gets there. We'll go in hard and fast."

Ten minutes later, the Escalade made a U-turn and next to a leaning mailbox that had the right address on it, it turned onto a crushed shell driveway. Bones had been quite proud of himself for getting the address of the guy who owned the boat. Tropical foliage enveloped the big SUV immediately.

Santiago sat forward in his seat as the vehicle emerged into a large parking lot alongside what looked like a restaurant—a low, metal-roofed building with many windows.

"This isn't a house, Bones," Santiago said.

"Look," Bones said, pointing off to the right. "There's a bunch of boats here. Maybe he uses this as his address and lives

on his boat. From what I was told, it was big enough."

"This complicates things," Santiago said. "There are a lot of cars here, so there's bound to be a lot of people."

"Should I turn around?" Julio asked.

"No. Find a place to park where we can see everything and let's just wait and watch."

Julio backed into a spot away from the other cars, where they could see the whole parking lot and the building.

"There's another place back there," Bones said, pointing beyond the metal-roofed building. "Looks more like a house."

Santiago dismissed the house and studied the bigger building directly in front of them, thinking that a man who owned a fishing boat as big as Bones had described wouldn't own a restaurant too.

He was sure that's what it was; it had all the markings of a restaurant, even beer signs in the windows, which stretched along the side deck. But there was no name anywhere that he could see.

"Julio, go walk the dock," Santiago ordered. "What was the name of the boats, Bones?"

"One was called *Gaspar's Revenge* and the other was *Sea Biscuit.*"

"Look and see if either of those is at the docks," Santiago said. "If not, my guess is that this McDermitt guy and his wife live in the house out back, but I'm betting this belongs to someone else."

Julio got out and walked toward the dock area. So far, there hadn't been any people outside, which was good. After a moment, Julio reached the end and returned, then went around to the other side and walked the length of the dock area. The two docks straddled a wide canal.

When he returned, he was walking faster. He got in and

turned around in his seat. "No boat called *Gaspar's Revenge,*" he reported. "But the last boat on the far side is *Sea Biscuit*—a big cabin cruiser."

"Was anyone on it?" Santiago asked.

"No, *jefe.* At least not that I could see or hear."

"We'll go inside," Santiago said. "Me and Manuel first. You two wait a minute before coming in. We'll find a place inside where we can see just what's going on. What does this man look like, Bones?"

"Real tall, *jefe,*" Bones replied. "Taller than Manuel and just as big as him. I was told he was clean-shaven and had dark blond hair. Oh, and a tattoo on his forearm—a skull."

"Let's go, Manuel."

The two got out of the back of the SUV and strode confidently toward the entrance. Just before they reached it, the door opened, and a man stepped out. He stumbled slightly and the door banged into his shoulder. To Santiago, he appeared drunk, but he held the door for them.

Entering, it took Santiago a moment for his eyes to adjust to the darkened interior. It was a restaurant. And it had a long bar against part of one wall. A short, fat man with a bald head and bushy beard stood behind the bar, talking to two men and a woman, who sat on stools in front of it. Both men had long hair and he noted that the woman was very pretty. Aside from them, the place was empty. This didn't fit with the number of cars and trucks in the parking lot.

Maybe they belong to people who were on the boats, Santiago thought.

"Have a seat anywhere," the fat man said. "I'll be right with you."

Santiago moved to a window table, where they could see the SUV parked in the lot. The two men sat down and looked

around. The interior was all wood, each plank a different shade, but all of them with knots.

The fat man arrived at their table quicker than Santiago would have thought he could move, sliding menus in front of them.

"What can I get ya to drink?" he asked.

"Just water," Santiago said, picking up the menu. "What's good?"

"Everything at the Rusty Anchor is good, *mi amigo*," the man replied. "I'm Rusty—the owner. We just had some fresh hogfish delivered by the guy who almost ran into you at the door. Dink's one of the local fishing guides."

"Sounds good," Santiago said, putting the menu down, and wondering just what a hogfish was. "We'll both have that."

"How do you want it? Platter or sandwich? Grilled or blackened?"

"Grilled sandwiches," Santiago replied. "Make it for four. We're expecting a couple of friends."

"That comes with fries and a pickle," the man said, picking up the menus. "I'll be right back with your water."

When the man left, Bones and Julio entered, spotted them at the table, and came over.

"I don't think any of those is the guy," Bones said, nodding toward the bar.

Santiago looked over. The man sitting next to the woman turned and glanced at them. He nodded a friendly greeting and turned back to the fat man. The woman was more than just pretty. She was tall, with long dark hair. She looked like she could be in movies or a model.

Santiago's lips curled slightly in a lecherous grin.

Behind the bar, a door opened and a tall, redhaired woman came out. The bartender said something to her, and she nodded, then went to work putting glasses on a tray. She filled a pitcher with ice and water, then brought the tray to their table. She was older, but still well put together, and, like the younger one, very tall.

"Rusty just put your order in, gentlemen," she said, placing the pitcher and four glasses on the table. "It should be up in a few minutes. I'm Sidney, if you need anything."

Santiago jerked a thumb toward the window. "Do you know who owns that boat on the end? *Sea Biscuit?*"

"I'm not sure," she said, without looking. "I'll ask Rusty. He knows everyone."

Santiago thought the woman was lying.

When she left, he leaned toward Bones. "Didn't you say the other boat was a fishing boat?"

"*Si, jefe.* One of those offshore fishing boats."

He thought about it a moment. "I think the man is out fishing," he said. "And I think the woman must be on that boat out there. The waitress was lying."

Slowly, as if he were just looking around at the décor, Santiago glanced toward the bar. The two men were turned toward each other, both looking over at his table, as was the dark-haired woman. The fat man was looking at him, also, and the redhead was leaning in and telling him something in a low voice.

"It is time," Santiago said, scooting his chair back and rising. He pulled his gun from under his shirt.

Manuel was a half-second behind him, then the other two came up, all of them with guns in their hands.

"Don't any of you move!" Santiago shouted, pointing the gun at the fat man behind the bar.

CHAPTER THIRTY-TWO

After lunch, we went back around to the other side of the shoal. It had been more productive, and the fish box was a little more than half full. As we drifted along, my phone chirped again.

"You ought to turn that thing off when we're fishin'," Tank commented.

It was Rusty's cell phone.

"Hey, Rusty," I said, answering the call.

"How's the fishing, you old dog soldier?" Rusty asked.

Dog soldier?

That was a slang term for an Army infantryman. Rusty and I had served in the Corps together, during my first tour. We'd arrived at Parris Island for boot camp on the same bus. It sounded like he had the phone on speaker.

I was instantly on alert.

"Just a typical day," I said, straining my ear for anything out of the ordinary. "How are things there?"

"A usual day at the old Roadhouse," he replied. "Jimmy said Savannah was with you on the boat. Is she available?"

Surely Jimmy had told Rusty that he'd called Savannah for a

ride. Something was wrong. *And Old Roadhouse?* I thought.

One of Rusty's favorite movies was called Roadhouse, with Patrick Swayze and Sam Elliot as bar bouncers. The bar in the movie, Double Deuce, was a wild and raucous place where fights happened every night and the band played behind a chain link fence. Swayze and Elliot were brought in to tame it. But the *old* Roadhouse was a dangerous place.

"Yeah," I said, getting Tank's attention with my hand. "But she can't come to the phone."

Tank was staring, ready. I gave him two signals—move up and hostage. He went into action instantly, first going to Alberto and whispering in his ear, then reeling in both their lines and stowing the gear.

"Down in the galley making lunch?" Rusty asked.

He also knew we were fishing from my skiff. Someone was listening who thought we were on the *Revenge.*

"No," I replied. "She's in the cabin. She got seasick on the way out here to the Gulf Stream."

"That's too bad," he said. "Happens a lot with her, though. When will you be back to the marina?"

Two more clues. Savannah's lived aboard for two decades and never gets seasick, and we keep the *Revenge* up at our island. I wanted desperately to know what was going on.

"We should be back there in a couple of hours," I said.

I suddenly realized that Savannah was on her way there now. And probably only fifteen minutes away. I stifled a gasp.

"Good," Rusty said. "We'll see you when you get here."

I looked down at my phone and the call had ended.

"What's going on?" Tank asked.

Alberto was up on the forward casting deck.

"Something's not right at the Anchor," I whispered, and started the outboard. "I think someone is there looking for me and Savannah and holding a gun or something on Rusty."

"Then let's go," Tank said.

"Both of you, move back here."

We sandwiched Alberto between us, and I hit the throttle, pointing the bow toward the southwest and Vaca Cut.

"I'll call Chyrel," Tank yelled. "Andrew and Tony were coming down to help move some stuff for her. Maybe they got there early."

He bent behind the small console to block the wind noise.

"What's wrong?" Alberto said, his voice sounding on the verge of panic.

"We don't know yet," I replied. "We're going to the Rusty Anchor to find out."

"She said they're in Layton," Tank shouted, over the engine and wind noise. "She's diverting them to the Anchor and will follow them as backup. Didn't Savannah say she was headed there? You should call her."

I let Tank reach over and take the wheel as I leaned behind the low console. Savannah's phone rang four times and went to voicemail.

"Don't go to the Anchor!" I shouted into the phone. "Something's going on there."

I ended the call and tried again but got her voicemail once more.

I put the phone back in my pocket and took the wheel, pushing on the throttle, though it was wide open.

"Should I try to call the police?" Tank asked.

"They won't get there for twenty minutes," I replied. "Are

you carrying?"

He nodded and I nodded back. I knew Tony and Andrew would also be armed, and probably Chyrel, as well. It was fifty/fifty whether Savannah was, but she also had Finn and Woden with her.

Slowing the boat a little as we neared the channel for the cut, I felt my phone vibrate and pulled it out. It was Tony.

"Where are you?" I asked, as we entered the channel.

"Just hit the four-lane," Tony said. We should be there in less than five minutes. Chyrel is behind us. What do you want us to do?"

"Head in normally," I said. "We're close, just entering Vaca Cut. We'll come in like a couple of fishermen just returning. Whatever's going on, they think we're two hours out."

We passed under the bridge and I slowed to a normal speed as we came out into Vaca Key Bight. I didn't want to attract any attention if anyone was watching. I just hoped we'd get there before Savannah. I had no idea what was going on, but I sure didn't want her in the middle of it.

We followed the channel until we reached Marker 7, then I turned right, staying just beyond the stick farm—a bunch of different colored wood and plastic poles marking the approaches to numerous private channels.

I knew the water was at least three feet deep and every fiber of my being urged me to mash the throttle. I tried Savannah's phone again. This time it went straight to her voicemail without ringing.

For a moment, my mind flashed back to Alex, and how she'd been abducted from Boot Key Harbor and murdered on our wedding night. I bumped up the speed just a little.

Still a mile from the entrance to Rusty's canal, I spotted the bow spray of a boat rounding East Sister Rock, off to the southwest. As we got closer, I recognized the familiar lines of my old Grady-White and angled to intercept.

As we neared one another, I pulled back on the throttle as Savannah dropped down off plane.

"What are you doing here?" she yelled across the thirty feet of water between us.

Finn and Woden stood next to her with their front paws on the gunwale. Finn barked a greeting.

"Something's wrong at the Anchor," I replied, keeping my voice low; sound travels well over water. "I've been trying to call you. Come over and take Alberto."

She pulled her cell out of her hip pocket. "My phone died. What's going on?"

We both shifted to neutral and I reached over and grabbed the midship cleat on the Grady.

"I'm not sure. But I think there's trouble."

I stood and, still holding the cleat with one hand, scooped Alberto up and lifted him over the Grady's higher gunwale. "Y'all stay out here until I tell you to come in. Come, Finn! Woden, *bewachen*!"

Finn leapt over the gunwale and Woden stepped down, turning sideways to Savannah and Alberto in a protective manner.

Without waiting for an answer, I put the Maverick in gear and headed into the canal.

Tank jumped slightly, then pulled his phone out of his pocket. "It's Tony," he said, stabbing the phone's screen with his finger and putting it to his ear. "We're just entering the canal."

He listened for a moment then said, "Good. Walk out to

Jesse's sailboat. We'll meet you there."

He ended the call and pointed toward *Salty Dog*. "Pull up here. I have an idea."

We tied up quickly and I saw Tony and Andrew headed toward us on the dock.

"Grab the four biggest fish," Tank said, opening the fish box.

I immediately realized what he had in mind and tossed his snapper and the big cobia up onto the forward casting deck, just as Tony and Andrew reached us.

"Where's Chyrel?" Tank asked.

"Blocking the driveway," replied Andrew. "What's the plan?"

"Grab a fish and head toward Rufus's kitchen," I replied. "Use the fish to conceal your weapon."

Removing my Sig Sauer 9mm from its holster at my back, I opened the cobia's mouth and looked inside. It was definitely wide enough. I thrust the Sig into the wide mouth and gripped the lower jaw with my thumb. It would take two hands, but as soon as I let go of the fish, my weapon would be up and ready.

The others did the same thing with the snapper and two big groupers, then we headed toward the back door.

"Finn, heel!"

He fell in beside me as we strode toward the deck. He must have sensed the urgency in my voice; his ears were up, and on full alert.

As we neared the back deck, I knew something was definitely amiss. Rufus was nowhere to be seen and he rarely left his little kitchen area, preferring the outdoors to the air conditioned interior.

The windows were streaked with rivulets of condensation; the AC was cranked up high.

A quick glance at the parking lot and the dock space where the guides kept their boats told me that there couldn't be more than a handful of people inside. Most of the boats were gone.

One vehicle in the lot stuck out like a sore thumb amid the pickups and Keys cars. It was parked away from the others, backed into a spot facing the building—a white Cadillac Escalade.

CHAPTER THIRTY-THREE

"Spread out a little when we get on the deck," I said quietly. "Tony, you open the door and lean in. Yell for Rusty and tell him we have some fish for Rufus."

The four of us moved up the steps and just as Tony reached for the door, it opened.

A Hispanic man stepped out. "What you want?"

"Dropping some fish off for Rufus," Tony replied, lifting a big grouper with both hands. "Who are you?"

I could hear the low rumble starting deep in Finn's chest. Dogs are a great judge of character and Finn could somehow sense that this man wasn't to be trusted.

Tank stepped past me. "Get outta my way, boy. This damned snapper's heavy."

The man in front of me pulled up his shirt and reached for a gun he had stuck in his waist band.

Already wary, Finn lunged instantly, sinking his teeth into the man's wrist in a vice-like bite as the man howled in pain.

We weren't visible from inside. With the AC cranking, it was unlikely that they'd heard the man scream.

"Off, Finn!" I whisper-shouted, dropping the cobia and cov-

ering the man with my Sig. "Don't move a muscle."

Finn let go but stood close to the man, just in case he didn't comply with my order.

I quickly rolled him onto his belly and put my knee on the middle of his back as I removed my web belt from my cargo shorts. I secured his hands behind his back, latching the buckle tightly against his wrists, as Tony tied his shoelaces together so he couldn't run.

Tank was still at the door, ready to go. Then, without a word or signal, he turned the knob and went inside.

The rest of us charged in after Tank, just as the first gunshots rang out.

I wasn't worried about the man Finn was watching; his innate sense of good and bad had been right. The man's gun hand would be useless for a while and the more he pulled against that belt buckle, the tighter the little teeth dug into the webbing. He was out of the picture.

Rusty and Sid were in front of the bar, along with Jimmy, Naomi, Rufus, and a guide by the name of Wilson. Two more Hispanic men had guns trained on my friends and a third pointed a smoking barrel to my left. The man with the smoking gun had a red stain slowly spreading down his shoulder.

Things seemed to move in slow-motion, as often happens in a terrifying situation. A part of my mind took all these things in and processed the information in a micro-second. The two gunmen wheeled to engage us, and the third man grabbed Naomi around the waist.

There was a fast succession of gunshots and two of the men went down. The man Tank had obviously shot held Naomi in front of him, shielding his body.

"Drop the guns," he ordered. "I will kill this *puta.*"

Without thinking or hesitating, I squeezed the trigger, just as another gun went off behind me. The man's head snapped back, and he fell to the ground, leaving Naomi unharmed.

"Mine hit the ground first," Tony said to Andrew, moving toward the two downed gunmen.

The mustachioed former Coastguardsman grinned. "Mine was taller."

Seeing my and Tank's bullet holes in the third guy's forehead told me he didn't need to be checked out. I turned toward Tank.

He lay on the floor, blood soaking his shirt at his abdomen.

"Tank!" I rushed to his side and knelt next to him.

Rusty came around the bar with a trauma kit in his hand, opening it as Tony knelt beside me.

Tony pulled a package of QuikClot from the kit and tore it open. Without a pause, he ripped open Tank's shirt, sending buttons flying, then poured the granulated contents into a bullet wound in Tank's torso.

I ripped open a large gauze bandage and handed it to Tony, then pulled another out of the white box and peeled the backing off.

Tony used the first pad to wipe the area around the wound, then I covered it with a self-adhesive bandage.

"Roll him," Tony ordered.

Tank grunted when we did. The exit wound was worse, as was usually the case. A bullet goes in small, but rapidly mushrooms as it passes through the soft tissue.

Tony poured another package into the wound, stopping the blood flow almost immediately. It took three gauze pads to clean the exit wound before I could put the bandage on. We rolled

Tank onto his back once more.

Sid produced a pillow and put it under his head. "An ambulance is on the way."

I leaned into Tank's field of vision. "Stay with me, Tank. We have a medevac on the way."

"Fifty-one years and I never got shot," he croaked. "Vietnam, Lebanon, Somalia..." He coughed hoarsely. "Only to get taken out by a gang punk. He got the first shot off and I missed my first one." He coughed again. "But I didn't miss the second one. Did you get them all, Gunny?"

"We got 'em, Master Guns."

He looked me in the eye and nodded. "Any friendlies hurt?"

"Zero casualties," I replied.

I could hear the wail of a siren. The hospital was less than a mile away.

Suddenly, the front door opened and Chyrel came rushing in. She saw Tank on the floor and raced to his side. "I heard the shots. What happened?"

"I got shot," Tank replied, grinning at her. "Ain't that kind of obvious?"

The back door opened, and Savannah and Alberto hurried in. "I know you said wait, but I saw Chyrel come in and—" Her hand flew to her chest when she saw Tank on the floor.

He started coughing again, harder this time, and Chyrel took hold of his hand. "Hang in there, Owen," she whispered. "Help's on the way."

Tank's head rolled to the side, eyes closed, and he was still.

CHAPTER THIRTY-FOUR

The flight from Marathon to Bimini took a little over an hour from takeoff to landing. *Island Hopper* would be kept in one of Armstrong's new hangars at North Bimini Airport, minutes from his shipyard on the west side of the island.

"There she is," I said, pointing at *Ambrosia* tied up at the new dock, next to Jack Armstrong's shipbuilding and repair facility.

"*Madre Dios,*" Alberto sighed, sitting up in his seat and looking over the dash panel. "She's really big."

Savannah had chosen to ride in back with Finn and Woden, so Alberto could enjoy the ride in the co-pilot's seat.

I brought the *Hopper* down to five hundred feet as we flew past and waggled the wings at several crew members looking up at us. I easily picked Nils Hansen out of the bunch. His white hair stood out among the others.

Switching to the airport's Unicom frequency, I announced my intention as we swung around and lined up with the runway. Once on the ground, I taxied toward the apron in front of three new hangars.

A white Ford F250 with the Armstrong logo on the front doors pulled out from beside one of them and stopped next to my

wingtip. Jack Armstrong himself climbed out of the passenger side as I shut down the big radial engine and went through my post-flight. Alberto enjoyed that part, repeating each check as I secured the bird.

Finally, we climbed out and Jack came toward us, extending his hand. "Good to see you again, Jesse."

"Good to see you, too, Jack," I replied, shaking his hand.

He turned to Savannah and gave her a light hug, then knelt on one knee in front of Alberto. "You must be *Ambrosia's* new deckhand."

Alberto looked up at Savannah, then me.

"Didn't I say work was going to be fun?" I asked.

Jack stood and looked me in the eye. "How's your friend?"

It never ceased to amaze me how much information the man had at his disposal. The shooting at the Rusty Anchor had only been three days ago, and news of it was kept to a minimum.

"He lost a lot of blood," I said. "But he survived the gunshot. It may have shortened the time he has left, though. Stage 4 cancer."

"That's too bad," Jack said. Then he turned to Savannah. "I came out here personally to deliver a fax the communications officer received just thirty minutes ago."

He reached into his jacket pocket, took out a sheet of paper folded in thirds, and handed it to her.

Savannah unfolded it and started to read. Her hand went to her mouth and her eyes moistened.

Jack smiled at me.

"It's from the Department of Children and Families," she said, looking up at me. "We've been approved."

"What?" I asked, taking it from her. "I thought it would take

weeks."

"I made a few calls," Jack admitted. "Hope you don't mind."

Savannah flung her arms around him and hugged him tightly. "Oh, thank you!"

When she released him, I took his elbow and stepped away from Alberto's ears. "I'm guessing you had something to do with the lack of fallout from what happened at the Rusty Anchor?"

"I did," he replied, simply. He winked. "But try not to make a habit of it."

I grinned at him, then knelt and showed the paper to Alberto. "Know what this means, little man?"

He looked at it. I knew he could read, but legal documents were probably too complicated for him. He shook his head.

"What this means," I began, "is that Savannah and I can now adopt you and you can live with us forever."

He looked up at me, then to Savannah. She knelt beside him and hugged him.

"It means you're my mother and father?" he asked.

"Nobody can take the place of a mother and father," I said. "That's a biological connection. But we can be a stand-in mom and dad for you. If that's what you want."

Finn and Woden joined our little circle, both nuzzling Alberto, as if they understood what was going on.

"Really?" Alberto asked, as a single tear dripped down his left cheek.

"It'll probably take a while for all the paperwork," I said. "But this letter approves us, and we can start the process right away."

He put his little arms around my neck and held on as if his life depended on it as he sobbed against my shoulder. Savannah leaned in and made it a group hug.

Finally, we stood and Alberto wiped the tears from his eyes, then looked up at Jack. "When do we leave, sir?"

"It's a rising tide," Jack replied. "And high tide's in an hour. The ship will be ready then."

"Well, we'd best not keep Nils waiting," I said.

We'd already shipped several things over and had only a couple of suitcases on the plane. We retrieved them, and a ground crewman wearing coveralls with the word ARMORED across the back and Armstrong's logo below it helped us load everything into the truck.

"ARMORED?" I asked Jack.

"Reorganization," he said. "You and *Ambrosia* have been assigned to Armstrong Research's Mobile Operational Readiness and Expeditionary Division."

"Still a mouthful," I said.

"Michael will put your bird in the hangar," Jack said. "She'll be secure there. Will the dogs be okay riding in the back of the truck?"

I lowered the tailgate and pushed our suitcases to one side. "*Oben*," I commanded Woden.

He instantly leapt into the bed of the truck, and Finn jumped in next to him.

"German commands?" Jack asked. "Very impressive."

Jack rode in front with the driver, and the three of us got into the spacious backseat. The ride to the shipyard took only a few minutes. When we arrived, the truck drove out onto the concrete dock to a large helipad and stopped.

Ambrosia's gangplank was flanked by several crewmen, with Nils standing at the gate. He came toward us as we got out of the truck, and two crewmen rounded the back to retrieve our

luggage.

"You don't know how happy I am to see you, Captain," Nils said, extending his hand for a hearty handshake. "And you too, Mrs. McDermitt."

"Nils, meet Alberto," I said. "Our soon-to-be adopted son." Then I looked down at the boy. "Alberto, this is Nils Hansen, Captain of *Ambrosia*."

Nils bent and shook hands with Alberto, who was obviously impressed by his uniform.

"I have some work to attend to in the yard," Jack said. "Nils will get you settled in and we'll be underway shortly."

"Please follow me," Nils said, as he walked up the plank.

We followed and I heard the click of a PA speaker onboard. The ship's bosun stood at the top of the plank along with four side boys. A fifth crewman held a microphone extended toward the bosun, who put his whistle to his mouth and piped the attention call.

The four crewmen at the top of the plank snapped to and the bosun piped the side, a series of low, high, then low whistles, and announced into the mic, "Captain McDermitt, arriving."

THE END

But really just a pause.

Jesse has a whole new adventure ahead of him in the next book in the series, Steady As She Goes.

AFTERWORD

I'm writing this on February 11, 2021, more than two months before this book will be released. My family and I were hit by the ChiCom Crud right at the end of 2020, all of us showing symptoms by New Year's Eve. It's always a struggle to work through an illness, but it's the only way I know. However, I wasn't equipped or ready when my wife had to be taken to the hospital in an ambulance. She developed Covid pneumonia and was hospitalized for four days.

I think those were the hardest four days of my life. She wasn't allowed visitors, and even the nurses and doctors only checked on her periodically, as they had to don hazmat suits to enter her room. Thankfully, her stay was short, and she received excellent care. We're all fully recovered now, and things are pretty much back to normal for us. But I don't mind telling you, on the day we brought her home, I sobbed with relief as I was able to hold her once more.

I fell behind in my writing in January but got a surge of renewed motivation when she came home. I worked in our new upstairs studio throughout January, to stay close. That's where our daughter, Jordan, and I livestream a monthly video podcast

on YouTube, called *Talk Write*. If you'd like to subscribe, go to www.youtube.com/waynestinnett.

So many of you wrote to me about Owen "Tank" Tankersley, who appeared in the first book in the series, *Fallen Out*, and later in *Fallen Pride*, as well as in the book just before this one, *Rising Moon*. Very few know this, but Tank is based on a real-life hero, right down to his comment, "They thought I knew where the mines were." The real "Tank" passed away seventeen years ago. His friends called him Mike.

As always, I give thanks to my family for their support and especially to Lowcountry Jack, who was the template for Alberto Marco in this book. They say that being around young people will keep you young, so I felt Jesse needed Alberto in his life. I know I have a lot of fun sitting in the sand pushing trucks around with Jack.

Tomorrow, which will be February 12th, my beta team will receive this manuscript. This motley crew is made up of a bunch of individuals, some of whom would likely never have known one another, had I not asked them for advice and brought them together via Facebook. Many thanks to Dana Vihlen, Rick Iossi, Alan Fader, Katy McKnight, Debbie Kocol, Drew Mutch, Glenn Hibbert, Rafael Olivieri-Geigel, Jason Hebert, Kim DeWitt, Chuck Höfbauer, Mike Ramsey, Tom Crisp, and Dave Parsons, the folks who ensure that all the details I know y'all enjoy are correct.

We're trying an experiment with this new book, turning more of the sometimes-tedious work of converting a manuscript into a novel over to Aurora Publicity. This simplifies things for me, as I only have to schedule a single entity to do what was done by three. Their team has done such a great job with many other tasks I've had them do on my behalf that I felt comfortable taking

this next step. The only thing I don't have them doing for this book is the editing, final proofreading, and narration of the audiobook. These tasks will stay in the capable hands of Marsha Zinberg, Donna Rich, and Nick Sullivan.

This novel is the twentieth in the Jesse McDermitt Caribbean Adventure Series. The first ten were quickly dubbed the Fallen Series by my readers and the next ten the Rising Series. But all twenty are part of the Jesse McDermitt Caribbean Adventure Series.

John D. MacDonald wrote twenty-one Travis McGee novels and for the last couple of years, I've struggled with whether or not I would match that number, out of respect for the man I consider the world's best storyteller.

I have decided that there will be a twenty-first novel in the Jesse series, and God willing, quite a few more. Randy Wayne White has already shattered the Travis McGee ceiling and I make no effort to hide the fact that I try to follow Randy's path in making decisions.

So, the title of the next Jesse book will be Steady as She Goes. But I'm not married to the idea of ten more with Steady in the title. We'll see how that goes.

Finally, I owe a great deal of thanks to you, my loyal readers. You've been with Jesse for—believe it or not—twenty-two years of his life, though it's only been a little over seven years in the writing of the stories. *Fallen Out* started in the spring of 1999, when Jesse retired from the Marine Corps. During the ensuing time, you've seen his daughters grow up, sometimes rather quickly, as I adjusted the time setting to catch up to current time. You've seen Jesse move from one relationship to another, sometimes with tragic consequences. For those of you who have stayed with us through it all, you have our undying gratitude.

Made in the USA
Coppell, TX
19 April 2021